SLIDING DELTA

SLIDING DELTA

DELTA

A NOVEL

ED BALDWIN

ISBN: 0989292797
ISBN 13: 9780989292795
Library of Congress Control Number: 2016933701
Brasfield Books, Hot Springs Village, AR

This book is dedicated to the memory of
Warren Wilson Baldwin (1945-1992)

Thirty years as a road musician

Chapter 1

The first time I heard Mississippi John Hurt play the guitar I was confused. He was finger picking a steady bass line with his thumb and an airy melody with his index and ring fingers. I'd never heard anyone play the guitar like that. I thought it was all a matter of which finger was doing what. I didn't know that a college sophomore who wouldn't need to rent a tuxedo to attend an upcoming debutant ball can't learn the Delta blues in a fraternity house sixty miles from Chicago. Especially not from listening to a record. The Delta blues taste like sweat and cheap whiskey; smell like jail; sound best in a concrete block club with no windows, set back along the river where there's no law after dark. I had a lot to learn. But, let's not get ahead of the story.

I picked up my grades on a Friday afternoon. It was snowing. My roommate had already left early for the weekend to get back to Chicago before the roads got bad. I dropped the envelope, unopened, on the desk and stood by the window. The falling snow disappeared in the mud and ice piles scraped from the roads and sidewalks after the previous storm a week before. That matched my mood exactly.

I could feel the presence of the envelope on the desk behind me. If there was a D in comparative anatomy, the fantasy of going to medical school was at an end. Three semesters of college, a lifetime of planning, and the expectations of the whole family that I, Douglas Spencer III would join the Spencer Cardiology Clinic of Lake Forest, Illinois, had come to naught, zip, nada.

I hated cutting up that shark in the first semester of anatomy, and now I'd been issued a cat for the second semester. I never liked cats, and now I had one – stiff and cold and reeking of the formaldehyde in which it had been immersed, possibly for years. And I'd been told in no uncertain terms to maintain that cat through the whole semester for dissection and study by myself and the rest of the class. Don't lose it, don't let it dry out.

Then a tiny light of optimism appeared. If I was truly out of the pre-med game, then I could drop comparative, turn the cat in and take something else! But I'd need to go home to break the news, and that was a problem. The parents were on the outs. Mother had hired a divorce lawyer, who had hired an investigator, who got pictures of Dr. Spencer and his office nurse having dinner at the Pump Room in the Ambassador East Hotel. Ethel, her name was. I had been down to the office a few times, and Ethel was really something: blond, buxom, friendly.

It wasn't fair. I had a vision of my father, a portly middle-age cardiologist, all tangled up with Ethel – Douglas Spencer II pumping a young honey half his age while Douglas Spencer III was still a virgin.

There was more. Stella had called two nights before.

"I hate it here," she'd said over the long distance line. "Let's run off and get married!"

That was a bit of a shock. Stella attended a girl's school downstate. A year younger, she'd been my prom date in high school, but there had been no exchange of jewelry, no exclusivity to our relationship. Stella was determined to play the field in college. The high point of our intimate relationship was an embarrassing stain that appeared after we wrestled, fully clothed, on the couch in her family room the summer before.

"Uh."

"Oh, I know this is sudden Doug. It's just so oppressive here. All the rules. We could just shuck it all and run off. There's a town in the next county that will issue a marriage license without a waiting period."

Well, that would solve the virginity problem.

"I've missed you." She knew I was thinking.

A veil of caution dimmed the vision of that first night in a motel somewhere in southern Illinois. "I thought you were dating someone."

"Oh, Vince."

Yeah, that's the guy. What about Vince? I wondered.

"Well, Vince and I didn't work out."

"Uh." So, Stella would drop out of school? Transfer? Get an apartment? Tell the parents? Oh, that was bad. I so didn't want to go to Chicago and face that frosty couple hewing and hacking with lawyers and accusations at a long-gone relationship.

"Oh, Doug. I'm sorry. I thought you would help." She broke down, sobbing over the phone.

"Help?"

"I'm pregnant."

"Oh." So it wasn't a longing for me that prompted this telephone call, just an inconvenient biological event; a successful insemination, fertilization, implantation.

"Vince?"

"Yes."

So, Vince is back in the scene.

"He's been so moody, Doug. We got along so well. We did everything together, and then, all of a sudden, he broke it off."

Apparently they did do everything together. Then it got worse.

"Oh, Doug, my life is such a mess. There's another problem."

"Oh?"

"The Presentation Ball is in two weeks," she said. "My parents are so proud, and they've gotten me sponsored by some of the board members. I had the final fitting for my dress last week. Really that was what finally broke it with Vince. He didn't want to rent a tuxedo and go to a debutante ball."

"So you need a date?"

"Oh, yes. Doug, would you?"

The snowflakes got bigger and began to overpower the mud, turning the campus white in the gathering gloom. I agreed to take Stella to the Presentation

Ball. I did not expect that date to rekindle our relationship. I opened the envelope. It was a D.

I took down my six-string guitar and began to run through some chords, warming up with no real desire to play anything. When my mother relented and let me trade piano lessons for guitar lessons in the sixth grade, she had insisted that it be the classical guitar and not the rock and roll electric. I dropped guitar lessons for baseball in high school, but by then my rudimentary skills allowed me to be a part of the folk music rage sweeping colleges in the early 1960s. I played regularly at fraternity parties and the occasional paid gig at a coffee shop. I hoped the guitar might bring solace on this dark day.

I ran through *Tom Dooley,* a song about the hanging of a man who killed his faithless lover, and *500 Miles,* a woeful tale about being stranded far from home. Then I strummed through *Nine Pound Hammer,* an old blues song about a railroad section gang. It got dark and the snow began to pile up, snarling traffic and trapping for the weekend any students who hadn't left already. I had no place to go and nobody to see.

On a whim, I retuned the guitar to open chord, intending to pick out some blues to match my mood. Authenticity was a key element in the folk music revival; all the artists talked about learning a song from "some old guy" or detailed when it was first recorded or performed. Folk music dominated the record market for a few years, and records from the old blues artists of the 1920s and '30s appeared in record stores. Muddy Waters, Howlin' Wolf, John Lee Hooker, Sonny Boy Williamson, Lightnin' Hopkins and "Mississippi" John Hurt became sudden celebrities.

I'd bought a record of "Mississippi" John Hurt that week, intrigued by his unique sound. Hurt's self-taught picking style using thumb to pick rhythm on the top three strings left his index and middle fingers to pick an airy melody on the bottom three strings. For the past two days I had been trying to play it, and couldn't. The recording of Hurt sounded like there were two people playing guitar. I got the record down and put it on the turntable and went through the whole side listening to Hurt pick, trying to understand which finger was doing what. I couldn't follow it. Then I started it again and listened while I read the liner notes from the album.

John Hurt's mother had been a slave. He lived his entire life within walking distance of the cotton plantation on which he was born, learning to play guitar by watching his aunt's boyfriend play. He played his music in obscurity for twenty years before a brief brush with fame in 1927, when he recorded in Memphis and New York for the OKEH label. Then he dropped back into obscurity until his recordings were rediscovered in 1963. He had recently played to rave reviews at the Newport Folk Festival, Carnegie Hall, and college campuses far and wide. If authenticity was important, then what I was listening to had to be the core of blues music, as Hurt had never had an opportunity to be exposed to anything else.

Blues fit my mood of the moment. Blues are supposed to be sad, doleful. I listened to *Nobody Cares for Me* wallowing in self-pity at the perfidy and superficiality of life. I played it again. Then I noticed that it wasn't sad at all. Though the words seem sad, they're accompanied by an upbeat melody, and the later verses are hopeful as the singer is returning home. I listened to *Spike Driver Blues,* which is about driving railroad spikes, backbreaking labor and dying. It, too, has an optimistic sound, plus a really unique back rhythm. Hurt's songs describe a harsh life in the Jim Crow South, with betrayal and murder, unrewarding work, whiskey, jail, sex and death as the usual themes, yet they made me feel better. Why was that?

The next track started with Hurt speaking at a concert and telling about his home in Mississippi that was on a small branch railroad line. He also spoke of living near the river and seeing a steamboat, the *Kate Allen,* transport people to New Orleans and back. Random notes while he was talking merged into a rhythm as he transitioned into his song *Sliding Delta*. It's all about the train running right by his door, his suitcase is packed, and he's leaving and never coming back. That driving rhythm picked me up, and John Hurt's optimism about the world waiting started me on a journey. On into that snowy Illinois night I picked, and listened, and dreamed, and when the sun came up my life had changed direction.

Chapter 2

Fragrant with honeysuckle, dead fish, mud and diesel exhaust, the heavy soft breath of the Mississippi River enveloped me as I stepped down from the air conditioned comfort of the Illinois Central *City of New Orleans* at Memphis Central Station on June 1, 1965. I collected my small suitcase, shouldered my guitar case and walked through the terminal onto South Main Street.

"Taxi?"

I had no plans yet, no idea of where I would tell a driver to go. I walked by the drivers competing for business in front of the train station. Only 12 hours removed from the Illinois Central Station between Michigan Avenue and Lake Shore Drive in downtown Chicago, I was there, at the jumping off point on my quest to find Mississippi John Hurt and learn to pick the Delta blues.

"A young man needs an adventure," my grandmother had said when I told her I was dropping pre-med and wanted to spend the summer traveling in the South. "Your grandfather went to Paris after the first World War."

"Oh?" I'd not heard about that before.

"Yes, he studied one semester at the Sorbonne before starting medical school. He was there with all the literary expatriates – Hemingway, James Joyce, Henry Miller, F. Scott Fitzgerald and Gertrude Stein."

"I never heard the Doctor talk about that."

"Well, you were young when Douglas passed away."

She sat for a moment, reflecting, then added, "It was a time of transition for Douglas."

She paused.

"He came back with a membership card in the Communist Party, and syphilis," she said brightly.

"Oh."

"It wasn't so bad. Arsenic cured the syphilis, and Joe Stalin cured his desire for a workers' revolution."

She laughed.

"He met all those famous people?"

"They weren't famous then," she said with a twinkle in her eye. "Go on your quest, Doug. You never know what you'll find."

She opened her purse and handed me three new $100 bills.

A sign for the Allenberg Cotton Co. caught my eye a block toward downtown. I stopped in the middle of the street I was crossing, the high-rise offices of downtown Memphis ahead and cotton warehouses to my left on Front Street, with the Mississippi beyond. I turned left and walked down Front. There were no bales of cotton piled in front of the warehouses or being brought up by mule wagons from barges docked along the river. No carts were taking bales up to the rail yard behind me. No colored porters struggling to load bales or coaxing stubborn mules up the steep hill. But, there had been at one time. The remnants were there. Front Street is cobblestone, worn by years of iron wheels and horse shoes, and as I walked a couple of blocks and turned to the west, the stones paved the bank down to the river.

Where had it all gone? Surely they still grew cotton in the South. I looked out into the great river to see a string of barges chugging upstream, propelled by a large tug spewing diesel fumes as it churned the muddy water. Behind the barge the Memphis-Arkansas Bridge brought two lanes of impatient cars streaming into Memphis from Arkansas to the west, including 18 wheel tractor-trailers. One was piled high with dozens of burlap-covered bales of cotton. Mystery solved.

"You a musician?"

I turned to see a colored boy about my age. The street was empty, so he must have followed me down to Front from the railroad station on Main.

"Sort of, I guess."

"You needin' a place to stay? Ain't no hotels down here."

"I thought I'd walk downtown."

"Big hotels mighty pricey, you need someone who know Memphis, sort of a guide. Keep things smooth," he drew this last word out as his hand, palm down slid across his chest in a slow controlled motion that left it pointing back up the bluff.

"I don't have much money."

"Don't need much money if you got someone who knows helpin' ya out. 'Sides, you might be makin' a record down at Stax or Sun, get in some of that big money.

"I doubt it," I said, smiling at the unbridled optimism. "How much does all this good advice cost?"

"Oh, we won't worry 'bout that. Depend on what I got to get for you."

"Get?"

"Yeah, a girl, whiskey, some Mary Jane. You know, stuff a man might want. No sense getting' into no trouble just to get what everybody else already got."

"Oh." The logic of this arrangement was beginning to appear. "OK."

"I'm Maurice," he offered his hand. Maurice, dressed in worn khaki work pants, a long-sleeve white shirt and shined black leather shoes, had an easy, winning smile.

"Doug."

"You got a cigarette?"

I pulled a box of Marlboros out of my pocket and handed it to Maurice, who took one and handed the box back, then went through an elaborate process of checking all his pockets for a light. I handed him my lighter.

"So, tell me something," I said, as we turned back toward Main Street. "Across the river there, how come nobody's built any houses there? Seems like a great place for condos, apartments, offices, perched right up on the river like that. You could just jump in the car and zip across the bridge down there and be in downtown Memphis in no time."

Maurice looked across the river and then at me and smiled. We walked a little farther up the bluff and he stopped and turned back to face the river.

"In the spring, that river be all the way to the levee in West Memphis."

"How far's that?"

"Five miles, maybe more."

"Why'd they put the levee so far over there? Couldn't they build one here to keep the river in check?"

"That ain't no ordinary river."

"It ever flood over here?"

"Naw. This the high side. That's why the cotton's all over there and the people's all over here. My granny said that when she was a little girl, it flooded all the way to Forrest City."

"How far's that?"

"Forty miles."

"You're right, that ain't no ordinary river. Where's Beale Street?"

"Right up there, cross from the Orpheum Theater."

"I want to hear some blues music. Any of that there?"

"Sure. Club Handy has a show most every night. Its rhythm and blues, more beat than just the old blues. You know, more like rock and roll."

"Anyone down there just play the acoustic guitar and pick, like Mississippi John Hurt?"

"Don't know him, but they all got drums and electric guitars, and sax, and electric organ. They put on a show, man, a show! That club be shakin' bout 10 tonight."

"Could I get in there?"

"You need someone knows the scene, see, make sure you get the service you need. Make it all smooth. You be with me? No trouble."

We walked down Main toward downtown and stopped in front of the Orpheum to look down Beale. It was pawn shops and a clothing store, and a couple cafes.

"Where's that Club Handy?"

"It's down there a few blocks. It's that two-story building on the corner. Club Handy's above the Pantaze Drug Store."

It was not an auspicious beginning to my quest. I'd expected to somehow just walk into a blues club and find legendary bluesmen standing around picking old standards and encouraging young white guys to learn their genre.

"You're gonna need a place to stay," Maurice said. "My aunt, she work down at the Lorraine. Get you a good deal. How long you gonna be here?"

"I'm in no hurry, but I'm really headed down to Mississippi. I might stay here a week. What's this Lorraine like?"

"It's a colored hotel, but white people stay there. My aunt, she worked at all the big places, the Peabody, the King Cotton, the Gayoso. She say the Lorraine just as clean as them. She change those sheets every day. No need to walk all the way downtown and pay no $20 for a night when the Lorraine right here for four."

I paid for a week in advance, $28. It was a fifties-style, two-story motel where each room fronted the parking lot, had two full length windows and a single room air conditioner. It looked like the standard small town Holiday Inn. The turquoise-color doors gave it a festive look, and it was well maintained. They gave me a room on the second floor and, as I was walking up the steps, I looked back to the office and saw the desk clerk hand Maurice a dollar. Just at the top of the steps, I walked around a corner to my room, facing the street, and paused to look up and down. There was a seedy two-story red-brick apartment building across the street with weeds growing up along the sidewalk, and I could see downtown Memphis to the north. Certainly not Chicago.

Maurice and I stepped up to the table at the top of the stairs leading to the Club Handy at 195 Hernando, at Beale and Hernando across from Handy Park. A line of young colored men and women stretched down the narrow stairs to the street. It was dark.

"This here's Doug," Maurice said with a trace of anxiety. "He's OK, down from Chicago to check out the blues in Memphis."

The man collecting the cover charge sat impassive, not seeming to care where I was from or why I was there. We were, after all, just two under-age boys trying to get into a nightclub.

"Two dollars. Each." He stamped the back of our hands with a star in red ink after I dropped a five on the table.

"See, I told ya, gonna be smooth," Maurice said, making that same sliding motion with his hand as we entered the club.

The Club Handy was a very large club, with tables around the side and a huge dance floor. Mine was the only white face in a crowd approaching a hundred, mostly young but some older couples dressed up for a night on the town.

"Now when the dancin' start, be cool," Maurice said quietly as we slipped onto bar stools at the end of the bar. "Some of the dudes here might get upset if a white boy be dancing with all the ladies. You want to dance, let me check with the bartender, make sure it be OK."

"I'm not much of a dancer."

"Hey, Maurice!" Two boys about our age crossed the dance floor and approached the bar. Introductions were made, and I become friends with Reggie and Nathanial.

"Four Schlitz here, and a pack of Marlboros," Maurice ordered, like he was paying. Then turned to me and said, "Can't be bummin' them cigs all night."

I pulled out another five.

The band set up: drums, saxophone, Hammond organ, bass, rhythm guitar and, last out of the case, a Gibson Flying V guitar. While I was admiring this modern instrument, the crowd at the top of the stairs parted and a huge colored man entered the room, which went silent for a moment. Dressed in dress pants, open-collar shirt and sporting a narrow-brim straw hat, he walked confidently across the dance floor, object of every gaze in the house. He waved, and the excited talk resumed.

"Hey, Sam," he said, approaching the bar

Fisst! Another can of Schlitz popped under the opener as Sam the bartender yanked the handle down and handed an open beer to the huge musician, who towered over everyone; six feet four inches tall and 300 pounds, at least. Albert King was the rock star of Beale Street.

"You boys alright?" he asked as he took a first sip. He looked briefly at me, then the other guys with me. He fished in his pocket and brought out a five and held it out to Reggie.

"You want to go down to that café across the street and get me a fried egg and ham sandwich?"

"Yes, sir, Mr. King," Reggie responded and was gone in a flash.

Albert King sat at a nearby table and addressed a line of well-wishers, signing autographs and bantering with his fans. Reggie returned with his sandwich. While the band warmed up, he wolfed it down and chased it with another Schlitz.

The lights went down. The crowd now filled the room, 200 strong, peppered with a few more white faces. They were all on their feet. The band started a twelve-bar blues rhythm, and Albert King strode to the bandstand. He picked up the Gibson and paused while looking out over the audience. Everyone in the room, including me, held their breath. I was astonished to see King playing the Gibson Flying V left handed and upside down, with the treble strings at the top.

The first note was a steel-string rifle shot amplified with reverb and, with the very next beat, the entire audience was in the groove with Albert King, dancing, swaying, led by that Gibson Flying V with the amps turned full up. The building shook as King tortured the strings of the Gibson, sometimes bending with his index and middle fingers, then using a steel thimble on his ring finger to slide down the frets. An exhibition of instrumental fury, it was just the warmup. And, unlike John Hurt, who picked the bass strings with his thumb and used his index and middle fingers for the melody, King picked the melody on the treble strings with his thumb and index finger. I realized there are a lot of ways to play the guitar.

"If it wasn't for bad luck," he sang, jumping right into the next song, singing a line and following with a guitar riff, like a question and an answer. The band kept the driving twelve-bar rhythm while King told his story, going into a long instrumental interlude before stepping back and letting his sax player wail for a bit before settling back into the story and finishing up.

The band played the standard twelve-bar chord progression while King improvised off the melody, wandering a half-step on either side of the chord by bending the strings, adding vibrato with his finger and sliding up and down the frets with the thimble. It was confusing to break it down to the musical parts, but the overall effect was magic.

For an hour, nobody in that room was aware of anything but a primordial, hard-charging, full-speed-ahead dance band. And Albert King, a giant playing a cut-down guitar that looked like a toy in his meaty hands, was the pied piper leading it all.

Then he took a break and lit his pipe. Lines formed at the restrooms and the bar, conversations started back up, and the big man, soaked with sweat, approached the bar.

Fisst! Sam handed him another Schlitz.

"Mr. King," I blurted out on impulse, "I'm a reporter with the Scimitar-Clarion. It's just a college newspaper, but my friend Maurice said you might let me have just a minute."

I made it all up. I was never on the newspaper staff, and I'm not even sure whether that's the name of the paper at my college. But it worked.

"Sure, have a seat," King said. He pulled out a chair and sat with his back to the corner, puffing on his pipe.

Fisst! Sam handed another Schlitz across the bar, the previous one already empty. I sat, and Maurice and Reggie and Nathanial joined us at the table.

"Sir, what made you decide to be a blues musician?"

King looked at his rapt audience, teenage boys, and smiled. He held out his left arm, pointing to his watch.

"When my grandfather died, my grannie gave me his watch, this watch." He paused. He'd told this story before. "You boys ever chop cotton?"

We all shook our heads, no.

"Well, across that river over there, in the delta, colored boys chopped cotton when I was your age. This time of year, cotton's 'bout this tall," he said, his fingers three inches apart.

"And the plants are about this far apart," he said, fingers an inch apart, "and there's some grass and weeds coming up."

He paused to take a sip of his beer and have a puff on his pipe.

"The man, he paid us five dollars a day to thin it out and get those weeds, with a hoe. Don't sound too hard, but you stand there in the morning and that row is a quarter-mile long. You start chopping and finish the row, then you turn around and chop the next row back, then turn around again. By noon that sun is on your back, and you're tired and thirsty. The man looks up at the sun, then he takes out a pocket watch and looks at it. We're all watchin' him, ready to take a break, eat lunch, get a drink. He takes his time, then he says, 'Stop, time for lunch.' Then he goes over to his truck and lights a cigarette while we're getting a drink and eating. He finish his cigarette, crush it out with his boot, and pull out that pocket watch. 'OK, lunch is over. Go back to work.' Well, I had this watch, and I looked at it. 'Sir,' I said, 'it's just been 20 minutes.' "

King pauses in his story for effect.

We're glued to it, waiting for the punch line.

"He walks over to me and says, 'Nigger, what use you got for a watch?' "

We nod, but say nothing.

Albert King raises his eyebrows and looks at us.

"That's when I decided to do something else besides chop cotton."

The band started up again, and Albert King returned to the bandstand. As I returned to the bar, I found that two colored men in their 20s had taken Reggie and Nathanial's seats. Reggie began to protest, but a stern look sent them both to the other end of the bar. Sam placed a shot glass of clear liquid before me.

"What about me?" Maurice asked.

Sam looked at the two men and one of them nodded. He served another shot from beneath the bar.

"That's moonshine," Maurice whispered as he took a sip.

It was fire with a smoky yeast taste, but I took a second sip.

"You lookin' for some action?" the man sitting next to me asked.

"What kind of action?" I'd had a couple of beers, and now this firewater was sinking in.

Maurice was strangely quiet.

"You want some pussy? We got black girls, we got white girls, whatever you want."

"We even got a Chinese girl," the other one giggled.

"No," I said, "I'm just here for the music."

The man held up his shot glass and drained it in one gulp. He looked at me.

"Whew!" I said, finishing my shot with bravado. Maurice followed.

"You gonna buy now?" the man asked.

During the next two hours I enjoyed the show with my two new friends while we alternated buying shots of liquid fire and chasing them with beer. My friend and guide, Maurice was steadily excluded from the merriment, and the drinks. He left. They continued to offer me the services of various women and

I declined. Finally I called it a night and stumbled out of the club, unsure which way the motel was. Riding the crest of an alcohol induced wave of optimism, I'd decided to buy a Gibson Flying V guitar and go on the road playing R&B. As I weaved down the street I marveled at how the streetlights seemed to circle in the sky above me.

A block south of Beale, two men grabbed me from behind and shoved me into an alley. A jolt of pain shot through me from a fist to the kidney.

"Put your nose on that wall, boy."

A heavy body pushed me to the wall and leaned on me. The bricks tasted like dirt.

Two hands felt my pockets, finding my wallet in my back pocket. They felt the front pockets and shirt pockets as well. The whole time, I was in the grasp of one of the men, who was breathing heavily into my ear. I heard a click and saw the glint from a switchblade knife with a red plastic handle held right in front of my face.

"Count to 20 boy, or I'll be back with this."

The weight lifted from my back. I kept my nose on the brick and counted to 20, twice. The men were gone. Timidly I stepped out of the alley and looked up and down the street; empty. I turned back to the south and could see the Lorraine ahead. I anxiously turned to look behind me and stumbled into a streetlight, spinning a full circle and staggering on. In my inebriated condition I struggled with the realization that Maurice might have set me up with the two guys at the bar and was in for a cut of what they'd found in my wallet, just like the cut he got from the desk clerk at the Lorraine. Or, maybe somebody else alerted them to an easy mark. I was just starting out on the blues road and had found it wasn't always a happy place.

Chapter 3

"That's a very nice watch," the old pawnbroker asked, examining it with a jeweler's loupe. "Where did you get it?"

"It was a gift, for my 16th birthday."

The muggers missed my watch, my only remaining possession other than my guitar, wisely left in the room. I'd spent a day in bed at the Lorraine recovering from the body blow and the hangover. I had 46 cents in loose change in my pocket, and I was not going to call my grandmother for more money. Three pawnshops were on Beale, and this one seemed the most reputable-looking. The wall filled with electric guitars told me the dream of going on the road with a blues band might have a low probability of success.

"Do you know how a pawn works?"

"No."

"I'll give you $50. The interest is 5 percent a month. If you don't redeem the watch in three months, with the accumulated 15 percent interest, I will sell it."

"OK."

The watch cost in the neighborhood of $400.

"Sign here."

I signed, and the pawnbroker gave me five tens.

"Where's a good place to eat?"

"Go down to Main, turn toward the train station. The Arcade is a couple blocks."

A plate of Southern fried chicken with mashed potatoes and gravy, a side of collard greens and ham, and two biscuits later, I was feeling better. I walked back to the Lorraine and, as I climbed up the steps to my room I glanced across the parking lot to see a white man leave one of the rooms downstairs and walk quickly to his car.

The maid was cleaning my room, so I leaned on the railing and smoked a cigarette. A 1958 Buick Roadmaster with chrome fender skirts, whitewall tires and a long whip antenna cruised slowly down Mulberry Street, turned around at the corner and slid into the parking lot. A young colored woman came out of the same room the white man had exited just minutes before and climbed into the Buick. There was a brief conversation, and they pulled out into traffic, headed away from downtown.

The room was small, and the disinfectant the maid had used covered a faint mildew smell, unavoidable, I learned, with air conditioning in the humid South. Still recovering from my first excursion into the blues, I took a nap, then walked back down to Beale and Hernando to the Pantaze Drug Store to get some aspirin for my various aches. I looked up the steps to the Club Handy, now locked, and pondered making another foray into the nighttime culture of the Delta blues.

I was pretty sure I was robbed by my two friends from the bar, and I was also pretty sure they'd be there if I returned. That thought made the pain on my right flank intensify. I wasn't ready for any more Club Handy just yet.

Exiting the drug store, I stood at Beale and Hernando and heard a guitar playing a basic blues song. I looked back up at Club Handy; it was still locked. The sound was coming from Handy Park across the street. I strolled over there to find a grizzled old colored man seated on a park bench playing a thoroughly worn out Gibson J-45. This old relic with the sunburst pattern on the front must have been the grandfather of my Gibson J-45. The battered case was open at his feet and there were three quarters in the bottom. I fished out some change and dropped it into his case. I sat down to listen.

This was the old blues I'd come south to hear. He sang softly in a worn voice, more like an accompaniment to the guitar that was keeping that haunting blues rhythm. It was the same call and guitar response I'd heard from Albert King, but much simpler, and the words were soft and muffled as to be barely recognizable. I leaned back and looked up Beale while he concentrated on his music. The street was virtually empty in midafternoon, and we had the park to ourselves.

"Hmm, mmm, mmmm." He stopped making words at all and just hummed the vocal.

Somehow, that made it easier to feel the music, and that calm that I'd first noticed listening to Mississippi John Hurt settled over me. What was that?

Beale Street looked shabby. Half the storefronts were closed, and the open businesses had little to offer. The busker's foot tapped with the rhythm, his old shoes broken down in the back so his feet slid in like slippers. His sweat-stained long-sleeve shirt was frayed badly at the cuffs. Handy Park was shabby, too. Pedestrians cutting across the corner lot had worn out most of the grass, and what little left was drying out. Weeds grew behind the bench we sat on.

The old man fit right in with the scene of a sad passed-over time and place.

"Not much going on here," I said, hoping to get some conversation out of the old guy.

"No." He stopped playing and nodded across the street.

"Club Handy over there, be rocking on the weekends, and the Hippodrome around the corner. Not like the old days, though."

"The old days?"

"Oh, yeah. Twenty years ago, right after the war, all the big bands came to Memphis. Duke Ellington, Count Basie and Louis Armstrong would come to town to play the Starlight Roof up at the Peabody. They'd play the Handy the night before or the night after. You couldn't find a place to stand on the street down here," he said, sweeping his arm at the corner and up Beale toward Main.

"But it wasn't just the big clubs, there were five or six bars along Beale, a couple pool halls, restaurants and clothing stores."

"All colored?"

"Oh, yeah. White people go uptown, to the Peabody and the stores up there."

"People had money?"

"A lot of money. After the war, everyone had a job, this town was rockin'."

He picked back up on his song for sixteen bars or so.

"There was nice houses down that way," he said, pointing south of Beale. "Big houses, cut into nice apartments, with porches and steps you could sit on in the evenin', 20 blocks down that way.

"That was all colored owned," he said proudly. "Back in the old, old days, when I was a boy, a man with a mule and a cart could make a good livin' moving cotton up from the river to the cotton warehouses and from the cotton warehouses along Front up to the railroad."

"I guess that's all gone now."

"Oh, yeah. I hear the white guys are still buyin' and sellin' cotton in those same cotton companies, but there ain't no cotton there. It all goin' from place to place on a truck."

"So, no guys with mules and wagons."

"Not since before the war."

"So, looks like you might have done some playing during those days."

"Oh, yeah," he said, resuming his music. He nodded back to the street.

"I played in all those places. Those were high times."

"What happened?"

"Well, the people left, moved up North, or out to East Memphis. Ain't nobody here now."

That was certainly true. A bomb could have gone off at Beale and Hernando and nobody would have been hurt. I asked him to give me a guitar lesson, and he said for a couple bucks he'd teach me as long as I wanted. I jogged back to the Lorraine and brought my guitar to the park.

"No, you been strummin' the chords on that folk music. For the blues, you got to shuffle. See? Like this," he said, demonstrating a shuffling two-beat rhythm, hitting the E and A string with a pick while damping the skinny strings with his index finger on the fret board.

"Sort of like riding a horse," I replied, trying again, nodding my head and feeling the shuffle.

"Yeah, that's it. You been playin' the E shuffle, now go to the A shuffle."

I alternated the chords, feeling bluesy already.

"Good, good. Now shuffle four beats in E, four in A, eight in E, eight in A, eight in E, four in B, four in A, four in E and finish up with four in B. Then do it again."

I worked on if for a couple minutes and some people came up to watch two guys playing the blues but began to lose interest when they saw it was a lesson. I pulled another dollar bill out of my pocket and dropped it into his guitar case to hold his attention a bit longer.

"OK, you got the chords, now you put it together like this."

He played the twelve-bar blues shuffle, then improvised on top of it. One of the onlookers dropped a dime into his case and moved on. He stopped and looked over at me. Not a novice guitar player myself, I was able to put some licks onto the basic shuffle, too.

After an hour I felt pretty good with what I'd learned, but I needed to practice it. I thanked him and packed up my guitar. He did the same and headed up the street toward Main. He said something about having a date with Rosie. I learned later that meant a bottle of Wild Irish Rose wine. I wished him luck.

Walking back to the Lorraine rehearsing the blues shuffle in my head, I encountered the colored girl I'd seen earlier. She was leaving the room again, now dressed in a miniskirt with calf-length imitation leather boots. She smiled over the top of a new Ford Mustang as she got into the passenger side. I couldn't see the driver as the car pulled out onto Mulberry headed downtown.

I practiced putting the shuffle into various songs I knew. My mother had tolerated my guitar as long as she heard only folk and classic Spanish-style playing, so I'd had practically no experience with pop music or an electric guitar. I'd been trying to copy Mississippi John Hurt by picking Spanish style, and it hadn't worked.

My music sounded different already. My acoustic Gibson played the shuffle just fine as I played in that stuffy little room, but I longed for a larger feel. The sun had dropped behind the two-story boarding house across the street, and it was cooling down some outside in the early evening, so I moved my chair outside and propped my feet on the railing of the balcony and continued playing.

The Mustang returned and the girl jumped out. She waved as the Mustang accelerated out onto Mulberry headed south toward the Arkansas Bridge. I nodded, intent on my playing and lost sight of her as she walked beneath the landing.

"You must be makin' a record over at Sun Studios."

She startled me, and I stopped playing and looked up.

"No, just practicing." I went back to my music.

"They stay here all the time," she went on, "the musicians, and some of the record company people who come to town. They record colored and white over there at Sun, and at Stax. You goin' down there?"

"Not right away."

I bent a string at the end of a phrase in a bit of Albert King improvisation.

"You're good," she said, leaning against the railing and nodding her head with the shuffle as she turned to gaze up and down Mulberry Street. "You gonna be here a while?"

"Few days," I said, pulling the pick from under the E string at the top and went into the only rock and roll song I knew, *Memphis.* That seemed appropriate for the moment. I finished it and looked up, "You staying here?"

"I do. If a boyfriend want to pay for the week, I stay here."

"Oh." I hadn't expected quite so much candor. I went back to the blues, eyes on the frets.

"That him in the Mustang?" Nosey, but she'd brought it up.

"No."

Well, that pretty much laid it out. I went on playing, and she left, returning to the room and giving me one last smile as she closed the door. I had already decided this was not the way to end my virginity problem. I packed up the guitar and walked down to the Arcade for some meatloaf and macaroni and cheese.

Five days later, the "Old Grey Dog" pulled out of the Greyhound Terminal in Memphis, heading down Highway 61 through the heart of the Mississippi Delta. I was in a row by myself with my guitar, practicing the blues. I never did go back to the Club Handy, though B.B. King and Booker T & the MGs played there the weekend after Albert King.

"You gettin' it," an old colored man said from across the aisle and one seat back. He nodded his head and tapped his feet to the beat, helping me to stay on it.

I picked my way to Moon Lake and then put the guitar up.

"Is that cotton?" I asked, nodding out the window as the flat, open landscape slid by.

The old man turned in his seat and glanced out the window.

"That's soybeans," he said. Then, a moment later, "That's cotton."

I didn't see any difference between the two fields, both planted with rows of small plants no more than half a foot high. There were a few tractors plowing in the fields, but nobody chopping, as Albert King had described.

My expectation of seeing labor crews of brawny black men chopping cotton and singing the blues was something from long ago. Times had changed. Then I noticed that the dozen riders on the bus were evenly divided between white and colored. I was sitting in the middle of the bus; all the white people were in front, and all the colored were behind me.

Nobody from the bus company had told them to segregate, but they had. I recalled the newspaper stories about the Freedom Riders a few years before. These had been colored and white college students from up North who rode interstate buses through the South challenging the segregation of seating and bathrooms in the terminals. I thought that had all been settled, but it seemed to be hanging on in Mississippi. Habit, fear, or a desire not to roil the status quo?

At an intermediate stop, a young colored woman got on, briefly surveyed the seating arrangements and sat in the front seat. Nobody seemed to notice.

"Cotton?" I asked again, trying to discern the difference in the fields.

"Soybeans," the man answered.

Then I saw it, a slight difference in greenness. The soybeans being iridescently greener.

The bus turned off the highway and proceeded into Clarksdale, dusty, hot, worn and poor. The bus passed the bus station, which was on the wrong side of the road for the riders to exit, and turned into a residential street to go around the block and turn around.

I was fascinated. No sidewalks, no curbs, and trucks and cars were parked in the front yards of these modest homes. I had assumed every neighborhood in America had sidewalks, curbs and manicured lawns like Lake Forest. Not so.

"Colored." The rusted sign pointed around the side of the bus station, but everyone ignored it and went inside to the restroom and to enjoy the air conditioning and get something from the vending machines. A Supreme Court decision a decade before had outlawed segregation in bus stations. The Freedom Riders had pressed the issue at some personal sacrifice, and it was no longer legally enforced. Yet, they left the sign up. My older companion from the bus joined me at the vending machines.

A poster proclaimed: "Delta Jim and the Blues Rockets! Playing one night only at the Stardust Club in Cleveland, Mississippi!"

"He any good?" I asked, biting off a piece of a Payday candy bar.

Cleveland was the next town, and my destination. The show date on the poster was that very day, June 7, 1965.

"He play the slide guitar," the man said and put a dime in the Coke machine. "He play on the radio."

"Memphis?"

"Helena. Across the river, in Arkansas."

"Live blues, on the radio?"

"Every day at noon. 'The King Biscuit Time Show.'"

"Now loading for Cleveland, Greenville, Natchez, Baton Rouge and New Orleans," the driver called out as he walked from the ticket window to the door. A fat middle-age colored lady carrying a suitcase held together with duct tape eagerly took her place first in line. The driver checked her ticket; me and my friend boarded.

"You going to Cleveland?" I asked.

A plan was forming. If I could get in to see Delta Jim, I might be able to get an invitation to get into the radio show in Helena. I could watch the show, maybe sit in for a song, just to play rhythm or something.

"Yes," he said warily.

"If I buy you lunch, could you tell me about this Stardust Club?"

"Well, my daughter be picking me up. She live over at Benoit."

"Oh."

"The Stardust Club, that be a colored club. You best stay away from there. You can hear Delta Jim on the radio."

"You ever hear of Mississippi John Hurt?"

"Sure!" The man's face brightened from the warning about the Stardust Club. "I heard him play over at Greenwood when I was courtin'. That was in 1930. I bought some of his records."

"He still around?"

"John Hurt from Avalon, Mississippi, that's over between Greenwood and Grenada. I heard he been sick."

"What was he like?"

"Oh, he pick, with his fingers, the old blues," the man said and demonstrated with a gnarled arthritic hand held across his chest. "Not like Delta Jim or the others you hear now with the electric guitars and all."

"Did people dance?"

I remembered the crowd at the Club Handy rocking with Albert King.

"Oh yeah, we danced," the old man smiled with a private reverie.

"Guitars weren't electric back then."

"No," he said. " I saw him sing at a club, and he held the guitar near a microphone and when he sang he leaned over and sang into it. We danced."

He smiled again.

Chapter 4

I almost told the cab driver, whose name was Henry, to turn around and take me back to Cleveland when I first saw the Stardust Club. It was a large concrete-block building set back in the pines behind a defunct gas station. Three small windows were set up high, and one was filled with an old air conditioner rattling against the humid night. The old man on the bus was right: This was not a place for me. But I had paid Henry five bucks to escort me out here, and he'd taken the rest of the night off and brought his wife along to dance. No backing out now.

"It be OK," he said, sensing my anxiety. "They know me here."

I had explained that I just wanted to hear some real blues. Besides, his wife, a plump middle-age lady, looked like she didn't get out that much and seemed eager to go in. A dozen cars were in the gravel parking lot.

"Dollar," an older man seated at a table at the door said, nudging an open cigar box. I dropped three ones into it. The door and frame were steel, bolted to the block wall like a vault.

"What's with the door?" I asked Henry.

"Ain't no law out here at night," he said quietly. "They kick that door down to get to the beer."

That didn't make me feel any better.

A tall, slender youth in work clothes carried in a bass drum, followed by an older man carrying a snare. They set up, walked back out to a pickup truck in the parking lot and brought in a bass amplifier. The club had no stage, so all this went in a corner. The youth, about my age, tuned up a Fender Precision bass guitar, then ran through some twelve-bar blues while the drummer finished setting up.

Delta Jim entered carrying his guitar case in one hand and a small portable amplifier with the other. He was a middle-age man wearing work khakis and a bright purple rayon shirt with full-cut long sleeves. Just two days before, I'd been in the Lansky Brothers clothing store on Beale Street in Memphis, and this same style of shirt was in the window, only the one I'd seen had been blue. I'd heard that Elvis Presley bought his clothes at Lansky. Apparently Delta Jim did, too.

He pulled a battered Fender Stratocaster out of its case and hooked up to his small amplifier. He tuned up and, without fanfare, began a twelve bar blues rhythm, and the bass player quickly joined.

"I'm gonna get up in the mornin'," Delta Jim sang, his steady, reassuring baritone launching into a tale of a woman who "wants every downtown man she meet." Though it wasn't dance music, the audience of 20 to 30 was nodding, tapping and swaying with the beat right from the start.

Like Albert King, Delta Jim sang a line and followed it with a guitar riff. He had a steel sleeve on his left ring finger that he slid parallel with the frets across all the strings. Keeping the twelve bar beat going while he sang, he slid the sleeve up and down the strings only on the response, adding vibrato mostly down the fret board and then wailing three and four frets at a time at the end of a verse.

"If I don't find her in Mississippi, she's in West Memphis, I know."

This first song was an old standard for warmup because, with the next song, the dancers started and the tempo picked up. No longer looking at the audience and telling his story, now he watched his hands as the slide wailed down the fretboard in increasingly complex riffs. I realized this was an evolution of the old Delta blues from John Hurt's style, and Albert King's playing was still further evolved.

Henry and his wife were dancing now. I was into my third beer and wondering whether I might find a way to sit in. I thought I could follow on the bass. I got up to buy another round and, as I dropped a five on the bar, the same man who took our cover put three more Buds under the opener and slammed down the handle to pierce the tops. No pop tops here in Mississippi, just old-style steel beer cans with "Mississippi State Beer Tax 5 Cents Paid" printed on the top of each can.

At the break, Delta Jim went to sit at the bar and talk with the owner. The bass player came over, and Henry introduced us.

"This Jerome," he said to me and turned back to Jerome. "Doug be down from Chicago, wantin' to hear some blues."

"Wish I's in Chicago." Jerome said.

"I'm just down here on vacation," I said. " I play a little guitar at home. Not professional or anything. You guys are good."

Jerome nodded, smiled.

After some more small talk, Jerome picked up his bass and showed me how Delta Jim liked his backup. I practiced a bit, and the first song in the next set featured me, Douglas Spencer III, on bass. I added a couple of ones to three lonely quarters in the tip jar.

Halfway through the second set, about 10 o'clock, we noticed a red flashing light outside the small windows. Response inside was instantaneous. The bartender slid a large cardboard packing barrel from behind the bar into the middle of the room, and all the patrons chugged their beers and tossed the cans into the barrel.

"What's the matter?"

"Beer ain't legal in Mississippi," Henry said, finishing his wife's beer and chucking the empty.

"Huh?" I thought,, recalling the Mississippi beer tax notice on top of the four cans I had consumed so far. I chugged mine down. Five minutes passed. Apparently, the cops weren't in any hurry. By the time the door opened, everyone was seated sedately with no booze in sight. Two sheriff's deputies entered, one white, one colored. They nodded at a few in the audience they knew and looked around the room. The band continued in a mechanical fashion. The colored deputy went to the bar and talked amicably with the owner. The white deputy came to my table.

"Who are you?" he asked.

"Doug Spencer," I said, standing.

"What you doin' here?" asked the deputy, a middle-age man with a spreading middle. He was not in a hurry.

"Listening to the music," I said.

I was only 19, way below the drinking age in any state except Oklahoma. My fake ID, good in some Chicago bars and most of the college town pizza joints, was in my stolen wallet.

"This here's a nigger club," he said, his eyes boring into me as he stood solidly in the middle of the club. The music stopped.

"Uh." I'd been worried about being busted for underage drinking but that, apparently, wasn't the problem. "Uh, I just came in here with Henry and, uh..." I'd forgotten his wife's name; big faux pas in Chicago, not so much here.

The deputy turned to Henry.

"You bring him in here?" he asked?

Henry stood his ground.

"Cab's out front. Meter's runnin'."

Henry's explanation covered his ass. Now it was back to mine.

"You got some ID?"

"Uh, no. You see, I was robbed in Memphis last week, my driver's license, draft card, all gone."

The deputy looked over at the colored deputy at the bar. The colored deputy looked beside the bar at the barrel filled with empty beer cans. This was all starting to make sense now. Mississippi was a dry state, but they allowed beer to be sold if the tax was paid. This club didn't have a beer license, because there were no beer licenses, but they were given adequate warning by the sheriff so they could remove the evidence of beer being consumed on the premises. No problem if everything else was in order.

But everything wasn't in order. They didn't care that I was an underage college student drinking beer in a nightclub. They did care that I was a white man in a colored nightclub.

"You got no ID?"

I shook my head.

"You got no ID, and you're drinking beer in a nigger club?"

I nodded sheepishly. How big a problem could that be?

"You from around here?"

"No."

"You got people here?"

"No."

"Put your hands on the table."

I complied. For the second time in a week, I was patted down and the contents of all my pockets were removed. He pulled my right hand behind my back, and I felt the cold steel of handcuffs.

Chapter 5

"Hey, white boy, you want to parteee?"

The jail in Cleveland, Mississippi, was a two-story affair with cells on one side and an open atrium with windows on the other. Men upstairs, women downstairs. As I was led to my cell, the women could glimpse my reflection in those windows.

"Oh, you cute!"

"Breakfast is at 6," the jailer said as he closed the door.

In addition to impounding my suitcase and guitar, they took my belt, shoelaces and cigarette lighter. They left me with half a pack of cigarettes and a book of matches. There was no fingerprinting, no mug shot, no discussion about lawyers or rights; just a lockup.

"Hey, white boy! You rob a bank?"

That went on for half an hour before they lost interest. There was not a sound from the half-dozen men, white and colored, who I'd passed in the two other cells on the top floor.

Scratched into the concrete wall by the lower bunk in my cell was an elaborate obscene drawing that someone had started and others had added on to, judging by differences in style and scraping techniques. The cell smelled faintly of urine, tobacco and sweat. Later that night, after I had drifted off to sleep, they brought in two more men. Apparently, the first two cells were full, I was in the third and there was one more. The same two deputies that had arrested me escorted a white man and a colored man to the last cell.

"Ray, I'm gonna put you and Harold in here together. Can you get along?" the white deputy asked one of the men. I couldn't see which. Apparently, they all knew each other; small town.

"Yeah."

"Harold?"

"Yeah."

"If you boys get into it, you're gonna have trouble with me and Clevon. Got that?"

They both answered in the affirmative.

"Clevon, they gonna be OK?"

"They better be."

I thought about that for a while as the two guys settled in. If race were the issue, they could have put the white guy in with me and given the colored guy the last cell. I realized I was an unknown; being white, reasonably well-dressed and well-spoken, they must have cut me some slack, worked it out with the local guys, colored and white, to prevent friction.

In the morning, the jailer said, "The sheriff's here." He opened my cell door and handed me a plate of grits along with a Styrofoam cup of black coffee. I assumed the comment about the sheriff being in to be a positive development, and I dug into the repast provided to me by the good citizens of Bolivar County, Mississippi.

The jailer came in after half an hour and brought me to the sheriff's office.

"Who are you, boy?" he asked.

Older than my father but just as portly, the sheriff had sun-damaged skin and calloused hands. He was wearing the same brown uniform as the deputies I'd encountered the night before, but his badge was gold instead of silver. His belly hung over the hand-tooled leather belt that held up a pistol and holster on one side and a black leather sap on the other. His question was neutral. He seemed genuinely curious.

"Doug Spencer, from Lake Forrest, Illinois. I'm just here on vacation, sir. I'm a junior in college."

"Where is that?"

"It's a suburb of Chicago, on the west side, sir."

I don't usually call anyone sir, but it seemed prudent in this situation to show as much respect as possible.

"Why are you in Mississippi?"

"I came down here to find Mississippi John Hurt and learn to pick the delta blues."

A smile broke out on his face and he leaned back in his chair.

"You did, huh?"

"Yes, sir," I said, nodding emphatically.

"Have you ever met John Hurt?"

I shook my head.

"Can you play that guitar?" he asked, nodding toward the corner of his office. I noticed for the first time my suitcase and guitar case sitting there.

"I can."

"Let's hear it."

I took out the guitar and tuned it up, then went into a twelve bar blues rhythm with a few simple flourishes I'd picked up from the street musician in Memphis and Jerome the night before.

"OK, put it up," he said.

A deputy had come in from the outer office during my brief concert and was leaning against the door watching.

"Now," the sheriff said, "tell me about how you come to be in Bolivar County with no ID and only eight dollars in your pocket."

I told him the whole story, while doing mental calculations to recall how my last fifty bucks was down to eight. It was down to eight.

"You got a lot of trust, boy," he said. "You put yourself into some places where you don't belong. Those niggers in Memphis could have killed you, and there's some down here will, just for that eight bucks and the guitar."

He looked sternly at me, leaning back in his chair.

"You're guilty of vagrancy — no visible means of support, no ID, nobody to vouch for you. We could put you in that jail and make your people find a lawyer here in town to get you out."

My heart plummeted.

"But, I'm sure they would find a lawyer and get you out, nobody with bad intent would be so stupid as you."

The sheriff leaned forward, elbows on his desk and said, "John Hurt lives in Avalon, between here and Grenada. There's a bus goes through there. It stops at Kinder's store. I'm going to give you some free advice. Don't let me catch you in Bolivar County without ID, or a job, or enough money for food and a place to stay. You understand?"

"Yes, sir."

"Get your stuff and go."

Chapter 6

Dust billowed up as the bus turned off the blacktop highway onto a dirt road.

"Avalon," the driver announced.

I jerked out of my reverie and looked down at the road to watch a dog running beside the bus, barking as if to establish territoriality over a 1947 GM "Silversides" bus. Another turn and we pulled up in front of a wood-frame store, a few feet ahead of the dog and our own cloud of dust.

"This is your stop," the driver said, opening the door and stretching. He descended the steps and opened the baggage compartment.

The whole town was one dirt road a quarter-mile long parallel to the county highway and fronting a railroad track on the other side. There were a dozen houses in various stages of disrepair. As I passed the front of the bus, I looked down the road to see a large corrugated metal building at the end. A small sign identified it as Avalon Gin. A cocktail crossed my mind before it registered that this was a cotton gin, not an advertisement for a British distilled spirit. The train depot was just a shack and appeared abandoned, a remnant of a long ago time when trains stopped at every little crossroads. I thought of the John Hurt song. *Sliding Delta* was written about a branch line railroad. Here it was.

A battered pickup truck passed and parked in front of the bus. Two dogs and three excited children jumped down from the back. The dogs engaged the one that had escorted us into town with much butt sniffing and posturing before they raced off to meet a yellow Coca-Cola truck just exiting the county road. The children ran toward Kinder's store.

"Watch for cars!" a woman called out as she climbed from the passenger side of the truck. The children ignored her and ran up the steps of the store.

Kinder's was a single-story, wood-frame building with a false front that made it look taller. It had a large front porch covered by a metal roof held up by six gnarled red cedar trunks someone had sawed off even on the ends and stuck there as roof supports. The foundation of the porch, and presumably the whole store, was large flat stones piled up about three feet off the ground on which sat the rough cut floor joists.

Two old colored men sat on a bench at the end of the porch, whittling and talking and completely oblivious to the bus and the children and the Coca-Cola truck now pulling in ahead of the three dogs and another cloud of dust. In front of the store was a single red Texaco gas pump, and on the side of the porch another, smaller pump with the same red Texaco logo. This one was labeled "kerosene." The whole front of the store was plastered with metal signs advertising everything from "Coca-Cola sold here" to "Chesterfield Satisfies," "Sweet Scotch Snuff, the Good Old Fashioned Kind" and "Nu-Grape Soda."

"Dadeee! He said he gets candy and I don't," cried a little girl bursting out the screen door just as I climbed the worn wooden steps, the couple from the truck right behind me.

"You kids sit down over there and behave," the father said, pointing to the end of the porch away from the two old men.

I stepped aside as the two other children were right behind the first one. The father stood pointing to the end of the porch while they assumed their assigned places, then stepped to the side of the porch and spit tobacco juice out into the yard, still with an eye on the children. He preceded me into the store.

"Sorry about that, Miss Addie," he said, stepping into the store. "Those kids been talkin' 'bout comin' into town all morning. How's your daddy?"

I stepped in, unnoticed.

"He's mending," said Miss Addie, who sat on a stool behind a high counter at the side of the store, cash register to one side, shelves of cigarettes, snuff, chewing tobacco, candy and notions behind her. "The doctor called this morning and said it wasn't as bad as we thought. Thank you for asking."

A beam of sunlight through the side window illuminated tiny sparkles of dust in the air and in Addie's long, chestnut hair.

"Mr. Rooney, those are lovely children. They were just fine. Why little Carole Sue said hello, and Johnny just stood there looking at the candy. There's not a thing wrong with looking at candy. Hello, Mrs. Rooney, I heard some good things about some jelly you made last month."

"You did?" With this talk of her jelly, half a decade vanished from Mrs. Rooney's worn face. "I never see'd so many strawberries as we had this year."

Mrs. Rooney beamed as she approached the counter. She wore a thin floral print cotton dress and men's brogan shoes. Her legs were unshaven.

"Well, you did 'em proud," Addie said. "Mrs. Carver was braggin' on your jelly just yesterday."

Her flashing blue eyes flicked from Mrs. Rooney to Mr. Rooney at the back of the store picking up a sack of corn meal, to the Coke truck out front, and back to Mrs. Rooney. Her smile captivated Mrs. Rooney. And me.

"Hello," she said. Just when I thought she hadn't seen me at all, she did.

I set my suitcase down and unslung the guitar case from my back.

"I just came in on the bus," I said.

I approached the counter, and Mrs. Rooney moved to the back of the store and began to put items into a basket.

"Welcome to Avalon," Addie said. "Is someone coming to pick you up?"

She had a few freckles on her cheeks, and I judged her to be about my age. She wore no jewelry. Her simple cotton blouse was blue oxford cloth with a button-down collar. Preppy for rural Mississippi, I thought.

"No," I said. " I'm just passing through."

It occurred to me that if there were an end of the road anywhere in America, this was it.

"Good morning, Miss Addie!" said the Coke route man as he came through the screen door, letting it slam behind him. I stepped back.

A moment later, his colored assistant rolled a hand truck backward up the steps and deftly swung it around, opened the door and pulled it in. Four yellow wooden cases of 12-ounce Coca-Cola bottles were stacked upon it. He went to the soft drink cooler beside the counter and began loading in bottles of Coke along-side Pepsi, Royal Crown, Dr. Pepper, NuGrape, Orange Crush, Chocolate Soldier, Sunrise Orange and Cream Soda, among others. He was careful to maintain Coke's dominant position within the cooler without taking unfair advantage of the others. Finishing, he pulled empties out of the mixed stack on the other side of the cooler.

"Heard Buck was in the hospital," the Coke man said while preparing the bill. "He doin' OK?"

"Yes, sir," Addie said. "The doctor said he was better this morning."

The route man looked down at the empty bottles being loaded into the now empty cases and recorded that.

"Looks like three cases this time, and two of empties," he said..

Miss Addie peered over at the total, opened the cash register and counted out a few bills and some change. She leaned over the counter toward the assis-tant, who was loading the last of the empties. "How's that baby, James?"

"Oh, he be growin' Miss Addie. He growin' big," James said, a huge smile breaking out as he nodded and began pushing the hand cart toward the door.

"OK, see you on Friday," the route salesman said heading out the door. " Tell Buck hello."

In a moment, the Coke truck started up and headed back to the county highway in a cloud of dust, chased by the three dogs.

The Rooneys came from the back of the store, he with a sack of cornmeal and she with a small basket of items. They set them on the counter. Miss Addie totaled the items on a hand crank adding machine and looked expectantly at Mr. Rooney. It was an awkward moment.

"Uh, work's been slow this week," he said, leaving the end of the statement unspoken.

"That's fine, Mr. Rooney, but with this your account will be $35.22. When you do get some work, you need to come in and put something on it."

"Oh, we will," Mrs Rooney exclaimed, relieved. "I'll have some egg money tomorrow. I'll come by."

Addie opened a drawer by the cash register containing rows of small ac-counts pads, found one with the Rooneys' name on it and added the new purchase. She put the pad back in the drawer and leaned over the counter to reach into a large glass jar of penny candy.

"Mr. Rooney, you tell those kids they were good," as if to rebut his admonishment of their exuberance on entering the store ahead of their parents, "and please give them these." She handed him the candy.

The dogs out front announced another arrival. I stepped back to see a shiny Buick sedan roll to a stop right in front of the steps and an older lady emerge. Climbing the steps with purpose and without a glance to either side, she entered the store. She wore a small blue hat perched upon gray hair meticulously groomed with a blue rinse. The hat sported a small bit of gauze to one side; formal for the location I thought.

Sweeping up to the desk she quickly scanned the store, ignoring me. She wore a starched blue dress with a bit of lace at the bodice, nylon hose and the same sturdy, low-heel, black leather shoes my grandmother wore.

"Aunt Emmabelle!"

Emmabelle leaned across the high counter and threw an arm across Addie's shoulder and gave her a hug and a kiss on the top of her head.

"Oh, child, I came as soon as I heard," Emmabelle said. "I was just up at the hospital, and Buck said he was feeling better. I want you to know that I'm here, and I'm staying as long as I'm needed."

Tears ran down Addie's cheeks, and she looked down at the counter.

"I just need to get my bag," Emmabelle said, turning toward the door.. " I can stay in Buck's room until he comes home."

Addie's eyes flicked to me.

"Uh, I could help with that, ma'am," I said.

"Who are you?" she asked, noticing me for the first time, her gaze indicating that she expected an answer.

Back in Lake Forest, my position in the social fabric was assumed and assured, never questioned. Boys of my acquaintance knew all the social graces but exercised them only when necessary, preferring to "go grubby" when at school and surrounded by our peers. However, with my complete lack of documentation and somewhat checkered recent past, this was not a moment for flippant informality.

"I'm Douglas Spencer, from Lake Forest, Illinois, ma'am. I'm in Mississippi on an eleemosynary grant from the Weathers Foundation to study the musical roots of the Mississippi Delta and their influence on the social structure and industrial development of the New South."

I affected a slight bow and held her gaze, adding, "I'm a junior at Stratmore College."

"Yes," she said, holding out her hand. I was momentarily confused but grasped it in a kind of hand shake. Her eyes searched mine. I felt like I was in the third grade.

"It's the blue suitcase and overnight bag in the trunk," said, taking the keys to the Buick out of her blue leather purse.

I retrieved her bags and followed her through the storeroom at the back of the store, out the back door and across a covered breezeway to a small house.

"Are you Addie's boyfriend?" she asked.

"We've only just met," I said, setting the bags just inside the door but remaining on the porch.

"Thank you, Douglas."

She searched my eyes again, nodded and handed me a dime.

I retraced my steps back into the store. Addie, recovered from her brief show of tears, was counting change on the counter as a tall colored man in worn work clothes watched.

"Thank you, Mr. Evans. Your account is down to just 12 dollars. This is your receipt," she said, smiling at me over his shoulder as she slid the paper across the counter to him.

He walked to the door studying the receipt.

"Well done, Douglas Spencer from Lake Forest, Illinois," she smiled as she sorted the money into the big cash register at her side. "Don't get too proud of your rhetorical skills. She's an English teacher from Jackson."

"The moment seemed to call for a bit of flourish."

"Weathers Foundation?"

"My grandmother gave me $300 dollars to come here over summer vacation to find Mississippi John Hurt and learn to pick the delta blues," I said, nodding at my guitar case in the corner.

"He lives a mile down that road there," she said, pointing out the front door and closing the cash register.

"Really! You know him?" I turned to look out the door, shocked that I'd actually gotten this close.

"Sure, I've known Uncle John since I was a little girl. He comes in here all the time, or did until he got sick."

"Sick?"

"Uncle John and Hennis, his brother, and Shack Pryor went down to Sharkey Bayou to fish, and John fainted. They carried him back here in the back of Hennis' truck. He was in the hospital in Grenada."

"Is he OK?"

"I think so. It's been a few weeks since I've seen him."

"You ever see him play?"

"Sure, he sits out on the porch there, and people come by and stand around and he plays."

"Wow, that's what I came down here to see."

"Where are you staying?"

"I have a bit of a problem," I said, and decided to lay it all out. "I went to the Club Handy in Memphis the other day, a colored club, and, well, I got robbed. I'm going to have to call my grandmother to get some more money."

"Delta blues can be a risky adventure."

"I'm learning that. Might be safer here."

"Maybe," she smiled as she turned around to slide a stack of W.E. Garrett Scotch Snuff onto the shelf behind her. Beside it were similar size cans of Copenhagen, Skoal, Peach, Tops and Tube Rose. The next shelf held pouches of Red Man, Levi Garrett, Beechnut and Mail Pouch.

"Chewing tobacco?" I'd never seen anyone chew. Kinder's seemed to be generously supplied with brands and types.

"And snuff, cigarette tobacco, pipe tobacco and cigars."

She stacked a fresh roll of Tube Rose next to the others.

"You want some?"

"Well, I could use a pack of Marlboros."

I fished out my wallet and flashed my last five.

"At least you're not a vagrant," she said, taking my five and giving me four ones and a half dollar along with the cigarettes.

"A vagrant?" Emmabelle asked as she came through the storeroom. She had changed into her work clothes — a cotton house dress with the same nylon hose and sturdy leather shoes.

"Mr. Spencer was just relating certain adventures he's had while pursuing his research project, Aunt Emmabelle."

"You're a musician?" she asked, nodding at my guitar case.

"Yes, ma'am."

"You ought to introduce him to John Hurt," Emmabelle said to Addie.

"He says that's why he's here," Addie said, grinning but looking down to hide it from Emmabelle.

"You came here to see John Hurt?" Emmabelle asked, a little smile breaking through the creases of sternness.

"Yes, ma'am."

"Was that eleemosynary grant a gift from your grandmother to get you out of Chicago for the summer?" Her smile was growing.

"Yes, ma'am."

I felt transparent and dropped my eyes to the floor to avoid her seeing any more. She pressed her advantage.

"How old are you?"

"Twenty in two weeks."

"Douglas was just going to call his grandmother," Addie intervened.

"I'd love to speak with your grandmother. May I?" asked Emmabelle, who was nothing if not forward.

"Uhh." I had no idea this was coming. "Why?"

"If you're going to be hanging around Avalon, listening to colored folk's music and making eyes at my niece, I want to know something more about you."

With great misgivings, I used their telephone to call my grandmother. I was embarrassed to have to ask for more money, doubly so in front of Addie and her aunt, but I'd had a brush with the law as a vagrant and didn't want that to happen again. Within five minutes, Emmabelle Kinder and my grandmother were friends, and I had a job for the rest of the summer working at Kinder's store, pumping gas, stocking and cleaning up.

Emmabelle shot Addie a glance while I was reciting their rural mail route address to my grandmother to send me a check, thanking her, and assuring her that my trip was going as planned.

"You're being very generous, Mrs. Kinder," I said.

"Miss Kinder," she corrected, as if it were a habit, stern again and looking at Addie.

"Douglas," Addie said, her smile gone as she bent to retrieve something from beneath the counter. As she sat back up, I heard a metallic click, and then another. She stood.

"I think we need to, ah, meet formally."

She came to the end of the counter and around to the front. Braces supported her withered legs, and she walked with crutches.

Chapter 7

"Gimme a dollar's worth," he said as he jumped out of his truck and handed me a dollar bill as he passed me on the step. He was a young man in his 20s, wearing a short-sleeve shirt, jeans and work boots.

I heard the pump come on as I walked to the side of the relatively new pickup. Mudflaps sported the stars and bars of the Confederate battle flag, and a gun rack hung across the back window, complete with lever-action rifle. Was that real? I'd never seen anyone carry a rifle in any kind of vehicle except a police car. It looked real. Was it legal?

I cleared the meter and removed the gas cap, inserting the gas hose nozzle into the tank. At 33 cents a gallon, it took less than a minute to dispense a dollar's worth. I replaced the hose and the gas cap and went to the windshield.

"Check the oil?"

"Naw, thanks," he said, extracting a cigarette from the pack he'd just bought inside. He lit it with a Zippo lighter, started the truck and was gone.

"That guy had a gun in the back window of his truck," I said as I returned to the store. "Is that legal?"

"I think so," Addie said. "Don't trucks come with a gun rack?"

So went my first week at Kinder's store. My wages were two dollars a day, which was somewhat less than minimum wage. But I got a cot in the storeroom, meals, three showers a week in the Kinder's only bathroom, and free access to the privy behind the store. Yes, an outhouse, pit latrine, little house out back – a shithouse. This one was a weathered, bare wood affair with a hand-sawed hole in the seat that someone, long ago, had thoughtfully rounded off with a wood rasp to prevent splinters. It did not have one of those half-moon windows in the door that you see in cartoons.

Sitting on the shitter early in the morning, sun not yet up, birds singing, flies not yet buzzing, smell not too bad before the heat of the day, I began to appreciate life at a more fundamental level. Delta blues are about the basics – love, work, jealously, happiness, retribution, jail and death – and nothing is more basic than taking a dump over a pit with the first cigarette of the day.

Buck Kinder came home the next week. Dr. Quinton Tarver drove his Pontiac Chieftain right up to the front steps and helped Buck out. He looked terrible.

"Daddy!" Addie leaned her crutches on the counter and stood unsupported as Doc Tarver and I helped Buck through the screen door.

Buck seemed to gain strength as he stepped away from our support and embraced his daughter. His worn work shirt hung on his once muscular broad shoulders as he lifted her feet off the worn wooden floor in front of the cash register. He buried his face in her long chestnut hair. His face had a gray look that seemed to foretell a cloudy future.

"You OK, baby?"

"Oh, yes. Aunt Emmabelle is here."

"Who's this guy?" he asked, turning to look at me.

"That's Douglas Spencer from Lake Forest, Illinois. Aunt Emmabelle hired him to pump gas and clean up while you're sick."

There was a momentary hesitation as he took it all in, then a look of resignation.

"Pleased to meet you, Mr. Kinder," I said.

We shook hands, and I understood that moment he'd just had. Probably for the first time in his life, he was forced to step back and let a younger man do the heavy lifting.

"Doctor, are you sure he's well enough to come home?" Emmabelle asked from behind the counter.

"Now, Miss Kinder, Buck's feelin' a whole lot better," Doc Tarver said, turning to Addie. "Addie, your daddy is gonna be just fine, yes, he's gonna be just fine. Don't you worry, he's gonna be just fine. Just fine."

He paused.

"He's gonna have to give up those cigarettes, though. Give 'em up, I told him."

Dr. Tarver, 50-ish, like Buck, heavy-set and dressed in a suit and tie, stepped to Buck's side.

"Got to get you back in the bed, yes, back in the bed. Don't want you to wear yourself out just yet. Back in the bed, Buck."

With his quick Southern accent he kept talking as he steadied Buck from one side while I held him on the other, and we all went through the storeroom toward the breezeway to the house.

"Now, Buck," Doc Tarver said as he opened his doctor's bag in the modest bedroom and took out a bottle of pills, "you need to take some antibiotic pills every day. This bottle will last another week. You take 'em all, y'hear? All of 'em. Miss Kinder, you make sure Buck takes all these pills."

He handed the bottle to Emmabelle.

"Now, I'll be back tomorrow. Yes, tomorrow, and I want him to stay in bed till then. You hear that Buck? Bed until tomorrow. Don't be gettin' up to go out to the store. Bed."

He turned abruptly and stepped to the bedroom door, still talking.

"Now Addie, don't you worry. Your daddy's gonna be just fine, yes, just fine."

He walked through the house and out to the breezeway, still talking.

"Who are you boy?"

"Uh, I'm Douglas Spencer, sir. Miss Kinder hired me to help out around the store while Mr. Kinder is sick."

The doctor's constant, rapid-fire patter was very different from my father's measured, academic speech. I'd heard Dad many times with patients on the telephone, and it was very different. Still, there was a certain utility to Tarver's manner. The visit only took a few minutes, everything he said was reinforced, and his constant talk drowned out any superfluous questions.

"Good. You take care of those ladies out here, Doug. Y'hear? Got to take care of those ladies, and don't let Buck do any work. Y'hear? I'll be back in the mornin'," he said, still talking as he closed the car door.

The lone streetlight in Avalon was across the street from Kinder's store, and it shone into my little corner of the storeroom. A few nights after Buck came home, around midnight, a shadow woke me. Someone shuffled through the storeroom and into the store. I recognized Buck Kinder by the wheezing rasp of his breathing. I lay still. It was his store, and he could roam around it at night if he wanted. I heard the crackle of cellophane and, a moment later the sound of a cigarette lighter. In a moment, I smelled the cigarette smoke. Emmabelle and Addie had taken all the cigarettes out of the house, per Doc's orders.

A minute later, I heard the unmistakable crack and whoosh of a church key popping open a can of beer. I got up.

"Mr. Kinder, you OK?" I asked quietly, entering the store. The lights were off.

"Couldn't sleep. Want a beer?"

"Yes, sir." A beer sounded like the best idea I'd heard all day.

"Call me Buck."

Whoosh.

"Yes, sir. Buck."

"Close that door back there, and let's go out on the porch."

He sat in an old ladder-back chair on the porch and leaned back against the wall. He set the six-pack between us as I took a bench at the end. Tree frogs filled the night with chatter from the big oak by the store, and they were answered by their buddies in the cypress across the street. Clouds obscured the moon. There was no traffic on the county highway and nobody visible in what was left of Avalon. In fact, looking down the street toward the Avalon Gin, there were no lights.

Buck had stifled a cough that came with the first drag on his cigarette inside. Now, he took a long draw and let the burn kick off a paroxysm of coughing that eventually brought up a big glob of phlegm that he deftly spit over the porch rail and out into the street.

"Ah, that's been sittin' down there since supper. You want one?" He offered me the pack; Chesterfields, unfiltered.

I took one, and he handed me the lighter. Harsh, flavorful, I felt the rush right away. I'd been smoking for only less than a year.

"College boy. What are you studyin'?"

"I was pre-med, but I dropped that. I'm in liberal arts now."

"Ah, English. Careful you don't wind up like Emmabelle, an old maid wrapped up in teaching high school kids to conjugate verbs they'll never use."

"Teaching is a calling. Don't know what mine is yet. I like music."

"Oh, yeah. Addie told me about that. You're down here to meet John Hurt and study the blues."

Buck took another long draw and choked through another round of coughing. It was dark, so I couldn't be sure, but the wad he spit over the rail this time might have been black or red.

Chapter 8

"They hang on low limbs, like that one there," Billy Ray Jenkins said, sculling a small, wooden, flat-bottom boat through the dark, still water of Sharkey Bayou two miles from Kinder's store. He and his friend Cooter Davis, recent graduates with Addie from the Holcomb Consolidated High School 10 miles from Avalon, had been discussing the hazards of fishing in a bayou infested with alligators and snakes.

"Gators stay away from people," Cooter said from the front of the boat, leaning over to push us off of a cypress knee as we glided through the shallow water. "But a cottonmouth will come after you, especially this time of year when they're breedin'."

I recalled the reproductive anatomy of reptiles from that fateful comparative anatomy class, the shoal on which my medical career had run aground. The image of the retracted fangs of a pit viper also came to mind.

Billy Ray said, "My uncle Newt knew a guy got bit by a big old cottonmouth. His leg turned blue, then black. His toes curled up. He got delirious one night with the pain and the fever, and they had to cut it off.

"They call him Stumpy now," he laughed.

A rangy six-footer with dark eyes and a ready wit, Billy Ray had taken the lead in welcoming me into the community of kids who hung around the store. The dozen or so "South County" kids were the ones living on the rural school bus route, and Kinder's store was their hangout. He'd been talking about going fishing since Addie introduced us the first day I worked at the store.

I'd had some misgivings about this whole venture. First, Sharkey Bayou was private property, owned by a duck hunting club and clearly marked as such. Second, I'd never been fishing and had no interest in whatever we might catch. The walleye, perch and lake trout fresh from Lake Michigan that we sometimes ate at home had completely satisfied any yearning for fish that I'd ever had. Still, the enthusiasm of Billy Ray's offer to take me out had spread through the group, gaining momentum.

"You want to learn about the blues? You've got to learn to fish," Addie had said, reminding me that John Hurt was going fishing when he fainted and had to go to the hospital.

So, reluctantly, I met Billy Ray and Cooter before dawn on a Saturday and we bounced down the rutted road to Sharkey Bayou in his father's truck with the small johnboat protruding from the bed. We lifted it into the water, stowed our gear – some minnows, worms, three long cane poles, a stringer, and some water and candy bars – and shoved off.

"They're out here in the middle this time of year," Billy Ray said as he sculled us out into the open middle of the bayou. "We'll fish at different depths 'til we find 'em."

And so we had. We loaded up with minnows and fished at different depths and, within five minutes, Cooter scored a fish identified by both of them as a black crappie. It was small by my estimation, but they pronounced it a slab. When we all lowered to the same depth, we caught a half-dozen more, relatives of the first one, no doubt. Then the bite stopped.

Billy Ray moved us twice more with no luck. As the sun rose to shine through the cypress canopy, we moved into the dark shallows at the edge, and the talk returned to reptiles; which ones lived in the bayou, and how many were poisonous.

Sweat stained Cooter's blue work shirt as he leaned out the front of the boat, grabbing cypress knees to pull us into a dark pool covered around the edges with duckweed, a light green plant that looks like leaves floating on the surface.

"There's a big ole' bass or a flathead cat in there," Billy Ray whispered, handing me a pole. "Put it right over there." He nodded at some open water off to the side.

I lifted the pole and swung the minnow out into the center of the pool and dropped it in, ready to see the bobber yank down out of sight.

"Snake!" Billy Ray yelled just as something soft hit the back of my neck and fell behind me.

I turned to see a thick, dark serpent with bright eyes lying just behind my seat in the bottom of the boat. The beast was six inches from my butt.

"Ayyyi!" Cooter yelled from the front of the boat.

I didn't know whether he was just reinforcing Billy Ray's warning or if he'd encountered another snake up there. It could be a nest of vipers. I jumped out of the boat.

Well, it wasn't really a jump, as in a clean leap from one point to another. No, it was more a stand straight up, hit head on overhanging branch, fall to the side while extending a leg to try to find something solid to stand on while still exiting the boat, then catching the other leg on the side of the boat and capsizing the whole enterprise, then falling face first into the bayou. I rolled upright and attempted to swim but before I could my feet found the muddy bottom. We were in only three feet of water. I stood up.

"Acchhh! Cheeew! Wow!" Cooter had gone down with the ship, so to speak, and was just emerging from under the bow of our capsized boat spewing water and flailing his arms to dislodge any creature that might be nearby. The minnow bucket and our half full water bottle floated nearby.

"Ha ha ha! Gotcha!" Billy Ray, soaking wet from falling off the back of the boat stood waving the rubber snake.

My anger lasted only a moment. We were all in the same boat, or rather, standing around the same boat, equally wet. I realized it had been a setup from the start.

"Let me see that thing," I said, anger giving way to laughter.

Billy Ray tossed it over. It floated. And it really did look real.

We righted the boat, retrieved the stringer of fish and our other gear, helped each other back in and went back to fishing, reliving the event a dozen times before a dark pool on the other side of the bayou yielded the flathead catfish that

Billy Ray had predicted before. Eight pounds on the scale he kept in the truck, slimy and a sickly yellow brown color, this was easily the most disgusting creature I'd ever seen. Billy Ray and Cooter were ecstatic.

"This makes a fish fry," Billy Ray said, laying the flathead out on the tailgate of the truck and plunging a fillet knife into the back of its head and jimmying it around, effectively pithing the fish, paralyzing it for the skinning and gutting that was to come. While explaining that the flathead looked terrible but would produce sweet delectable meat, he nailed the head to a board, cut a circle around the beast's head and pulled its skin off in strips with pliers. Then he gutted it, throwing the head and guts back into the bayou.

Cooter, meanwhile scaled the half dozen crappie with his pocket knife, tossing them into the minnow bucket, now filled with bayou water.

When he was finished with the catfish Billy Ray retrieved the scaled crappie and, with the larger knife, cut off the heads and pulled the guts out. In 10 minutes, we were bouncing back toward the store.

"Whoa! Stop! Stop!" Buck Kinder yelled, stepping out on the porch of Kinder's store. "You can't light a fire over there, you'll blow the place up."

Billy Ray and Cooter and I had filled a ceramic charcoal bucket about the size of a 10-quart pail and doused it with lighter fluid. Cooter held a book of matches. We were right in front of the store and had taken no notice of the bright red Texaco gas pump not five feet away. We moved to the side of the building while Addie and a couple of her girlfriends watched from the porch.

Word of our expedition to Sharkey Bayou and my experience with the snake had spread rapidly. I wondered whether this crowd had gathered to eat fish or to witness Billy Ray and Cooter and that college boy from Chicago try to fry them.

The catfish had been filleted and the thick fillets cut into smaller pieces, which were now soaking in a quart of buttermilk in the dairy cooler inside. The crappie were whole without their heads, also in the buttermilk. Cooter had gone home to get some of his mother's famous seasoned fish breading and promised "the best fish you ever tasted." We stood around retelling the snake story while the charcoal heated the ceramic bucket to red hot, then Cooter produced a large cast iron frying pan and a can of Crisco. I moved to the porch.

"You sure you want to sit next to a guy who smells like the bayou?" I asked as Addie scooted over on the bench at the end of the porch to make room for me. Saturday was one of my shower days, but not until later.

Her shy smile as she looked down into her lap answered that question.

"You knew, didn't you?" I asked, sitting next to her.

"Billy Ray's had that snake for a couple of years," she said. "He pulls it out on anyone who goes fishing with him. As soon as anyone heard he'd asked you to go fishing, they knew you'd get the snake. I hope you're not mad."

She smelled fresh and happy. Happy? How can a smell be happy? I pondered that while I turned around behind her to check out Billy Ray and Cooter's progress with the fire, and to get another whiff of her. Happy.

"No. I'm not mad. Hell, they got as wet as I did." I chuckled at the memory of all three of us soaked, muddy, laughing in the bayou.

"I asked Daddy to see if Uncle John could come play his guitar and sing for my birthday next month."

"Wow! That would be wonderful, thanks." I hugged her, a bit awkwardly. As I did, I looked over her shoulder. Everyone was smiling.

Billy Ray had backed his truck beside the store, and the open tailgate was again the table on which the work was done, this time cutting up potatoes and onions and breading the fish. Soon the Crisco was hot and smoking and Cooter dropped a piece of fish into the fat. The grease splattered, boiled up over the side of the pan and dropped down into the burning charcoal. The whole enterprise burst into flames 4 feet high.

"Whoa!" Cooter jumped back.

I recalled reading somewhere that you should cover a grease fire with a lid, but that didn't seem feasible here, as the fire surrounded the pan. What to do? It was their show, and I stayed put. Buck Kinder stepped out the screen door from the store. A dog barked. Two colored boys riding by on a bicycle stopped to watch.

Nonplussed, Cooter grabbed a towel and approached the towering inferno. He crouched low, bending to the side so his face was below the fire and took hold of the handle of the cast iron pan. He stepped sideways as he rose and flicked the burning grease out into the gravel drive. It flared, sputtered and died. The grease in the charcoal bucket burned out.

"Better start over," he said, setting the hot pan on the truck tailgate.

The dog approached the hot piece of fish and sniffed from a safe distance, marking it, no doubt, for some future exploration. The two colored boys got back on their bicycle and wobbled down the street.

I'd lifted that frying pan when Cooter first brought it over, and it was heavy. I took another look at Cooter. He was stout, and it wasn't fat.

"Good thing you boys moved that fire or we'd all be in trouble," Buck said, stepping to the side of the porch in front of Addie and me. One of Addie's friends, sitting in the ladder-back chair got up, and he sat down. Actually, it was more of a collapse, just from the effort of walking out the door. Buck was not getting stronger.

The grease was reheated and more fish put in, this time before it got too hot, and the fish fry progressed without incident. The first plate was offered to Emmabelle, who declined, and then to Buck, who didn't. Addie was next, and she shared hers with me.

"You ever eat any crappie?" she asked, picking up the single fried crappie we'd been served, crispy and hot.

"Never saw one before this morning."

"First, pull this top fin off," she said, pulling on the dorsal fins, which came off with the bones that supported them.

"Then these," and she pulled the pectoral fins, which came out with the attached bones, then the tail, which came easily off.

"Then flip it over," she said and took her fork and inserted it from the top and flipped one side off of the spine and ribs. "And, there it is," she said proudly, indicating I should eat it. It was a boneless fillet, crispy and spicy on one side and soft and flavorful on the other.

"Oh, that's good," I said.

The problem was, we'd caught only six crappie, and there were 8 people at the fish fry. Somehow, the six little fish were distributed in a manner that didn't cause any fights. Then the catfish was fried. Addie's two friends had prepared side dishes or desserts, and there was a mountain of fried potatoes, sliced with the skins on. Another first for me.

"Any bones in this?" I asked, picking up a piece of catfish about as big as two fingers together, breaded and steaming hot.

"Nope." She looked expectantly.

"Wait," Billy Ray said, rushing up the steps. "First, you got to put some hot sauce on it," and he doused it with some Louisiana Hot Sauce. "Then, you take a bite and follow it with a bite of onion."

"Oh, that's good. He was ugly, but tasty."

We ate all the fish, all the potatoes, and all the sides and desserts. The dog went back to the first piece of fish. The sun dipped behind the trees, and shadows advanced from the big oaks at the back. The tree frogs started in. The two colored boys came by again headed back from where they'd come. I went inside and retrieved my guitar case.

"Come all of you cowboys …" I sang, opening up with Woody Guthrie's *Ranger's Command.* It's an easy song because you can just strum the chords with a simple *doom tum tum* rhythm, no fancy picking needed. Addie slid to the edge of the bench to allow me to swing sideways and lean against the wall so the guitar faced out from the front of the store. The others paired up. Billy Ray sat on the tailgate of his truck with his girl and Cooter and his girl were on the steps. Buck opened a beer.

No college party of the day was complete without someone bringing out a guitar and singing, and I'd starred in my share of gatherings. I always opened with *Ranger's Command* because it's easy, and because of the wonderful visual images of cowboys and a pretty girl who agreed to go on the roundup and, when the rustlers hit, "she rose from her warm bed with a gun in each hand."

I ran through my repertoire of folk songs of the day popularized by Peter, Paul and Mary, the Kingston Trio, the Weavers and Pete Seeger. I played the twelve-bar blues song I'd learned from the street musician in Memphis, and closed with *Red River Valley.* This had always worked for me, because everyone knows the words and tune and can sing along. I'd sung this song since music class in the third grade. This time was different. When I came to the last verse, sitting there on the bench with Addie ...

So come sit by my side if you love me
Do not hasten to bid me adieu
Just remember the Red River Valley
And the cowboy that loved you so true.

Chapter 9

Finishing up in the privy one morning, I walked out in front of the store, admiring the straightness of the cotton rows in the field across the highway. In the couple of weeks I'd been there, the plants had grown to be nearly knee-high. I decided to go have a closer look. The morning was cool, and the air was soft and fragrant with the scent of magnolia and tupelo.

The little plants were only 6 inches or so apart. I had watched Cooter Davis' father carefully drive his Ford tractor down the rows a few days before, taking out the emerging weeds and grass. I walked down the rows just taking it all in, enjoying the morning. I heard an airplane approach.

Looking up, I saw a biplane, like an old World War I fighter. He circled the field and I watched, thinking there must be an airfield nearby. I thought it might be fun to drop by there sometime and see this old relic. Then he came over low, and I waved to him. He rose to clear the trees at the end of the field and dropped a wing, turned and came back, lower still. He was waving at me, so I waved back. He crossed the highway and turned, coming back over a little higher. Just overhead, he cut the engine and shouted something to me. I couldn't tell what he said, but I waved again. He restarted the engine, exited the field, turned and came back. This time he was really low, just above the cotton.

I had a flash of memory. The movie *North by Northwest*, starring Cary Grant and Eva Marie Saint, had been a favorite date movie when I was in high school. There's a scene in that movie in which an airplane, a biplane just like this one, chases Cary Grant, almost running him over. The plane was coming right down the row where I was standing. I panicked, turned and began to run back toward the store.

Zoom! The airplane roared over my head. I kept running, dashed across the highway and sprinted up the steps to the store. He turned again, came in low over the privy, and started spraying just at the edge of the highway. I watched in amazement as he painted the field with a mist in a dozen quick passes and was gone.

A white pickup pulled into the drive a couple of hours later, "Ace's Aerial Applications" painted on the door.

I had a sense of apprehension as I descended the steps. A man in white coveralls got out and stood there eyeing me, chewing on the unlit stub of a cigar.

"You the guy that stood in the cotton field over there and waved at a crop duster?" he asked. "Malathion will take the starch out of your shirt collar."

"I'm sorry. I never saw a crop duster before."

"Really. Where you from?"

"Chicago. I'm sorry, uh, I guess I owe you a Coke or something for not just spraying over me."

"OK. I accept. Fill it up first, though."

He seemed to lighten up some and went into the store. The pump came on as soon as Addie saw who it was.

I filled the tank, cleaned the windshield, checked the oil and jogged up the steps into the store with the total. Addie and the man were having a laugh as he related watching me running down the cotton row and across the highway.

"I owe, uh, the gentleman a Coke," I said, taking one from the cooler and fishing a dime out of my pocket. "I kind of got in the way of spraying the field over there."

"You're learning all sorts of new things since coming to our fair state," Addie said.

"Ace McNutt," he said, taking the Coke and shaking my hand. "You certainly seemed fascinated."

We walked back out to the truck. The air still smelled like garlic from the spray.

"You know, you can't go back in that field for two days," Ace said.

"So, what were you spraying?"

"Malathion. Ervin Davis called me yesterday. He's got boll weevils in that field."

"Really?"

"Yeah. Well, he had weevils last year, and we thought we had the upper hand, but he found some when he plowed the other day."

"I'm really sorry. I didn't know I was waving at a crop duster, and then when you came in low all I could think of was that movie, *North by Northwest.*' I guess I panicked."

"You looked just like the guy in the movie," he said. "When I came over those trees I was doing 85 miles an hour, and it looked for a moment like you were going to out run me."

He got a big laugh out of that.

"You shut the engine off to yell at me. Isn't that kind of risky?"

"I pulled the throttle back and, yes, it is, but I only pulled it back for a moment," Ace said. " If the engine stalls, that would be a big problem."

"You smoke cigars? Maybe I owe you a cigar, too."

He smiled and chuckled again. I loped up the steps and grabbed an El Producto, our top-of-the-line cigar, and slapped a quarter on the counter. Addie just smiled and shook her head as she dropped it into the cash drawer.

"So, you must have an airfield somewhere close by," I said as he lit up the cigar. "I'd like to come by sometime and see your plane up close."

"Sure. We work mainly in the morning. Once it gets hot, the wind picks up and the spray won't settle right. The field is just west of the road to Greenwood, down about five miles. You'll see the sign. Stop by anytime."

He turned to get back in his truck.

"Sunday is my only day off. Do you spray on Sundays?"

He paused and looked me over before replying.

"We work seven days a week in the summer," he said. "You want a job on Sunday? I need to let my helper off occasionally. I need someone to help me load the sprayer."

And so, on the following Sunday, I had a new job.

The eastern sky was just beginning to glow when we pushed the aircraft out of the hangar. It smelled strongly of gasoline and chemicals. Though it seemed a large aircraft, it was easy for the two of us to push. It was made of painted cloth fabric over a wood frame with wires holding it all together, so it wasn't that heavy.

"That's a Stearman," Ace said proudly.

"It looks just like the crop duster in the movie."

"It is. That was a Stearman. The Army bought something like 10,000 Stearmans to use as trainers during World War II. It's a good, reliable aircraft. This one was built in 1943."

"Older than me," I said, admiring it.

"Oh, and it's had some mileage," Ace said. "After the war, you could get one of these for next to nothing. It was the first really good crop duster. People would pull the front seat out and put in a hundred-gallon tank attached to sprayers on the underside of the wings. I bought this one in west Texas at an auction. It had been dusting down in Mexico for 10 years. It was all I could afford at the time. I overhauled the engine, replaced most of the cloth, added some supports to the struts and around the tank, and flew it up here. I don't know who the fool was that flew it before me, but if he filled up that hundred-gallon tank, he must have been a hell of a pilot. It flew like a concrete aircraft with that 800 extra pounds. I only filled it up about three-quarters full."

"When was that?"

"Fifty-six. I had been out of the Air Force for a year and couldn't get an airline job. Didn't want one really. I flew for a year, dusting with a partial tank, to make enough to upgrade it. Malathion had just come out. It was less toxic than DDT and killed boll weevils better than anything else. Boll weevils were bad then, and everyone wanted their fields sprayed. I made a little money and flew it up to Mid-Continent Aviation in Hayti, Missouri, and they replaced the 220-horsepower engine with a Wright radial 450, and put in a 200-gallon tank. I love this airplane."

Ace let me climb into the cockpit, which was the area of the back seat. It had virtually no instruments, just a radio, airspeed indicator, oil pressure, attitude indicator and fuel gauge. I sat there and wiggled the stick and depressed the rudder pedals, watching over my shoulder as the rudder turned.

"OK," Ace said, "time to get to work. I write up a work order when I schedule a field. It has the location and the size of the field. I keep them in there."

I climbed down and followed him over to his office adjacent to the hangar and a small warehouse.

"While I'm out spraying, you get ready for the next field," he said as he opened the schedule book on the counter, then walked through to the warehouse.

"This is Malathion," he held up a plastic gallon jug from a pallet. "Each one has five pounds of Malathion in it. We spray a half a pound per acre.

"You figure out how many of these to put into the tank, remembering that we dilute every gallon with three gallons of water from that hose over there," he said, pointing out the window at a hose stretching across the taxiway as he turned and walked back through the office.

"Then you write it down on this invoice," he said as he took a pad of blank invoices out of a drawer and dropped it on the desk. "You go over it with me before I take off."

"OK." I was struggling to keep it straight.

"Anytime" – he started, then paused for emphasis. "Anytime there is a notation on the schedule there" – he pointed to a work order – "there." He paused again.

"Anytime you see something written there, be sure to remind me. Look," he said, picking up a work order. "See, it says there's a new power line next to Lester Hudgins' north quarter section."

He looked at me sternly.

"And here," he said, picking up another one, "cattle next to Luther Dees' field."

"What do you do about cattle?"

"Run dry over 'em, and they move to the other side of the pasture."

"Like you did with me."

"Yeah."

It was only half a day, but I earned my five dollars. We sprayed two half-sections, a quarter-section, and two eighth-sections, 960 acres. That's 96 gallon jugs hoisted into the tank, 288 gallons of water and about 50 gallons of 100 octane aviation gasoline that I pumped. I envied Ace, who swooped up into the cool air on the way to the next field and left me sweltering on the ground to carry out another load of jugs.

Ace dropped me off behind Kinder's store by the breezeway to the house. I was soaked with sweat and smelled of gasoline and Malathion.

"Don't come in here, Douglas Spencer," Emmabelle said "There's a hose around the back of the house. Wash off first."

I stripped off down to my boxer shorts, feeling like the whole world was watching, and hosed down. Addie was standing on the porch when I finished. She handed me a towel, smiling shyly. I dried off and walked through the house to the bathroom for a shower with soap.

The next Sunday, I pitched watermelons.

The driver of the flatbed 18 wheeler cut the stem with his pocket knife, and I picked the watermelon up and handed it to a colored boy named Jessie, who handed it to Billy Ray, who handed it to Cooter, who pitched it up to the farmer who had grown the melons standing in the back of the pickup. When we had a load, we drove over to the tractor-trailer and took turns pitching the melons up to the driver who stacked them, just so, on the flatbed. He expected to have them at the Central Market in Chicago the next afternoon.

"Big money, huh city boy?" Cooter teased.

Now I knew where his big arms came from. I'd signed on to pitch watermelons because the $2 a day from Kinder's wasn't covering expenses and I needed to have a little bit to get back to school in the fall. The $8 a day to pitch watermelons had seemed to be a good deal. Now I was so tired I could hardly stand, and there was still a quarter of that flatbed to stack.

"It's buck night at the drive-in over at Grenada," Billy Ray said, stepping in front of me to take over pitching up to the driver on the flatbed. "Whole carload for a buck. We'll take the truck, put a bunch in the back and get in for a dollar. Plus, it's a double feature – *Rio Bravo* and *Thunder Road*."

"Westerns?" I'd never heard of either movie.

"*Rio Bravo* is a Western. It has John Wayne, Dean Martin, Angie Dickinson and Ricky Nelson. They run it again every summer, and it always fills the house, especially when they show it with *Thunder Road* – fast cars and moonshine."

Billy Ray paused to pitch another watermelon, then added, "You could take Addie."

"She was valedictorian of our high school class," Cooter said, as if I needed additional information.

"She was president of the Student Council, and Homecoming Queen," Billy Ray said, "and you'd never guess who the Homecoming King was. Our own Cooter Davis!"

Cooter said, "Yeah, we rode through town on the Homecoming float, band playing, people waving and cheering. It was fun. We got to dance the first dance at the gym that night."

"She danced?" I asked, curious.

"Sure," Cooter said. " I had to hold her up, but, she danced. Just the slow ones."

He paused for a moment, then added, "We drove around after, then I took her home. We didn't do nuthin', or anything."

That seemed to be a sort of due diligence indicating that her reputation was clean.

"We all care a lot about Addie," Billy Ray added, pitching a watermelon.

"Yeah," Cooter said.

So I'd gotten a suggestion, some due diligence and a warning.

Two hours later, Billy Ray dropped me off at the store. I was exhausted, sweat-soaked and sticky with watermelon juice from eating the ones that broke when we dropped them. I felt rich with eight dollars in my jeans.

"How about a nice slice of watermelon?" Addie asked, smiling when I came through the door.

"No thanks. How about a date tonight? Billy Ray says the drive-in at Grenada has a double-feature. He and Cooter are taking their girlfriends and invited us to go along."

"OK." She beamed.

"If I were you, I'd ask Aunt Emmabelle to let me break the routine and take a shower before we go."

"I'm sure Aunt Emmabelle would want you to be clean. The shower is all yours."

Later, after supper, there was some pushback from Buck.

"No. Addie can't go to the drive-in in Billy Ray's truck. You take her in my truck," Buck said, handing me the keys. "Fill it up out front."

When Billy Ray drove up in a cloud of dust, I was just lifting Addie into the passenger side of Buck's truck. She wore yellow shorts with a blue blouse, and her hair was in a ponytail. She laid her crutches beside her on the seat and immediately began chattering out the window with the other two girls. They had been in almost constant telephone contact since I'd asked her out.

"Have fun, baby," Buck said, coming to the passenger side window to give her a peck on the forehead.

"Stay out of the cigarettes," she reminded him.

And, we were off. She waved back to him as we turned onto the county highway. A mile down the road, she turned and looked back, then picked up her crutches on the seat between us and moved them to the other side. She scooted over next to me.

Billy Ray and Cooter and their dates were all crammed into the front seat of his truck. We drove in right behind them, paid our dollar and followed them to the last row. Billy Ray turned the truck around, pointed away from the screen. I parked next to them. All six of us got in the back of Billy Ray's truck.

Rio Bravo was the first feature, and they'd seen it more than once. The guys loved Dean Martin's nifty fast-draw scene and then commented on Angie Dickinson's seduction of the straight-arrow sheriff, John Wayne. The guys thought Dean Martin's song was cool, and that Ricky Nelson's song was lame. The girls liked everything about Ricky Nelson. At the intermission, I carried Addie back to our truck to get her crutches, and we accompanied the group, girls chattering away, to the concession stand.

"Want to put a little kick in your Coke?" Billy Ray asked as we got back to the trucks, showing a half-pint of whiskey.

"No," I laughed. "I'm not going to take Buck Kinder's daughter home with booze on my breath."

"Wise. He was a Marine. Got a Purple Heart during World War II," Cooter said. "When he was younger, nobody messed with Buck Kinder."

Thunder Road was more of a guy's movie, with Robert Mitchum shooting Cumberland Gap in a souped up '57 Ford, driving moonshine into Knoxville and Memphis. We split up, with Cooter and his date in the back and Billy Ray and his girl in the front of his truck. Addie and I repaired to the privacy of Buck's truck.

Two hours later, we turned off the country road back at the store.

"Better comb your hair," Addie said, brushing back my hair. "Don't want Daddy to think we've been making out or anything."

Doc Tarver's car was parked in front of the store. He and Buck were sitting in the dark on the front porch, smoking cigarettes and drinking beer.

"Daddy! Are you OK?" Addie leaned over me to speak out the window.

"Sure, baby. Doc just came by on a social call. You better check in with Emmabelle, she's been out here twice asking why you aren't home yet."

"Daddy! The movie just got over. We didn't even stop for a Coke on the way home."

Addie's virtue seemed to be a topic of considerable importance in Avalon.

"I know, baby," Buck said. "Check in so she doesn't come out here again and I have to throw away another perfectly good Chesterfield."

I drove the truck around to the back and lifted Addie out, an act that was taking on significant emotional impact each time it was repeated. I learned later that she could get into and out of a truck unassisted, but I wasn't complaining.

Addie had managed to give me one chaste kiss and then one that wasn't so chaste before the light blinked and Emmabelle was there in the door.

"You're right on time, Mr. Spencer," Emmabelle said as she opened the door to the house. "I like a young man who can be depended upon."

I said goodnight and was left standing in the breezeway. I walked through the storeroom and dark store to the porch.

"Take a seat, Doug," Buck said as I opened the screen door. He was leaning back in the ladder-back, his usual spot, and Doc was on the bench at the end. I got a chair from the other side of the porch.

Whoosh! Buck handed me a beer.

Two hours passed. We talked briefly about my date with Addie, the St. Louis Cardinals and their prospects for the pennant in 1965, the Game of the Week to be played on CBS the following day and broadcast by Mississippi hero Dizzy Dean. Then, as the beer began to take effect, they asked me what I thought about the college kids coming down from the North over the summer to register colored voters in rural Mississippi.

"Do they need any help?" I asked, innocently.

"A lot of them can't read," Buck countered.

"Do you have to read to vote?"

"Ah, Doug," Doc jumped in. "You are a bright boy. Bright boy, yes you are. There are a lot of adults in Mississippi who can't read. Nobody is suggesting that the white ones shouldn't vote, but they claim the colored aren't qualified. It's racial prejudice and bigotry, and it's wrong. Wrong, dammit, and those college students are welcome to come down here and bring the colored to the polls. Bring 'em on."

Buck said, "Some don't think people from up North should be coming down here interfering in our business. Some people feel very strongly about that, Doc. Very strongly. I've had some people asking about Doug, asking what's he doing down here. Some of those people are in the Klan."

"I'm just trying to learn how to play some blues on my guitar," I said. "And now I've met a girl."

I threw that last in, just on a whim. It was the beer talking. It got a laugh and another round of beer. Then Buck went through Addie's considerable accomplishments in high school and how their rural school might not have all the fancy equipment of the city schools, but the kids who studied could go to college and make something of themselves. He was proud that Addie had already been accepted at Millsap's College in Jackson for the fall semester. Doc threw his weight behind that endorsement of the local school system, then they got quiet for a moment.

"Do you still remember that night, Doc?" Buck asked, pulling another Chesterfield out of his shirt. He lit it and blew the first drag out and looked out across the road and the field beyond.

"Like it was yesterday," Doc said, looking at the floor. This was Buck's story and he was going to let Buck tell it.

"She was just 5," Buck said. "The prettiest little girl you've ever seen. Fun, active, full of life."

He paused and looked out across the field again.

"Then, one day, she came in from playing, right out there," he said, pointing to the parking lot by the store. "It had rained, and there was a big mud puddle, and she'd been running through it. The next day, she had a fever and a headache, and she vomited and felt bad. Her Mama was already gone, it was just the two of us here at the store. She looked sick. I called Doc."

He looked down at the floor, unable to continue.

Doc picked up the story.

"We had a polio epidemic in 1952, all over the country. We'd had half a dozen cases here in Carroll County, and the County Health Department was on high alert. Summer was polio time, and every parent dreaded hearing their child didn't feel good in the summer. Any fever, and they'd be on the phone right away. It was a busy time. When I got here, Addie was already drooling, because the nerves controlling her swallow mechanism were affected. It was bulbar polio, affecting the part of the brain at the top of the spinal cord. I took her in my car to the hospital."

"Doug," Buck said, "you don't know what it's like to sit there in the hospital and watch your little girl …" He sobbed. "They had this machine they'd turn on when her spit was building up, and they'd suck it out. She couldn't swallow, and she couldn't talk. Her eyes would get big, and we'd know it was time for the nurse to turn on that machine. Then, about midnight, she started gasping for breath. She'd lie there real quiet for a half a minute and all of a sudden she'd give a big gasp, and her eyes were wide and, just, just, looking at me."

Reliving the experience gave him a desperate look, as if he were there again.

"Then, she got real quiet and her eyes just kind of …"

He sobbed again.

"She just opened her eyes and looked up, like at God or something. I shook her and she gasped, and then she gasped again and came out of it. She looked at me again. That's when the iron lung got there."

Doc said, "There weren't enough iron lungs for every child. Some died."

Doc sat straight up and set his beer on the floor.

"I called the health department from here, as soon as I saw Addie, and they called the Mississippi State Department of Health. They found one that a child had been using in Greenwood, but the child died that afternoon. They put it on a truck and it got to the hospital in Grenada just in time."

Buck said, "It was like she couldn't remember to breathe, and she'd just drift off. I was shaking her and hugging her and holding her. Then they rolled this big cylindrical tank into the room and plugged it in. They opened one end and slid out the bed, and I lifted my baby onto it. They closed it up and just her head was sticking out the end. When they turned it on the motor started to whir, and this big bellows thing underneath began to move and … and … she breathed."

Chapter 10

"We go to church on Sunday."

Addie had followed me out to the porch to sit while I ate my supper later in the week. Meals were part of my pay, but I wasn't part of the family, so I ate in the store.

"Good." I was digging in to baked Spam with a pineapple glaze, macaroni and cheese, sliced tomatoes and crowder peas, which are like black-eyed peas, only better. I had learned how to swab up some of that pea juice with a biscuit, and that's what I was doing at that moment.

"I'm in the choir," she said.

"You sing?"

"Yes."

"I didn't hear you sing the other night when we were all out here on the porch."

"You were doing just fine. You go to church in Chicago?"

"You think we Yankees are all a bunch of pagans, worshiping idols and sacrificing virgins in some kind of big city ritual?" I asked in mock indignation. "I go to church. Well, sometimes. I belong to the First Presbyterian Church of Lake Forrest."

"We're Presbyterians, Southern Presbyterians."

"I didn't know there was more than one kind."

I hadn't been in a church since my grandfather's funeral, five years before.

"You a soprano?"

"Yes," she said, looking down modestly. "I'm not as good as you are, so don't ask me to sing for you."

So that's how I wound up in a rural Presbyterian Church on a Sunday morning in July. If I wanted to hear Addie sing, this was the only way. It was a small clapboard affair with 50 congregants and a dozen in the choir, including Addie, who sang lead soprano and was, actually quite good. The choir's anthem that morning was *Come They Fount of Every Blessing,* an old standby that even I, recently exposed as a heathen, remembered from my long ago church days. I found myself humming the traditional American tune as we exited the church. I shook the minister's hand and was waiting with Buck and Emmabelle for Addie to shuck her choir robe and join us in Emmabelle's car for the ride back to the store.

"Buck," I blurted out on impulse, "would the church let me borrow a hymnal, just for a couple of days?"

I'd been thinking of guitar chords and wondering if I could put something together.

"Sure, just go back in and get one. I'll talk to the reverend."

The tune is in D major, not a bad key for a guitar, and I studied it on the way home, fending off some ribbing from Addie, who said that if I'd go to church more often, I wouldn't find the music so exotic. The words begin with Old Testament images of battles and victories, so they wouldn't make a typical folk song, but it is a catchy tune. Back at the house, Addie and Emmabelle worked for a couple of hours, and we had a tasty fried chicken dinner. I was invited to eat with the family.

A few days later, I drove Addie into Greenwood to buy a thank-you gift for Emmabelle, who was packing up to go back home. Southern ladies, and Addie was very much being raised to be one, are big on giving each other doilies, curios and bric-a-brac all done up in frilly packages. A department store in Greenwood had a whole section of such stuff.

"Oh, this is cute, what do you think?" Addie asked. She held up a small ceramic swan with open wings that made a small cup or cavity.

"She needs one of those. She could put toothpicks in it."

"Toothpicks? No, silly. It's just for decoration. Go someplace else, and I'll do this myself, Mrs. Gregory can help me." She laughed and shooed me away.

Freed from the bric-a-brac mission, I walked across the street to a drugstore and bought a birthday card for Addie. The selection took a few minutes. I wanted friendly without too much in the way of romantic overtones. Returning to the department store, I came upon a developing drama.

Mrs. Gregory was just finishing wrapping the gift, and Addie stood at the counter watching. The store was run by Mrs. Gregory and another lady, who had emptied the merchandise from a cabinet of shelves and pushed it into the aisle in front of the cash register.

A man entered the front door right behind me. After the usual greetings and "how's so and so's," they clustered around the cabinet. The ladies had decided they didn't need the cabinet any longer and had given it to the man's wife, and he was there to pick it up.

"Do you need any help getting it into your truck?" Mrs. Gregory asked.

"No," he said as he looked out the glass front window and walked to the door. He opened it and looked up and down the sidewalk outside and yelled,. "Hey! Boy!"

Two young colored men in their early 20s came into sight from further up the sidewalk toward the courthouse. "Yes, suh!"

"You work out at the MacDonald farm?"

"No, suh. We work for Mister Hedges."

"Oh, yeah. Out south of the Mandeville Gin."

"Yes, suh."

"Come in here," he said, turning and walking into the store. "Mrs. Gibson wants to move this cabinet. You boys take it out to my truck."

"Yes, suh!"

They followed him into the store, anxious and submissive, and nodded politely to the ladies. They picked up the cabinet.

"Careful with that, now," the man warned.

"Yes, suh."

The two men carried the cabinet gingerly out to the truck and then returned. "Anything else, suh?"

"No." He handed each of them a dime. "Ya'll go on now," and he dismissed them with a wave.

I couldn't believe what I'd just seen. Those were not boys, they were grown men and older that I was. If someone had flagged them down on State Street in Chicago, using "Hey, boy," it would have been an entirely different kind of drama. Anywhere in the country, two young men walking down the street and greeted with some polite sort of hello, and properly asked to do a lady a favor by carrying some item to the curb, would cheerfully help out. This had not been that at all. I'd been seeing what I thought were the remnants of segregation, but this wasn't a remnant of anything, this was clear evidence of a profound, systemic intimidation.

Then it grew more troubling. The cabinet wasn't that big. The man could have easily carried it out with the help of one of the women, and I was standing right there perfectly capable of pitching in. I was ignored. It wasn't about getting the cabinet out to the truck.

I pondered this mystery as Addie and I climbed into the truck, and it began to clarify as I thought back over the event. He'd gotten the hook into them right at the first, when he determined where they lived and worked. They didn't know him, but after that hook, they knew he knew where they lived. Why would some random white guy who knows where they live make them so afraid?

Then I thought of all the pickup trucks I'd gassed up in the past month. Virtually all of them had gun racks in the back window, and fully half had guns. It wasn't hunting season, and there were no dangerous animals in the region that one would need a firearm for protection. What did they need guns for?

"You're awfully quiet," Addie said as we pulled out from the curb and headed back to Kinder's store.

"That guy back there, in the store. Did he know those two colored boys?"

"I don't think so."

"So, just two guys walking by."

"As far as I know."

"Did they seem afraid, to you?"

"Well, they were respectful …"

She was sensing that I was disturbed by what I'd seen.

"In their place?"

"He was a bit harsh."

"And, he put them," I said, pausing and looking at Addie, "in their place."

She didn't respond, and we rode in silence for a bit.

"You don't do that in your store," I said. "You show respect for every person who comes in."

"I try to. I was taught that way. The colored are our customers."

"Why did he do that? Was he showing off in front of the ladies?"

"No. Some people have been taught … uh, the old ways, that the colored have their place and we have ours."

"And those people who have been taught that way take every opportunity to reinforce those old ways?"

"I guess so. I'm sorry, Doug. I don't even know that man."

That pretty much killed off the happy mood of a shopping trip and we drove in silence while I pondered how "some people" were able to intimidate a whole society.

Before long I would find out.

Chapter 11

The guitar is a versatile instrument that allows a novice to sing along to simple, strummed chords. A player can embellish by plucking the strings and providing a more complex multinote rhythm, like John Hurt.

Advanced beyond simple strumming but way short of Hurt, I could do some of both. Sitting on the porch in the evening after supper with my guitar and using the hymnal from Addie's church, I worked out the D-major chords for *Come Thou Fount of Every Blessing* and found it to be well-suited to the guitar. I began to sing it. A decent song strummed and sung, but with some simple improvisation it became much more interesting.

Addie joined me on the porch, taking the other side of the bench, which had become my favorite spot to sit and play. Leaning against the building in the evenings, I sang out into Avalon's single, deserted street.

"Sing it with me?" I asked, hitting a D chord.

And she did. A crystal clear soprano with relative pitch, Addie was a natural musician. On the very first verse, she hit the notes exactly, adjusting to the imperfectly tuned guitar, then, without effort, adjusted her pitch and timing to match mine in a duet.

"Whoa! Do you take lessons?" I asked when we had finished.

"Only in choir," she said, smiling modestly. "Mrs. Jenkins has given me some books to work with."

"You sing it, I'll accompany."

She was even better without me. Well, she was better with the more elaborate accompaniment I was able to provide by not singing myself. No, she was better without me.

"So, what's an Ebenezer?" I asked afterward with a mischievous grin, referring to the first line of the second verse:

Here I raise my Ebenezer;
Hither by Thy help I'm come;
And I hope, by Thy good pleasure,
Safely to arrive at home.

"That's from the book of Samuel," she said.

And the men of Israel went out of Mizpeh, and pursued the Philistines,
And smote them, until they came under Beth-car.
Then Samuel took a stone, and set it between Mizpeh and Shen, and
Called the name of it Ebenezer, saying, Hitherto hath the Lord helped us.

"So, it's a rock, something hard?"

She gave me a disapproving look.

"How do you know that?" I asked, over my little joke and wondering whether all of these Southern Presbyterians could snap off a Bible quote like that.

"It was the Old Testament scripture we read in church on Sunday, how come you don't know it?" she asked quickly, responding to my challenge with another.

"OK," I said. "I remember something about Philistines being 'smote,' but I must have missed the other part. Maybe I was wondering what it might be like to be smote. Is that a really common passage, for you to remember it verbatim like that?"

"If I read something, I can remember the page. I see it later. I read along in the pew Bible while Reverend Abernathy was reading it."

"And so, just now, you were reading from the pew Bible again, in your memory?"

"Yes. I can read music that way, too."

"That first day I came here, while I was waiting, and since then, I've heard you quote what somebody's account balance is without looking at their ledger."

"If I made the last entry, I can see the ledger," Addie said. "Of course, if Daddy has made an entry, I won't know about that."

"That's amazing! Have you always been able to do that or did you learn it from working here?"

"Well, spelling tests were always pretty easy. I wondered how other kids had trouble spelling. If I had written it down, then later I could see the word. I could remember accounts from the very first time Daddy let me write in the ledgers."

"I've heard of a photographic memory but never met anyone who had one. You are one exceptional lady."

I picked up the guitar and strummed a G chord. "Would you sing *Red River Valley* for me?"

And she did.

"Can you sing baritone?"

I knew that would come when Addie asked me to take her to choir practice the next night. The choir, besides Addie, was nine women, most of whom were competent singers, and two old men who couldn't carry a tune. I joined them and anchored the baritone part. The two old men could fix to my voice and stay, more or less, in the same key. The whole choir sounded better, and the choir director proposed that Addie and I begin to work up a duet for an anthem in a week or two. She suggested *Lonesome Valley*.

A detour on the way home after choir practice is a long-established Southern tradition in the courting of a young lady. Addie pointed out a farm road half way back to the store, and we pulled up under a big oak beside a bean field.

Buck's '59 Chevy Apache half-ton pickup had a good radio, a three-speed manual transmission with the shift on the column, and a bench seat.

As a gentleman, let me assert at the outset that Addie's virtue remained pristine. But after half an hour on that bench seat, it was clear that, though her legs were crippled by polio, Addie's womanly virtues were wondrously intact. That settled, we slipped in under her curfew with two minutes to spare.

Chapter 12

The harmonica moaned a long, single note that rounded into a wail. It stopped me half way up the steps from pumping a dollar's worth of gas. The radio was tuned to station KFFA in Helena, Arkansas, to catch the King Biscuit Time broadcast at 12:15, but instead of starting out with the voice of the host, "Sunshine" Sonny Payne, there was just this call, followed by a rhythmic song that could only have been played by Sonny Boy Williamson, a regular on the show I listened to every day.

Usually, Sonny Boy was backed up by his band and played and sang in the traditional call and response form. This day, the radio played a recording of Sonny Boy without backup —only his haunting harmonica, each note rounded and nuanced as he adjusted his embrasure and his hands around the instrument, making the rhythm and the melody. Then he sang a brief verse of *Bye Bye Bird* in that gravelly old voice before resuming the light rhythm.

I could sing on key. I could keep on a beat, but I was never able to make a tune into an emotional experience the way this guy did. What was it that an old man with gnarled hands and big lips did with a three dollar instrument that elevated simple music that way? Shaking my head, I walked into the store, deciding that was why I had come to Mississippi in the first place, and I'd seen it and heard it but I hadn't found out what it was yet.

"Your show's on," Addie said as I slapped the dollar I'd just collected on the counter.

"That's good," I said, listening to the song.

"Yes," she nodded, tapping her hand on the counter with one hand to Sonny Boy's beat while filing the bill in the cash register.

Bye Bye Bird went on with its few words, mostly about a bird being gone. When it was finished Sonny Payne came on and announced that Sonny Boy Williamson had died that morning.

"Gonna need some help," Buck said, appearing from the back one afternoon in July.

I followed him through the storeroom to the breezeway where his truck was parked. He'd been to town to the distributor, and the truck bed was filled with supplies, including five 50-pound bags of sugar.

"That's a lot of sugar," I said after I'd unloaded everything else. We sold sugar in 1- and 5-pound bags. I'd never seen 50 pounds of sugar.

"Yes, it is. Stack it just inside the door," he said without further explanation.

He moved the truck back to the side of the privy, where he usually parked it. An hour later, another pickup pulled by the front of the store, and I went out, thinking they wanted gas. The truck pulled to the breezeway and backed in, just like Buck had. We didn't see that many Studebaker trucks in Chicago, especially not an old one like this.

It was a '53, I was to learn later. It had a rakish look to it as the front end seemed to be large for a truck that size, suggesting a more powerful engine. This one was battered pretty badly and covered in mud.

"Mister Buck in?" a slender old colored man asked, getting out and closing the truck door. He was dressed in work clothes and muddy boots.

"Ah, Hennis," Buck said from the door of the house. "How ya doin'?"

"Tolerable," he replied, as Buck descended the two steps to meet him.

"Anyone besides Addie in the store?" Buck asked me as he looked over my shoulder at the highway.

"No," I said.

"Load that sugar into the back of this truck, then throw that tarp over it," he said, pointing to a tarp in the truck bed. "Tie it down with those straps there," indicating some strips of canvass tied to eye bolts on the sides of the truck.

Curious as to how Buck knew so much about this stranger's truck, I loaded the five bags while Buck and Hennis talked about Hennis' brother, who had apparently been sick. As I tied the weathered tarp over the sugar, Hennis was saying that his brother was good as new and would be home in a few days.

Was this Hennis Hurt, John Hurt's brother?

I jumped down from the truck. Hennis counted out four fives and five ones, and Buck stuck all but a single in his pocket, then walked over to me and snaked an arm around my shoulders.

"I can't help Hennis with this, and he's been down in the back. I want you to go with him, unload that sugar, and forget where you go and what you see," he said quietly into my ear.

He stuffed the dollar into my shirt pocket.

"It just down the road," Hennis said as we backed into the drive. "If someone see us, tell 'em I showin' you where I caught a big catfish."

"OK."

I'd had enough contact recently with the law to know these two men were probably involving me in something illegal, but I couldn't see how 250 pounds of sugar fit into that.

"So, your brother's been sick," I said, as we turned onto Highway 7, trying to clarify if I was indeed getting this close to John Hurt.

"He had a heart spell, the doctor said. But he told me to tell Mr. Buck he'd be here for Miss Addie's birthday next week. Don't you be tellin' her," Hennis said. "It might be a surprise."

"Who's your brother?" Could it be?

"John. John Hurt. He my baby brother."

Some quick mental calculation put Hennis' age at 75, then. No wonder he couldn't lift the sugar. Less than a mile down the road, we turned off onto a farm road and went for a half a mile sloping gradually downward toward the Little Tallahatchie River. We pulled off into the yard of an abandoned farmhouse, its windows gone and roof sagging, and drove back toward a barn. Strange, I thought. The house was abandoned, but there was an electric line to the barn. We drove down a grassy strip, avoiding the muddy drive from the house, pulled around behind the barn to a grove of trees and stopped a hundred feet from the barn. Hennis dropped the tailgate and pulled back the tarp.

"Grab a bag and follow me. Stay on the grass. Don't want to leave no tracks," he said as he stepped toward the barn.

"Oh!" I said as I entered the barn. Now I understood. A shiny copper pot, about 50 gallons, was perched on a steel rack over a burner attached by a long hose to a 100-gallon propane tank in the corner. Dismantled, but lying beside it on the floor, was a coil of copper tubing. A garden hose connected to a spigot in the other corner was draped across boxes of various sizes of glass bottles. The smell of yeast was very strong, coming from five 55-gallon steel drums in a row by the side.

"Put it in this one," he said, pulling a pocket knife from his pocket and cutting the string holding the top of the bag. He pulled the lid off the closest barrel.

The white cornmeal bubbled slowly, and the yeast smell, not unpleasant at all, was stronger. I hefted the bag and poured it into the barrel.

"That jump it up," Hennis said. "Tonight, them bubbles be poppin'! 'Bout four days, we be cookin'."

Then he lost his enthusiasm for a moment and turned to me.

"Mr. Buck said you was cool. Got to keep quiet 'bout this."

"Yes, sir," I said earnestly, but I was thinking about when I got back to Chicago. What a story this was going to be!

Hennis picked up a wooden boat paddle and began stirring the mixture while I unloaded the other four bags. As we traced our way back along the grass by the empty farmhouse, I saw the wisdom of this arrangement. There were no tracks or indication anyone had been there. The secret was safe with me, for now.

After Hennis dropped me back at the store, I rushed in the back door.

"Addie!"

Her finger shot to her lips and her brow furrowed, stopping me in midsentence. She glanced over at the side of the store. A colored woman with two children was picking out some canned goods.

"Miss Addie, you have some mo' a this hominy for a dime?"

"Why, yes, Mrs. Lofton, we have another case in the back. Doug, the hominy is next to the wall behind the crackers."

And so it was. Not only did she have the accounts in her head, she had inventory, too. I brought it out and restocked the shelf.

"So, what is this?" I asked, holding a can of hominy as the woman and children left.

"It's corn, treated some way to soften the shell. That's what your grits come from."

The first time I'd seen grits, I thought they were oatmeal, and thought it strange to put a big glob of oatmeal right next to a fried egg. Then I tasted them and now, halfway through my Mississippi sojourn, was stirring grits into runny eggs and piling them on top of sausage or bacon every time I could get Addie or Buck to cook them.

"So, you know who that was?" I asked, referring to my mysterious trip down by the river.

"Of, course. Hennis Hurt has been a customer here as long as I can remember."

Her smile told me she knew what Hennis was up to.

At that moment a truck pulled into the drive by the gas pump, and I recognized it as Billy Ray Jenkins' truck as I pushed through the screen door.

"Fill 'er up," Billy Ray said as he climbed out of the cab. Cooter stepped out from the other side. Billy Ray strode to the back of the truck and reached in to produce a cane pole about 5 feet long with some sharp metal spikes on the end.

"Know what that is?" he asked as I cleared the meter and pulled off the gas cap.

"No."

"That, my friend, is a frog gig. And tomorrow night, we have an adventure planned, and you're invited."

"No more rubber snakes," I laughed. I heard the pump go on and started filling the tank.

"No, this is on the level, well, at least as far as you're concerned."

He turned and nodded toward Sharkey Bayou, several miles down the road and visible as a line of large trees.

"There's about a million bullfrogs in the bayou over there, and tomorrow night we're gonna take some gigs out there and get some."

"What for?"

I had dissected my share of frogs and hoped that phase of my life was finished.

"Frog legs, man! Fry 'em up, better'n chicken," Cooter said..

"That's just the excuse," Billy Ray said, stepping close, dropping his voice and casting a wary eye up at the store. "The hunting club has their annual meeting Saturday night. Bunch of rich guys from Memphis and Jackson come down here every year for the weekend. They leave their wives at home and spend the weekend drinking and playing cards. Last year they had some women up there."

Cooter's leering smile suggested the women may have been there for salacious purposes.

"Women?" I asked, as the automatic shut-off clanked the pump off.

"Yeah," Cooter said, stepping closer. "We snuck up there last year, through the bayou, and you could see 'em through the windows. This one gal put on a cooch show!"

"A cooch show?" I replaced the gas cap.

"Doug, you dumbass, she took her clothes off!"

Chapter 13

BOOARRH!
The night was filled with the moaning exclamations of a dozen bullfrogs, deep, guttural, placid.   Hundreds of smaller tree frogs in the cypress canopy above chattered in their own world, oblivious to us and their larger cousins below. An occasional splash indicated a crisis for some creature as a large fish grappled with something in the shallows or on the surface. The sun had set, and the pale glow in the western sky had been just enough to launch the boat without using the light.

The boat slid silently through the dark water, propelled by Billy Ray sculling with his paddle in the rear. Cooter manned the bow, watching for cypress knees and stumps beneath the spreading carpet of water lilies, blooming now in August. I sat in the middle, thinking about reptiles and amphibians, and how this whole primordial place reflected the development of the more sophisticated vertebrate class Reptilia, characterized by laying already fertilized eggs that can live on land while the embryo develops, as opposed to the Amphibians, which must lay unfertilized eggs in water to be fertilized by the male.

The smells of mud and rot and the fragrance of the water lilies and giant tupelo mingled with the cypress trees in the water. A large magnolia at the edge of the bayou added to the sense that, at any moment, a giant dinosaur could raise its head out of the water and stare at us while blandly chewing on a mouth full of water hyacinth.

UUAAHHHHH! It was a deep, visceral growl out there in the dark someplace.

"Gator," Cooter said.

"Oh, great!" I said.

Before, when they pulled the rubber snake caper and I'd jumped out of the boat, I'd worried I'd drown or get bit by a snake. Now I had to worry about being eaten by an alligator.

"Shhh! He's lookin' for a girlfriend. He don't care about you," Billy Ray whispered. He sculled us over to a large cypress knee sticking four feet out of the water, and Cooter tied us up.

Tap, tap. Whoosh!

It was a ritual – hitting the top of the steel beer can with the church key, or opener, twice before opening it. The explanation was that the tap would break the bubbles at the top and prevent a blow out of beer when the can was opened.

"They're just starting to drink," Cooter said, peering through the darkness at the silhouette of the hunting lodge ahead. I handed the first beer forward.

We had pulled out of Kinder's store just before dark and drove by the bayou and several miles down the road before turning off on a gravel road that led to the Satellite Club, a backcountry colored nightclub, like the Stardust Club where I'd been arrested. We stopped in front, and a young colored man about my age walked over to greet us.

"How y'all?"

"Doin' good," Cooter said, nodding to the club. "Looks like a party here."

"Maybe later," the colored man said, not turning around. He knew why we were there.

"We need some beer," Billy Ray said, taking over from Cooter.

"What's in it for me?"

"A beer," Cooter responded.

"What'ya want?"

"Six pack of Schlitz."

"Two dollah."

The cans had that Mississippi State Beer Tax notice printed on the top.

Tap, tap. Whoosh!

Later, I took a long pull and leaned back against the side of the boat. A half-moon was peeking through the trees, throwing a silvery streak across the bayou.. The croaking of the two species of frogs was now joined by the buzzing of about a million mosquitoes. I lit a cigarette. Billy Ray and Cooter lit up wood-tip Swisher Sweet cigarillos.

"That ought to keep 'em back," I commented, referring to the thick smoke rising from both ends of the boat.

"Gotta do something, or they'll eat you up."

"So, what are you guys going to do at the end of the summer?" I asked quietly, starting in on my second beer.

"I'm off to Mississippi State in two weeks," Billy Ray said, popping his second beer. "Incoming freshman are supposed to show up early. Indoctrination."

"How about you, Cooter?"

"Just waitin' for the draft, I guess." He was already half way finished with his beer.

"Just waiting for it?" I asked.

"I've talked to the recruiters. I just turned 18 last week. No need to get in a hurry. I'll hang out till all you college boys pull out, then see what my options are. This is the party time!"

We sat there and drank the beer and swatted mosquitoes while it got darker and the parking lot filled up over at the lodge. Late-model pickups and expensive four-door cars rolled in until about eight. All the chairs on the broad veranda were taken as men milled about talking, smoking, drinking and greeting the late arrivals. Then they all went inside, and we cautiously pulled in to get a closer look.

"Look," Cooter whispered excitedly, "there's a woman."

A middle-age woman carrying a tray of salad passed by the window.

"A waitress, shithead," Billy Ray said.

As we waited in the boat, a hundred feet into the bayou, we could smell steaks cooking on the other side of the lodge. The waitress reappeared and passed out plates of steaks. Then there was half an hour of various people stand-ing up in front of the group; probably that was the business meeting. Then they all sat down.

"OK, this is it," Billy Ray said suddenly and sculled toward the bank.

The boat ran aground and Cooter stepped out into calf high water and pulled us in. He tied it to a cypress knee, and I followed, stepping off into ankle deep mud. Billy Ray, coming from the back of the boat knocked over the lan-tern we'd brought for the frog gigging.

Thud!

We all froze. Frogs, mosquitoes, the faint sound of music from inside. We crept forward. A woman appeared at one end of the large dining room, dressed in a long, formal evening gown. We could hear applause. The music got louder and she began to prance about the room. Clustered behind the last large tree in the bayou we could see her as she passed by the half dozen windows on our side of the lodge. And we could see only her top half.

"Lemme see!" said Cooter, the shortest of our group, putting a foot on the tree and grabbing my shoulder to lift himself up.

The woman threw her big, wide hat into the audience, then her feather boa, and made another circle. When her skirt came off, Billy Ray tried to climb up my back.

"We gotta get closer," Cooter said, giving up on climbing the tree and step-ping out into the yard.

Being in the middle of a swamp, the lodge was built up from ground level. We could see in the windows from a distance, but as we got closer we could see less. We were going to have to climb up onto the veranda to see the show.

Billy Ray started to giggle.

"Shut up, dumbass!" Cooter whispered, intent on seeing the show.

Creak!

The first step was loose. We froze. The music inside was louder. She passed by the window right above us, breasts covered only by pasties with tas-sels, swinging in alternate circles. The room was loud with applause. Another garment went flying across the room. We crowded to the window.

"Get outta here!" A frenzied shout erupted from the door, and a man in work clothes emerged holding a shotgun.

Cooter vaulted the railing, Billy Ray and I ran to the end of the veranda and leaped down the steps there.

Boom!

I could feel the heat of the blast and hear the shot rip the air over our heads. The caretaker chambered another round. We were running flat out.

Boom!

The first big cypress rattled as the shot tore through its lowest branches.

I expected to be killed or crippled at any moment. Billy Ray and Cooter were convulsed with laughter as Billy Ray leaped the length of the john boat and Cooter pushed me across the muddy first step to tumble over onto the second seat. He lifted the bow and shoved us into the bayou, then jumped in and grabbed a paddle.

Bang!

Now 50 yards away, the sound had a sharper, less visceral sound. I could hear the shot falling into the water around us. We weren't going to die. I began to laugh as the little boat fairly leaped through the water with Billy Ray and Cooter paddling frantically.

"And don't come back," the caretaker yelled as we pulled away into the darkness of Sharkey Bayou.

"We got closer this year," Cooter said triumphantly, "I thought we were going to see the whole show!"

"Yeah." Billy Ray panted. "It was the same girl."

"You guys got shot at last year?"

"Hell, yeah!" they answered in unison.

"You crazy fools! This is worse than the damned rubber snake!"

Our laughter stopped the frogs for a full minute. Then ...

UUAAHHH!

Chapter 14

Alone figure walked down the dusty county road that abutted State Highway 7 in front of the store. I was sitting on the porch with my guitar practicing the slide technique after hearing Delta Jim on the King Biscuit Time show. He played the same songs I'd heard at the Stardust Club, and I could tell Jerome was still playing bass. I was using a short piece of copper pipe for a slide. It was not as good as the nickel plated slides you could buy in a music store, but Avalon had no music stores, and I didn't have any money.

It wasn't unusual to see people walking or riding bicycles down the rural roads around Avalon. A lot of people still lived on the farms then, and many of them didn't have cars or trucks. That's why a small outfit like Kinder's store could survive. As the lone figure got closer, I recognized Cooter Davis.

"Hey, Cooter!" I called out as he loped across the highway.

"Evenin', Doug. Is Buck in?" he asked somberly as he climbed the steps.

"Sure, I'll get him."

I set down my guitar and stepped to the door. Cooter's demeanor indicated he had something serious to discuss and it wasn't the time for the usual light-hearted banter. Buck broke away from fixing supper with Addie when I told him Cooter needed to see him. He didn't seem surprised. I assumed it had to do with the Davis family account.

"You can stay, Doug. You might need some of Buck's advice yourself," Cooter said when I moved to retrieve the guitar.

Buck took his seat, I took the bench and Cooter leaned against the post.

"I got my draft notice yesterday."

"Well, you knew it was coming," Buck said, lighting a Chesterfield. "No way to dodge it now."

"I know. I'm not trying to dodge it."

He looked out across the highway, back toward his family's farm on the county road.

"Mama cried all night," he said. "Daddy said I should just go down there and do it, like a man."

"When you goin'?"

"Bus leaves in two weeks, to the processing station in Memphis, then on to Fort Leonard Wood in Missouri."

"Not much time," Buck said, blowing smoke from the first drag. He began to cough, cleared his airway and spit into a can he carried with him.

"You were a Marine," Cooter said. "Should I go in the Marines? My uncle was in the Navy. He said that was the way to go."

"Well, the draft is for the Army, and it's only two years, then you're out," Buck said. "The Marines is for three years. You can join the Navy or the Air Force, which would be for four years. You'd get some training there, electronics, mechanics on airplanes or big diesel engines, stuff like that."

"Yeah, I talked with the recruiter. I sort of wanted to get into it, you know, do some fightin'."

"Yeah," Buck said. "Young guys want that."

"That's why I wanted to talk to you. You've been in the thick of it. What's it like, you know, what's it really like?"

"I'm not going to tell you what to do, except to talk with your dad."

"I know. I didn't tell Dad I was coming down here."

"If you don't, I will."

"OK."

At that moment, a horsefly careened across the porch, circling around among the three of us. Cooter and Buck ignored it. I swatted at it and it flew out across the gravel lot. After the interruption, Buck sat motionless for a good minute before beginning his story.

"Marine Corps training is fourteen weeks. Army training is about half that. Then they both do some advanced infantry training. All Marines are infantry riflemen first, and any technical skill they might acquire is secondary. The Navy handles the support for the Marines, so there aren't any cooks or clerks or supply technicians. Marines spend all their time learning to fight."

Buck stubbed out his cigarette.

"The Marine Corps is very focused. If the Marine Corps has an opinion about how something should be done, every Marine knows it and agrees. When the time comes to move, Marines move as one. And that, Cooter, is what saves lives. I joined the Marines in 1943. After boot camp at Parris Island and advanced infantry training at Camp Lejeune, we shipped out."

A truck pulled up in front of the gas pump.

"Fill'er up. And I need some milk and bread," a farmer said, climbing out of the truck and heading for the steps. "Hey, Buck."

I slipped into the store and turned on the pump then jumped down the steps to fill the truck.

"Hey, Charlie," Buck said, his sickly pallor and the fact that he was in the middle of something with Cooter kept their greeting brief.

"Check the oil?" I asked.

"Naw, it's fine," Charlie said, entering the store. He had the milk and bread at the counter when I came in. He paid cash and left.

"I hit the beach on Saipan with the 4th Marine Division at dawn on June 15, 1944. The Navy had 15 battleships bombarding the island for 24 hours before that."

"Fifteen battleships!" Cooter exclaimed. He'd taken a seat on the bench.

"Yeah. We could hear those big shells roaring overhead all night. We figured the Japs would all be dead by the time we got there. When the sun came up, we couldn't even see the island for the smoke. There were 300 LVTs in the first wave. Hell, we thought we were invincible sitting in that thing behind the armored ramp with two 50-cal machine guns blazing away at the beach. Then the Jap artillery started in on us, and we wised up fast. They blew the LVT right next to us to pieces with a direct hit. Killed everyone, including a guy I'd been through boot camp with. One second they were there, and the next it was just a big noise and a column of spray."

I leaned against the post and lit a cigarette with a wooden match, which I flicked out into the drive. I'd taken to keeping a penny box of matches in my shirt pocket since my lighter was stolen in Memphis.

"Did'ja have to wade in to the beach?" Cooter asked.

"No, the LTV had a track, like a tank, and that carried us through the first line of sand dunes and machine guns. After that we were on our own. We hit light resistance. When we'd hit a bunker or a line of dug-in Japs firing at us, we'd take cover, return fire, send guys out to flank 'em and shoot 'em from behind, or lob in grenades. We made pretty good time with minimal casualties. Then they started runnin' when we got to 'em.

"We got three miles in from the beach the first day. Then, that night, with us dug in and dog tired, they hit us with an all-out banzai charge. That's where the training paid off. Before it got dark that night, and before we got chow, the lieutenant had us dig in, place our machine guns and fields of fire just so. He walked around and inspected every gun, every hole, every squad. When they hit, about midnight, they broke through some of the other units, but not ours. It was a turkey shoot. In the morning, there were a lot of dead guys lyin' around. Most of 'em Japs."

He took a drag from his cigarette.

"But, not all."

I waited on a couple more customers while Buck told of the advance across Saipan and the final battle. I was trusted now to use the cash register, but not to enter accounts in the ledgers.

"... and this Jap had me down and was about to run one of those short daggers the officers carry into my chest when my buddy Jerry Etheridge swung his rifle butt around and knocked him over. One good thing about the M-1 Garand, if you run out of ammunition, it weighs 10 pounds and makes a fine club. We both jumped on him and finished him off pretty quick."

"Daddy," Addie said at the screen door. "Supper's ready."

"OK, honey. Be there in a minute."

"I guess I better be runnin' on," Cooter said, getting up. "Thanks, Buck."

"No. Sit down." Buck pointed to the bench, then he turned to Addie still at the door. "I'll be there in a minute."

She got the message and turned back to walk through the store to the house.

"Cooter, there ain't nothin' tougher than a Marine Corps corporal, except a Marine Corps lieutenant. If you go into the Marines, you're more likely to see combat, but if you do see combat, you want a Marine lieutenant standing right behind you deciding what to do next. And, if you get into it – combat, I mean – it's total chaos, exciting, scary. It's the most intense thing you will ever do. If you do that, something gets into you."

Buck paused, looking at us both.

"And it don't ever leave."

Chapter 15

He shuffled through the storeroom just after midnight. The wheezing told me it was Buck and not an intruder. I lay there quietly until I heard the beer open and his cigarette lighter click. I got up.

Whoosh! He opened the second beer just as I entered the store.

"Come on out here," he said, leading the way. He handed me the beer as I closed the screen door quietly. He leaned back in the ladder-back chair.

I took the bench, lit a cigarette. Waited.

"That talk with Cooter?" he said. "That wasn't the whole story."

He took a long pull and went through the coughing fit, spitting into a cup he carried with him.

"You need to hear the rest of it."

I tipped up the beer can and let a good third of it drain down into my stomach. I felt the cold hit bottom.

"After we secured Saipan, they sent us back to Pearl Harbor to rest and train replacements. I came back home on leave. I got married. Then, I went back to Pearl and, just after Christmas, we shipped out in troop transports. They never tell you where you're going, but we figured it was someplace bad, because every Marine in Hawaii went with us. We hit the beach at Iwo Jima on February 19, 1945, 30,000 Marines. It was hell. It took five weeks."

He emptied his beer.

I jumped up and went inside to get two more. He went through another paroxysm of coughing, using the freshly opened beer I handed him to wash it down.

"Sit here," he said, motioning for me to move.

I got the other ladder-back chair from the other side of the porch and sat right in front of him.

"Doug," he said, leaning right into my face. "I died on that island. Everything that's happened since then has been a bonus. Me and Jerry Etheridge fought up the mountain with our squad, taking turns carrying the dead and wounded to the aid station and getting more ammunition. One night, they rushed us, threw grenades into our trenches and overran our position. The Marines behind us counterattacked and pushed them back. In the morning, all that was left of our squad was a pile of dead Marines, and me at the bottom. I was unconscious for three days.

"I don't remember anything, but they told me later that Jerry was right on top of me," he sobbed.

I could think of nothing to say.

"The hospital ship got back to Pearl at the end of April. By then, I was up and around. I got my mail and learned my wife, Alice, was pregnant, due in September. I was elated, of course. But, we went right back to training, expecting to have to assault the home islands of Japan. We shipped out again in June and sailed west. We got off the coast of Guam and just circled. We could see all the other troop transports out there. The ships parked off the Marianas went from horizon to horizon, and every day there were more. Then, sometime in July, they all turned back east. The second week in August, we learned that we'd dropped the atomic bomb on Nagasaki and Hiroshima and that the war was over."

Buck finished the second beer, and I jumped to get another.

"I wasn't the same after Iwo Jima," he said. "I felt guilty. Why Me? Why did I come back and Jerry and the other guys didn't? Then I found out."

His eyes pierced me, there in the dark.

"Before we got off the ship at Pearl, they called me out and gave me a telegram. Alice had died in childbirth, and I had a daughter."

Chapter 16

One was named Jasper and the other was Jarvus. Jasper was 10, and Jarvus was 9, or maybe it was the other way around. It's been a long time. They had one bicycle, and it seemed like every time they rode by the store, they were in a different configuration – Jarvus peddling with Jasper on the handle bars, or Jasper peddling and Jarvus balanced on the back axle holding on to the back of the seat waving to one and all, or Jasper facing backward holding on to the handle bars and feet balanced on the front axle. They lived in a tenant house with their mother and grandmother just behind the cotton gin at the end of the street and came by the store every day.

"Mornin', Jarvus," I said one morning when the young colored boy leaped off as the bicycle flashed by the steps and his brother braked it to a sliding stop in the gravel.

"Mornin', Doug," Jasper said, topping the steps at full stride and pulling the door open, "he's Jarvus." I knew it but deliberately confused them to a get a rise. They had come to accept it, as nearly everyone got them confused, even their granny.

Their father was in town. He was an auto worker up north and came home only a few times a year. It was always an event. Addie told me he would show up in a late-model car, flash some cash, pay off bills, buy clothes and cram his fatherly duties into a long weekend, and then drive all night to get back to the assembly line. He'd given them each a half dollar to spend at the store.

"How much is that?" they asked a dozen times as they picked out their purchases – sodas, candy, ice cream. It was a tough choice.

"The sodas are a dime, the Popsicles 15 cents, the Dixie Cup ice cream and Drumsticks are a quarter," Addie said, leaning over the counter to pull open the top of the ice cream chest. "You pick out what you want, and I'll tell you how much you have left."

They built two small piles on the counter in front of Addie as they made their decisions. I went to the back and leaned against the door to the storeroom to watch. I thought back to the Economics 101 class I'd taken instead of the second semester of comparative anatomy. Wealth, we'd learned, was the power to choose. Here was the surest proof of that. It wasn't so much the prospect of eating the ice cream and candy that excited Jasper and Jarvus, it was the novelty of being able to choose from among the many alluring items on display.

Jarvus, or maybe it was Jasper, chose a Coke, an orange Popsicle, a bag of peanuts and a Snickers bar. His brother chose an Orange Sunrise soda, a Dixie Cup vanilla ice cream, which came with its own little wooden spoon, a Tootsie Roll and some hard candy. After the sales tax, which was 3 percent, they each had a few pennies. When Addie handed them their change, they looked confused. Paying with cash and getting some back was unexpected.

"Put the pennies in your pocket. You can come back tomorrow and get some candy," Addie said with a laugh and laid her hand on the penny candy jar on the counter.

That was almost too much to comprehend! All these goodies and the prospect of more tomorrow! They let out a whoop and bolted for the door.

Bling!

Bang!

"Goddammit!"

The "bling" was the bell on the door activated when it opened. The "bang" was the door hitting the side of the building. The curse was from the middle-age white man the boys ran into at the top of the steps.

"You niggers get outta here or I'll skin your ass!"

Jasper, or maybe it was Jarvus, slid under the railing at the side of the porch, his brother did the same at the other end and they disappeared around the side of the building.

"You let niggers run wild around here?" he asked in a fury as he let the door slam behind him.

"They're just boys," Addie said placidly.

"Niggers come and go through the same door as whites?" His bulging belly strained the front of Big Smith bib overalls as he sauntered to the counter, scanning the store – looking for another outrage to find.

"Yes, sir. We only have one door."

"You have toilets?"

"Yes, sir. One. Out back."

"Niggers use that?"

"Anyone can use that, Mr. Hoagland."

Her benign smile was unchanged from the beginning of the conversation. I hadn't seen this man before, but Addie apparently knew him.

"Fill the tank, check the oil, the tires and clean the windshield," he said pulling a Pepsi out of the cooler by the counter.

I went out the screen door and down the steps to find an old pickup, complete with gun rack, lever-action rifle and Confederate battle flag mudflaps parked by the gas pump. I removed the gas cap and waited for the pump to come on. It didn't.

"Bullshit! Lemme see that?"

I trotted back up the steps to the door. He was leaning over the counter. Addie's placid smile was gone, and her eyes were wide with fright as she leaned back on her stool to get away from him. I stepped behind the counter.

"Lemme see that," he repeated, pointing at the account book.

"Daddy marked the Hoagland's account," she said, handing the book to me, "for no more credit until they pay something."

"Pay $25" was written in red pencil on a slip of paper beneath the cover of the book. I opened it to see the recent entries for gas and food, and the total, more than $50.

I stepped closer to the counter, putting myself between Addie and Mr. Hoagland and confronting him face to face. Realizing that the ledger, obviously a source of conflict, was the only record of his debt, I kept that safely out of his reach.

"You'll have to pay something," I said.

"Who are you?" Fury was in his eyes.

"Doug Spencer."

I didn't consider myself a tough guy, but I was pretty sure I could handle this fat old farmer. On the other hand, I'd had a brush with the law and knew very well how outsiders were treated in Mississippi, and Hoagland could be the sheriff's cousin or something. Tact was called for here.

"You work here?"

"Mr. Spencer is the assistant manager," Addie said.

I almost smiled. Addie's face was behind me so I couldn't tell if she was inflating my position to make me more credible, or if she was attempting humor by saying Kinder's store had an assistant manager. Whatever the intent, it worked.

"Well, how much do I owe?" he sputtered.

"Fifty-eight dollars and twenty-two cents," I responded.

"How'd it get to be so much? We don't buy that much here."

"It's mostly gas," she said.

"Gas is a nickel cheaper in Grenada."

He stepped back from the counter and replaced the Coke in the cooler.

"Yes, sir, Mr. Hoagland," Addie replied, recovering some now that he was no longer right in her face. "But you have to pay cash there."

He regrouped and trained his gaze, now getting hot again, at me.

"You live here?" he sneered, "with her?"

That did it. Fortunately for us both, the counter was between us. I handed Addie the account book and stepped toward the front. Dr. Douglas Spencer II of Lake Forest, Illinois, was going to have to bail his son out of a slammer in Mississippi and probably find some big city lawyer from Jackson to get me out of this. I was already looking forward to a month of grits and black coffee for breakfast in the Carroll County jail. Hoagland had hit a hot button I didn't even know I had, and in about 10 seconds he was going to learn some manners.

"Doug, stop!" Addie's voice had a shrill element to it that caused just enough pause to let Hoagland retreat behind the soda cooler.

"We'll put a dollar's worth of gas on the account and you can pay when you get your check," she said quickly.

Bluster gone, I saw a desperate man. Desperate, not because he was about to get his ass kicked, but because he was ignorant, unemployed, flat broke, and without property, skills or prospects. Addie was throwing him a line, a reprieve so if he were out of gas, he wouldn't have to walk home.

Hoagland wouldn't take it.

"I don't need no charity," he said, eyes blazing. "I'll settle up with Buck later."

I let him pass. We heard the truck start, the gears grind as it started to move, then the brakes squeaked, and the gears ground again as the truck moved again.

Crunch!

He ran over the bicycle.

Chapter 17

The song *Come Thou Fount of Every Blessing* is one of the oldest American traditional sacred songs, dating from 1757. Though the tune is familiar to most people, even heathens like me who rarely went to church, it hadn't been made secular by new lyrics. Unlike *Lonesome Valley, Amazing Grace, Morning Has Broken* and *Farther Along,* it hadn't made its way into the popular songbooks of folk musicians of the day such as Pete Seeger and Joan Baez.

To me, that was a major attraction, and I'd been working on the guitar chords for a couple of weeks. I had suggested it instead of *Lonesome Valley,* and the choir director had agreed but wanted to hear it at choir practice that week.

"There's no room to play the guitar up here," I asserted from my position in the back row of the choir. "We should step down in front to do the anthem."

I knew Addie didn't like to walk in front of a crowd on her crutches, but I reminded her that she'd be going off to college in a couple of weeks and that crutches would be her only mode of transportation. It was best to get over being self-conscious about it. We'd been debating it all week. She had finally, reluctantly, agreed.

"Addie? Do you want to step out of the choir loft?" Mrs. Jenkins asked skeptically.

This whole idea of doing an anthem with a guitar accompaniment was a huge break with tradition.

"Yes," Addie said.

She was resolute. The transition from high school and her rural life to the new world she hoped to step into was well underway.

I relished my role as catalyst for change. Young people of the day saw themselves as breaking down the old ways and forging our new world, and I was very much a part of that. This was early in the "Make Love Not War" movement that would lead to the riots and social turmoil of the late 1960s.

It was fun to see Addie blossom, and I looked forward to this small congregation expanding its concept of sacred music. On this night, two thirds of the way through my summer in Mississippi, I saw myself as Johnny Appleseed planting the seeds of progress, after which I would go back to my privileged life in Chicago. But somewhere in the back of my consciousness was a tiny doubt that it might not turn out that way.

"OK, let's try it," Mrs. Jenkins said.

We'd asked for a chance to do it our way, and she wanted to see how it would work.

I stepped back from the second row in the choir loft, took two steps to the end, picked up my guitar, stepped down to the front row and held open the gate that opened beside the organ. Addie slid sideways through the gate on her crutches, which were mostly hidden by the choir robe she wore, and took the two steps to the middle of the front of the church. Right beside her, I did a quick strum to check the tune and started.

I'd worked out eight bars of the tune, which I fingerpicked for an introduction, and then Addie came in solo for the first verse.

Come thou font of every blessing
Tune my heart to sing Thy grace;
Streams of mercy, never ceasing
Call for songs of loudest praise
Teach me some melodious sonnet,
Sung by flaming tongues above.
Praise the mount! I'm fixed upon it
Mount of God's unchanging love.

I was stunned. We were all stunned. Addie and I had practiced that song all week. She was good – relative pitch and clear, true soprano voice – but it was different now. Performing in front of the dozen people of the choir brought out something in her singing that wasn't there in practice. She felt it, too, and it showed in her face as she connected with her audience. The verse is about music carrying God's message.

I came in to sing the second verse with her, the one about raising the Ebenezer, and then she finished solo. At the end, there was silence. Mrs. Jenkins had tears in her eyes.

That night, on the much anticipated detour home from choir practice, under the big live oak by the bean field, Addie took off her braces. There in Buck's '59 Chevy Apache truck, with the interior lights on, she took off her shoes, to which steel rods connected with the hinges at her knees, which she locked to stand. Above the knee, two more rods connected with a leather pad that supported her pelvis. She piled all that on the floor with her crutches, pulled up her skirt and laid her bare legs across my lap.

"Here I am," she said.

I rubbed her small feet, rigid because there were no functioning muscles there, and her calves, small for her size and strangely inert. I could feel muscles in her thighs, but not enough to make up for the lack of anything below; hence, she needed the braces. Her butt muscles were normal and well developed. She directed my hand to callouses from the braces at her knees, and rolled over to reveal more callouses just below her panty line in back. Her arms and shoulders were very strong because they performed much of the work normally done by the legs. After 14 years of rehabilitation therapy, she was like a gymnast from the thighs up.

"Any questions?" she asked, lifting herself quickly to a sitting position with those strong arms and leaning against the passenger door.

We got in five minutes late. Buck didn't say anything.

The church was packed the following Sunday. Word had gotten out from the choir members who witnessed our practice for the anthem. When the time came, she moved quickly to the front of the church and stood there with a big smile. The song was even better in front of 75 people. With the last chord, there was a murmur, then a sort of a cheer and then applause. Applause in a Southern Presbyterian Church, bastion of restraint and control? Yes.

The next night, Addie and I were seated on the bench out on the front porch watching the dark creep in.

"Your dad told me about the war, and about your mother dying in childbirth. How'd he get here, in Avalon?"

"You mean running a little store in the middle of nowhere?"

"Well, I didn't mean for it to sound like that. I suppose family in the area would be the reason."

"You're right. Grandfather Kinder's family were farmers and merchants all around Grenada and Greenwood. Lloyd Kinder – that's Daddy's name, by the way, Lloyd Kinder Jr. Lloyd senior was an engineer on the Yazoo and Mississippi Valley Railroad, the one that ran through Avalon, and then he drove on the Illinois Central. Daddy was born in Cleveland, Mississippi, when his father was an engineer on the Yazoo.

"My grandmother, I called her Memaw, was a Leland. Her father, Grover Leland, owned a large farm, including that land over there," Addie said, nodding across the road.

"The Davis farm?"

"It used to be the Leland farm, and then the Kinder farm."

"You owned it?"

"Daddy and Emmabelle did. The Lelands had three girls, and none of them married farmers. Grover Leland died in the 1930s, and his wife shortly after. The three daughters split up the farms, and Memaw got that 360 acres over there."

"Farms have a history."

"Of course they have a history," Addie said. "You Yankees think the South is just a bunch of big anonymous plantation owners with vast tracts of land they've inherited since before the Civil War. It isn't like that at all – well, except for Senator Eastland. Each farm has to be farmed by someone, and it works better if there are several family members cooperating, like Cooter and his dad.

"If there's nobody to work it, then you rent it to a neighbor or someone who can work it. That's how farmers get a start, renting someone else's land. If they're good at it, they buy equipment and land and get bigger. That's how Mr. Davis started. He was a farm manager for Senator Eastland over in Sunflower County, saved some money, borrowed some money, got some money from his parents, and bought that farm from Daddy."

"So Buck decided to get out of farming?"

"Daddy got too sick to farm. If the dust was bad while he was plowing, he'd come back to the store coughing and wheezing and have to sit to catch his breath. We sold the farm to the Davises five years ago."

"Farming's a tough business."

"Yes," Addie said, leaning back into me. "You don't want to hear all this stuff about farms and railroads and people you hardly know or people who died before we were born."

"No, really, I do. All my family lives in and around Chicago, and my grandparents and great grandparents were all there, too. It's not a very interesting group, and aside from a crazy old uncle, they were all doctors and lawyers and business executives."

"OK, you asked for it," she said, sitting back up and moving to the other end of the bench. She turned to lean against the post. She took her braces off and put her feet up on my lap.

"Rub my feet and I'll tell you the whole thing."

I started rubbing the hard little nubbins that were her feet.

"Oh, right there," she said, indicated an area midfoot.

"So, you can feel, even though there's no movement?"

"I can feel, not as much as you can, probably, but I do feel. The problem with not having muscles down there is that there is no substance to the foot. When I walk, the bones kind of grind together. It's like cracking your knuckles. Billy Ray used to crack his knuckles in class, and it drove the teachers crazy because they couldn't tell who was doing it. I think about that sometimes when I walk."

"So this feels good?"

"Oh, yes. Be my bestest friend and do that some more!"

I went back to the foot massage, and she went on with the story.

"When Grover Leland and his wife died and my grandmother inherited part of her family's farm, Grandpa Kinder retired from the railroad, and he and Memaw moved here to Avalon to open this store and farm the land across the road. Daddy finished high school in Holcomb and farmed with his father. When the war came along, Daddy enlisted in the Marines. All the young men left for the war, including a lot of railroad men, and the railroad recalled retired engineers, including my grandfather. He was stationed at Grenada and drove trains from Memphis to Jackson. My grandmother ran the store."

"That subject, the railroad, keeps coming up."

"The railroad was really important. My grandmother Memaw was born in Teoc, a little town over there somewhere," Addie said, motioning to the south. "She told me that when she was first married, in 1910, the roads were passable only about half the time. They'd get muddy, bridges would wash out, and horseback was the only dependable way to get around.   She still remembered how excited they were when the Y&MV built a branch line from Greenwood to Grenada."

"Where'd she live then?"

"Here," she said, indicating the back of the store.

"That same house?"

"Same one."

"Same outhouse?"

She laughed.

"They had a well and plumbing and a septic tank before I was born," Addie said. "It's no problem to dig a well here. The water table is only about 10 feet. The privy is for the customers at the store, so we don't have to maintain a toilet and all that."

She mused for a moment.

"You know, that might be the original privy from when the house was built."

"When was that?"

"My great grandfather bought the farm about 1910 and moved here from Teoc. When Memaw married Lloyd Kinder, he worked for her father on that farm across the road and together they built the house, and they had the privy."

"Forty-five years of shit in that one pit?"

"I don't know. I never thought of it that way."

"So, you could just dig down there and find some, uh, remnant of your great grandfather?"

"I'll loan you a shovel, and you can dig if you want. No telling what you might find in there."

She wiggled her feet to indicate I should get back to the task at hand.

"What's a branch line railroad?" I asked. John Hurt's song *Sliding Delta* was named after a branch line railroad.

"It was a smaller railroad," she said. "The engines and cars were smaller and couldn't carry as much as the main line of the Illinois Central that went, well, still goes, through Grenada."

"They built it to carry the cotton?"

"There was cotton, but it was mainly to carry trees to the big sawmill in Grenada. All along the river here, and around that swamp over there," she said, pointing south again.

I turned to look.

"Your swamp, dummy. Sharkey Bayou," she laughed, slapping me on the shoulder as if I had forgotten my adventures on the bayou.

"Oh, yeah."

"Timber was the main reason for the railroad at first, then cotton. But there were several passenger trains every day, and everything people here on the farms and in the little towns along the line ate and wore, and worked with, came from the railroad."

"So, your grandfather went back to driving trains, and your father was off fighting the Japanese. He comes home on leave, gets married and you're born."

"No."

She sat up, pulling her feet off my lap.

"No," she said. She put her hands in her lap and looked down at her feet.

"This is so sad. Daddy cries every time we talk about it."

She paused as if to collect her thoughts and turned to look up at the moon just coming out from behind a cloud.

"My grandfather was killed in a railroad accident."

"Oh, I didn't know."

The mellow glow of the foot rub was gone now.

"He was driving a troop train from Memphis to New Orleans on April 30, 1944," Addie said. "His train had priority over all traffic as the soldiers were to embark for the war in Europe as soon as they got to New Orleans. There is a passing track east of the main line at Vaughan, just north of Jackson. A passing track is a siding that a train can pull off on to wait for another train to pass.

"On this night, there was a northbound double-header freight – that means it had two engines – that pulled onto the passing track to let the troop train through. A southbound freight also pulled onto the passing track, and their combined length was 10 cars too long for the passing track, so the back of the southbound freight was blocking the main line north of the station at Vaughan. This happened a lot during the heavy railroad traffic during the war, as this was the main Illinois Central Line south to the Gulf.

"The station manager at Vaughan had the northbound freight back out of the southern end of the passing track to let the southbound freight pull all the way off the main line. Then, when the troop train came through the station it would slow down and they could back the southbound freight onto the track, move the northbound onto the passing track and the troop train goes through."

"Whew, complicated."

"You have to have the whole picture: troop train, rainy night, fog, lots of train cars, small station."

"Got it."

"Just as the northbound train backed out of the passing track south of Vaughan, an air hose on the southbound freight broke and the brakes locked, leaving four cars blocking the main line north of Vaughan. My grandfather was ahead of schedule, going 75 miles an hour coming off an unrestricted straight section of track as he came into the final turn before Vaughan and encountered a flagman and flares warning him the track was blocked.

"He had a thousand soldiers on that train," she sobbed, " and two freight trains blocking the main line right in front of him. He hit his whistle to warn the station, threw his wheels into reverse, opened the throttle and told his fireman to jump."

Addie sobbed again, looking out at the gravel road.

I remained silent.

"His engine shattered the caboose, then plowed through two flatcars loaded with lumber, then hit a flatcar loaded with an army tank. That knocked the engine off the rails, and it hit an embankment and the boiler exploded.

"My grandfather had slowed the train so that only the engine and the baggage car behind it derailed. The troop train had just a jolt, and everyone was OK. They took the engine off the southbound freight and backed it up to the troop train. The soldiers were astonished to find that they'd been in a train wreck when the troop train pulled out of Vaughan less than an hour after the crash, and they passed by the crushed engine, still steaming from the boiler explosion, and ... and ... my dead grandfather."

"Oh, that's sad." I scooted over and put an arm around her.

"So, to answer your initial question, Daddy came home from the war to run the store, farm the farm and take care of his mother, daughter and sister."

"Bob, bob, white!"

"There! What's that bird?"

We were sitting on the porch, Addie leaning against me as we watched the shadows spread across the parking lot. It was the week after the railroad accident story. I had heard this bird call, usually in the mornings and evenings. This one came from the brush behind the store.

"That's a quail. You really are a city boy. You never heard a quail before? They're called bobwhite quail because of their call. It sounds like 'Bob White.' "

The first call was answered by one across the highway in the tall grass by the cotton field.

"So, is that a girlfriend?"

"Could be, or just another lonely quail."

The screen door squeaked as Buck stepped out onto the porch. Addie sat up just a bit, then relaxed and leaned back into me as before. He took no notice and sat in his chair. The quail called again. Without hesitation Buck put his first two fingers into his mouth and blew a perfect "bob, bob, white," in answer to the call. Within moments, the quail across the road answered.

"How do you do that?" I asked, incredulous.

Buck made a circle with his thumb and index finger and put that circle under his tongue and blew another quail call. This time he got an answer from down the road toward Greenwood, then one from behind the house.

"They're feeling social tonight," he said. "My grandfather taught me to call like that, and I was the envy of all the boys 'til some of them learned how to do it. I'd go out with my .22 rifle and set up in a fence row in the morning and call 'em in. They'll come right up to you. I'd pop their heads off with the rifle."

"Doug was asking about how we came to live here, in Avalon. I told him about Grandfather Kinder's accident," Addie said, after a pause.

"They lived right here when that happened," Buck said, "and before Dad built the store, the house back there was where my grandparents lived. It was more than a year after the accident that my mother and Emmabelle ran the store alone. They had some sharecroppers on the land, but most of the young men were gone. The women and old men got the crop in that year, and in '45 Emmabelle drove a tractor with the men to get the ground ready to plant."

"Wish I could have seen that," I said.

"Me, too." He laughed at what must have been a vision of his proper sister sweating on the seat of the tractor, shrouded in dust. "Then I came back from the Pacific, and Emmabelle could go back to finish college."

The quail called out again, and we sat quietly as they answered each other.

"So," Buck went on, "I sat on the porch of that house back there and called in the ancestors of these same quail when I was a kid visiting here in the summer."

He took a last pull from a Schlitz and held up the empty, indicating he wanted another. He leaned forward and looked down the street toward the defunct cotton gin.

"Was a dozen houses here then. More than a dozen, maybe two, counting the ones that were down there," he said, pointing south. "Get a beer for yourself. Addie, you want one?"

"No, Daddy."

I got up and got us each a beer.

"Could you teach me to do that call?" I asked as I handed him the beer and sat down on the bench.

"Sure," he said. He set the beer on the floor and turned toward me. "Make a circle with your thumb and index finger. Like this."

I made the circle.

"Now pull your lips down over your teeth and touch the roof of your mouth with your tongue. Then put the circle against the bottom of your tongue and blow. Like this."

He made a loud quail call.

"Or, if you want to get someone's attention, whistle like this," and he made an ear-splitting shriek that would alert a man halfway across a quarter-section of land.

I tried it and got only a harsh rush of air.

"No, the whistle doesn't come from your lips, or your tongue. It's the air rushing around your fingers. See, like this," he said and whistled loudly again.

We talked for a while and then Addie helped Buck back to the house and bed. I stayed out on the porch another hour, trying to whistle.

Chapter 18

He came in Hennis' '53 Studebaker truck, the same one I'd loaded with sugar for the drive to the still. A dozen people lounged around the porch, colored and white about evenly mixed.

I craned to see him, the man I'd come to Mississippi to meet: a small man in a bowler hat cocked rakishly to the side and wearing a worn blue work shirt and pressed khaki pants. Mississippi John Hurt looked like an elf next to his older brother Hennis.

"Hello, John!" Buck stepped down the two steps to meet him. They shook hands and Buck slipped a pint of Old Grand Dad Bourbon into his hand. "Heard you were sick."

"Had that spell down by the river last month, thought it was the end," he laughed, "but I guess it wasn't."

John Hurt slipped the whiskey into a pocket with a self-conscious grin and approached Addie sitting on the porch.

"Happy birthday, Miss Addie. You be about 20?"

"Nineteen, Uncle John, just 19," she said. "Thanks for coming to my birthday party. It's a real treat."

"John, this here's Doug Spencer, from Chicago," Buck said, stepping back and letting me step up. "He's come all the way down here just to meet you."

"Mr. Hurt, I'm delighted to meet you."

His shy smile showed pleasure at meeting me, as if he were just a country musician doing a favor for a friend on her birthday. I recalled he'd played Carnegie Hall, the University of Chicago and the Newport Folk Festival all in the past six months. This man didn't have swagger and aloof in him.

John greeted each of the colored on the porch as old friends. Billy Ray and Cooter and their girlfriends showed up in Billy Ray's truck, and he nodded in recognition of them. The Coke route driver with his colored loader pulled off the highway and parked at the side, bringing a case of cold Coke to the party. Aunt Emmabelle, up from Jackson, stepped out from the store.

The introductions and small talk went on for half an hour. Then John made his way to the end of the porch and laid his guitar case on the bench and pulled out a Guild F-30 NT Sunburst guitar. This was a popular acoustic guitar with blues musicians. He took a sip of whiskey, followed by a swig of Coke, and tuned up.

Musicians usually have a play list before a performance. I'd had enough performance experience at fraternity parties and coffeehouses to know how annoying it is for someone to start making requests right at the beginning. I leaned against the side of the porch next to Addie and waited. John started off with *My Creole Belle*. The simple arrangement was perfect for an arthritic old man to warm up his fingers. He'd added words to a tune played by jazz bands and orchestras for 50 years, turning it into a simple love song.

My creole belle
I love her well
My darlin' baby
My creole belle

Even this simple song was anchored by a driving rhythm played with his thumb, while his index and middle fingers picked a melody. Right off, that separated his playing from mine. I had to think of the rhythm like it was part of the tune – John didn't, it was automatic. He proved that later in the evening when he played *Talkin' Casey,* which was an original performance piece of his where he played the rhythm while delivering a monologue about Casey Jones' wife asking him not to drive the train that fateful day, punctuated by using a steel slide to create sounds on the guitar to mimic her pleading voice, the train whistle, the wheels on the track and the brakes. It was a masterful tour de force where he spoke, sang, played rhythm, melody and made sound effects all at once. You can't teach that.

He took a pull from the Old Grand Dad bottle and went into *Spike Driver Blues,* one of the standards from his 1927 recording. This is a true Delta blues tale of driving railroad spikes and being killed by the hammer, meaning the hard work.

> *Take this hammer and carry it to the captain*
> *Tell him I'm gone. Tell him I'm gone. Oh, tell him I'm gone*

He was hitting his stride now with that much more spirited piece based on the story of John Henry but with a different tune and story line. When John sang of swinging that hammer, it wasn't a fantasy, it was a memory. Hennis told me he and John had worked on the original Yazoo & Mississippi Valley Railroad in the 1920s, and later the Avalon and Southeastern Railroad spur that went to a nearby gravel quarry.

But, building railroads is not a steady job. John's primary occupation during most of his younger years was logging cypress, oak and gum to make railroad ties. He'd cut the trees with a crosscut saw, split them with a steel wedge and sledgehammer, plane them to size by hand and haul them by mule wagon to the nearest railroad siding to be inspected, bought and loaded by the railroad. He got a dollar a tie.

What must it have been like, I mused, to haul a load of ties to the railroad siding after a week of backbreaking work, and have someone like Mr. Hoagland be the railroad inspector. A man like that might reject a tie just for spite, just to rub a colored man's nose in the dirt. And there would be no recourse. How many of John's white neighbors had been Hoaglands, and how many had been Kinders? How many had been like the man in the store in Grenada, reinforcing a rigid social structure by casually imposing a menial task on a complete stranger just because his skin was black?

Tap. Tap. Whoosh.

Buck handed me a Schlitz from the six-pack by his chair.

Hurt's voice was old and withered, and it cracked at certain points, but his sincerity and shy smile made you want to scoot your chair up to be closer, to hear every nuanced note.

When he got to *Avalon Blues,* his fingers fairly flew across the strings as the rhythm had feet tapping and heads nodding. A story about the very place we were sitting, and when he got to the part about "pretty women in Avalon," I wondered what the place must have looked like 40 years before, when he wrote the song. The only pretty woman living in Avalon now, I thought, was Addie Kinder.

Jarvus and Jasper were leaning against the corner foundation rocks just below the bench where Hurt sat with his guitar. Their mother and grandmother found places on the porch. He took a break, took a healthy pull from the Old Grand Dad and smiled down.

"You boys all right?"

A late model pickup came up Highway 7 from the south, toward Greenwood, and the driver used his engine to slow down, producing a deep roar and banging backfire from the pickup's dual glass-pack mufflers that diverted everyone's attention.

The truck pulled off the main highway onto the gravel in front of the store. Two men were inside and stared as they drove slowly by. The truck turned around down the street by the gin and came back, accelerating in front of the store, throwing some gravel. When it got back to the highway, it turned north with a rubber-burning squeal as the tires spun and the mufflers roared away into the night.

"Hennis told me you play too," John said, nodding at me as he took another healthy pull from the Old Grand Dad. He leaned back against the wall, taking a break. Several people got up to go around to the side of the store to the privy or to get some refreshment from inside the store.

I jumped to get my guitar and tune up. I went right into the simplest song, *Creole Belle,* trying to get the rhythm line right. He corrected my fingers, then showed me again how he did it. For about 10 minutes, I had a lesson from the master.

After the break, he tuned up again and went into *Frankie,* his version of the old blues song *Frankie and Johnny.* In John Hurt's version, it was Frankie and Albert. Then he went into *Big Leg Blues,* an account of a man asking his lover to move her big leg off of his, it apparently being so large as to "make a good man change his mind." Then he played *Sliding Delta,* the song that brought me to Mississippi.

"Is this the Sliding Delta?" I asked after he'd finished, pointing behind the store.

"Sure. Railroad ran right back there," he said, turning to nod in that direction. "The station was over there," he said, indicating the abandoned building a half-block toward the Avalon gin.

"Must have been more people then," I said.

"Oh, yeah. There was houses all up and down this street, a church, another store down the road there," he said, pointing down the gravel road abutting the state highway. "And people lived all around the fields here."

Buck reached under his chair and pulled out a pint bottle with no label on it and passed it over to me. Not realizing at first what it was, I took a sniff.

"Whoah!" I exclaimed at the yeasty smell I'd encountered at the still, now accompanied by the strong scent of ethyl alcohol.

Buck's hand pushed the bottle down out of everyone's sight as he gave me a sly grin. Hennis was watching, too.

No stranger to whiskey straight, I expected the burn. Oh, and I got it. I'd turned sideways away from the crowd to take a swig and was facing the red Texaco kerosene pump, so that's what I thought of when it went down and kind of burst in my midsection, sending out waves of fire. I'd taken a deep breath before, and when I released it the fire burned my nose.

"Whew! Umm. Uh, good," I said, my eyes watering.

Buck and Hennis laughed. John, still playing, smiled. Addie looked down to hide her smile. Billy Ray and Cooter were huddled up with their girls in the back of the truck and didn't notice.

I took another swig before handing the bottle back to Buck and chased it with the beer. John went into *Farther Along* as a mellow glow spread up from my stomach.

Farther along we'll know more about it,
Farther along we'll understand why,
Cheer up my brother, live in the sunshine,
We'll understand it all by and by

John seemed to be looking into my very soul, and he was answering the question he found there. How could a man work his whole life for the comfort and profit of people who trip, cheat and humiliate him, and not be bitter?

Buck handed me the bottle again, and I took a healthy swig.

The old gospel song about injustice, toil and pain turns hopeful, promising that the toil will be for only a little while longer before we all "sweep through the heavenly gates," and finally we'll "understand why."

A downtrodden people grasping religion to ease their sorrow, or patiently serving as examples to the rest of us? I didn't know, and for the first time in my life, I wondered.

"This is the first song I learned to play, when I was 10," John said shyly. He began picking and, at first, I didn't recognize the tune.

"Lead Belly recorded it years later, and it was a big hit, but this is how I learned it," John said.

The song was *Goodnight Irene,* and it was the last one he played. We all knew it, and by the end were all singing along.

He packed up and said his goodbyes. Going down the steps, he was a bit unsteady, and I helped him put his guitar in the truck. He took the Old Grand Dad out of his pocket and held the remaining half of the pint on his lap.

"Jessie will be waitin' for some o' this," he smiled as I closed the door.

"His wife don't leave the house much," Hennis added as he climbed in and started the old Studebaker.

I thanked him again and shook his hand and then they were gone. Going back up the steps I was a bit unsteady as well and thinking about having another slug of Hennis' lightning. Addie and Emmabelle were picking up empty bottles and other decidua from the guests. Buck sat pale and glassy-eyed.

"Buck, you OK?" I put my hand on his shoulder.

He slid to the side and fell to the floor.

"Buck!" I sat him up.

"Blurrpp!" He vomited a quart of black coffee grounds material that reeked of whiskey and beer onto the worn wooden floor.

Chapter 19

Flames woke me. Fighting through confusion, I came up from a deep alcohol-induced sleep. I heard the guttural rumble of a motor running outside the store, and I could see flames flickerng through the door to the front. I leapt up and ran into the store, trying to remember whether we had a fire extinguisher someplace. The fire was out front. Peering through the windows as I unlocked the front door, it appeared that something was burning in the parking lot – a car on fire?

It was a cross. I rushed onto the porch to confront a cross 6 feet tall and wrapped in rags soaked with kerosene. It was anchored in the driveway, and flames shot 10 feet into the air. Flanking it were three men in white wearing peaked hoods with a white cross in a red circle. They stood silent, holding clubs. Behind them, the pickup we'd seen pass earlier in the evening sat idling. Were these guys for real? Was this a joke? Did this stuff still happen? Yes. No. Yes.

"What do you want?" I called out, trying to be as intimidating as possible.

They stood, silent. The crackling of the flames and the light flickering across the parking lot and out onto the highway and the fields beyond was their answer.

The sheriff's deputy for this part of Carroll County lived in Holcomb, 10 miles away. There was no 911 system in Mississippi in 1965. The only neighbors were Jasper and Jarvis and their mother and grandmother, and a few older white families along the road to the gin. They wouldn't be of any help even if they were alerted. The Kinders didn't have any firearms that I knew of, and I had never handled one anyway.

I was on my own here, but I began to gain some composure. Unlike Negroes confronted by the Klan burning a cross on their front yard, I wasn't in any danger of being lynched. I was pretty sure of that, though not certain.

"Are you that college boy from Chicago?" the one in the middle asked, his voice a derisive sneer.

My composure evaporated. Three college students had died the summer before, apparently killed by the Klan for registering colored voters. The FBI was still investigating, but no charges had been filed. That happened in Neshoba County, not 50 miles from Avalon. Was I next?

"Mississippi is still part of America, isn't it?"

I held my ground.

"I work here."

My patriotic response led to another minute of silence. Out of the corner of my eye, I could see Buck's ladder-back chair beside the door. It was light enough to pick up and sturdy enough to be a weapon. I could do some damage if they tried to climb the steps.

"Niggers been mixin' with whites at this store. We seen it last night."

"This is a retail establishment. We sell to whoever has the money to buy, same as Sears."

"They was singin'."

"People sing at football games," I said.

I was winning this debate, and I was getting cocky. Another minute passed.

"By the order of the Grand Dragon of the Klu Klux Klan of the state of Mississippi, we have orders to burn this store."

He stepped back and held his club up to the burning cross. It was wrapped in rags and burst into flame.

"We was just gonna give 'em a warning," one of the others turned and whispered to the leader.

"The Dragon said to burn it," the first one responded and took a step forward.

"But, hey, that crippled girl lives here," the other one said.

"Let smartass up there save her." He took another step.

My mouth had gotten us into this. Obviously this was someone from out of the county brought in to give a warning and backed up by two locals, and I had pissed him off. Kinder's store was wood frame with wood shingles on the roof, a wooden porch, 50 gallons of kerosene in a tank on the end of it, and 500 gallons of gasoline in a tank almost beneath their feet. That kerosene soaked torch would easily set it afire, and it would spread quickly. Addie was in the back, and it would take her 10 minutes to get her braces on. Buck was immobile on his deathbed; he couldn't walk even with help. It would take two to get him out.

"Wait! Buck Kinder's in there, and he's too sick to walk! Addie's crippled! You can't do this!"

"The people of Carroll County are gonna remember this for a long time," he said, stepping forward. The other two shrank back.

I grabbed the chair and leaped from the steps, catching him by surprise. He poked the torch at me as he stepped back. One of the others regained his resolve and swung his club low, catching me on the kneecap. I went down and dropped the chair. He swung, and the club came down toward my head. I dodged and it hit my right shoulder. As he raised it the leader aimed a kick at my head, glancing my jaw. I saw stars.

"Stop!" Addie Kinder stood above us on the porch, her white nightgown glowing with reflected light from the cross and the torch. "291KG3! Lowndes County, Mississippi."

The Klansmen froze. The one with the club about to brain me looked back at the third man and whispered, "You took the plate off didn't you?"

"Yeah, it's under the seat."

"291KG3, Lowndes County, Mississippi," she repeated. "I saw it last night. And you," she said, pointing at the man with the club, "you sound familiar. I know you."

He shrank back.

"This wasn't supposed to be no murder," the third man said. "Let's go."

The man with the torch hesitated as his two backups headed to the truck. Then he tossed the torch toward me and turned, snarling back over his shoulder, "I'll remember you college boy!"

I rolled from the torch and tried to stand. My leg gave way and I fell on my face. The truck doors slammed shut. Gravel sprayed as they backed up, swerved down the road to the highway and turned toward Greenwood, tires spinning and mufflers roaring into the night.

Two days later, on August 4, President Johnson signed the Voting Rights Act of 1965. Back in April while I was planning my trip to Mississippi, I had followed news of the battles in Congress to get it passed. Sen. James Eastland of Mississippi was chairman of the Senate Judiciary Committee, in which the bill was crafted, and the majority of his committee was in favor of the Voting Rights Act. Eastland had opposed it at every turn, and it had taken action by the whole Senate to force him to release it from committee and allow a vote by the whole Senate. Eastland owned 6,000 acres of the best cotton land in Mississippi, and it was spread out along Mississippi Highway 3 not 30 miles from Avalon.

Addie and I had driven by the huge, white, antebellum-style manor house surrounded by cotton fields. No trees or sloughs or rivers to work around on James Eastland's land. Just cotton.

Chapter 20

"You got a pick sack?" Cooter asked Addie as he came up the steps. We were sitting there after supper watching it get dark.

"We don't have any new ones, but there are some used ones in the storeroom."

"Good. Doug, want to make some more big money?"

"OK." I had a feeling I might be going down another primrose path.

"No, I'm serious. I need your help. This cotton field across the road here is 160 acres," he said, nodding to the field I had run out of just ahead of Ace McNutt's crop duster. "Ace will spray it next week with a defoliant, and the leaves will drop off and the bolls will open. In two weeks, Dad will run the cotton picker through it – get it all in one pass."

"I'll be back in college by then," I warned.

"Right, and I'll be in Marine boot camp. We have another field, just 10 acres. It's got the highway on one side, a ditch on the other and trees at both ends. Dad can't get the picker in there. Ace sprayed it last week, and I promised I'd get it picked before I leave. Can you help me? We're payin' three cents a pound."

Addie said, "The pick sacks are in the closet behind the canned goods. There's a nine-foot and a 12-foot."

"You take the nine-foot," she said to me.

"Oh, I'm not man enough to handle the 12-foot?"

"Go ahead, big boy," she said with a laugh.

And so it came to pass that I stood there at dawn on Sunday at the first row dragging a 12-foot pick sack and contemplating 10 acres of freshly defoliated cotton. That row was 540 feet long, and there were 278 of those rows planted 3 feet apart. Jessie, the colored boy who had pitched watermelons with us, his brother, a cousin and three other friends of Cooter's were all there, enlisted for the picking. Ervin Davis pulled up on the tractor, pulling a cotton trailer. He set up the scale, grabbed a pick sack and started in on the row beside Cooter.

"Put the strap over your left shoulder with the open sack at waist level behind your right arm," Cooter said, demonstrating as he started down the row next to mine. "Pick with both hands. Pull the cotton out of the bolls and stuff it into the sack. Pull the sack along behind you."

Soon they were all well ahead of me.

The fluffy white cotton seemed so clean and wholesome. It was bursting out of the dried husks and hung there with promise, seeming to invite being plucked. Easily plucked, it was soft, and one could feel the seeds buried within, attached to the fiber. The gin would remove the seeds using a comb mechanism.

Nothing to this, I thought, plucking bolls with both hands and shoving them into the sack.

"Doug, you missed some," Cooter called out from the next row.

I looked back to see a couple of open bolls low on a plant on the other side. I stretched around and leaned down to capture them. Ten minutes later, with the sun beginning to get hot on my back, aching from leaning over to get those bolls close to the ground, hands smarting from encountering the sharp ends of those dried husks, the novelty began to wear off.

An hour later I finished the first row. Cooter and Jessie and the others were halfway back to the truck. I stood up straight, stretched my aching back and pushed the cotton down in the sack. It was almost half full. I bent over and started picking again.

"Here, wrap it like this," Mr. Davis explained patiently at the end of the row.

He showed me how to wrap the shoulder strap around my pick sack to make a bundle to be weighed. I wrapped it as he demonstrated and lifted it up to the scale, which hung from a tree branch.

"Seventy-eight pounds. Good start, Doug. You might be missing some, the other guys are getting 85 out of their two rows."

He jumped up onto the end of the cotton trailer, and I lifted the sack to him. He dumped it into the trailer and tossed the sack back to me. Turning back, I looked back down my row and could see some cotton still on the plants. Cooter's and Jessie's were bare. I got a drink of water, shouldered my sack and started down a fresh row. I had made $2.34.

In another hour, I heard the truck horn honk and turned to see the other guys back at the truck and breaking for lunch. I was just finishing my row. So, leave the sack and eat, then fill it up coming back, or drag 40 pounds of cotton back to the truck to weigh?

"Bring the sack!" Cooter shouted, seeing my hesitation.

I bundled the sack and hefted it onto my shoulder and walked toward the truck down the row I had just picked, eyeing the row I would have to pick after lunch. It did not seem the least bit clean or wholesome. Halfway there, I stopped to shift the weight on my back and saw myself from a distance as if in a painting – a lone figure bent under the weight of a cotton sack trudging through the late summer heat.

"Makes you appreciate that ol' well water," Cooter said, lifting a cup filled with water from the water thermos in the back of the truck.

"That it does," I said.

I'd thought all the water there had an iron taste, but it sure tasted good that day. After my second cup, I sat and unwrapped the sandwich Addie had thoughtfully prepared for me.

"What you got?" Cooter asked, looking over at my lunch, comparing.

I opened it up. White bread, two slices of bologna, mustard, pickle and a slice of cheese.

"Oh, Doug gets cheese on his baloney," he announced to the others.

"Then you want to trade, I guess."

"No, I was just wondering if Addie had put something special in your lunch. And she did. Good thing about baloney is it stops a guy from thinking about food for the rest of the day. What's a sandwich for if not that?"

"Wisdom from the fields of toil," I said.

I dug in on my sandwich. I've always liked a bologna sandwich. And, I had something special in mine.

The afternoon wore on, and I was determined to keep up with the other guys. The hotter and more unpleasant it got, the more determined they seemed to get the job done. I realized that this was subsistence for them. Quitting wasn't an option, nor was knocking off early because it was hot. I redoubled my efforts. The scion of the Spencer family of Lake Forest, Illinois, should be able to at least keep up with Cooter, the scion of the Davis family of Avalon, Mississippi. By cutting my water break at the next turn and weigh in, I caught up.

"How are we doing?" I asked Cooter, hopeful that there was some predetermined stopping point.

"Good. We've got about 2,000 pounds. Dad said we're gettin' 45 pounds a row, which will make a bale an acre. He'll let us quit when we get thirty-six hundred pounds. That'll fill the wagon, and he can take it to the gin tonight. The gin at Holcomb is offering a hundred-dollar prize for the first bale ginned, and we may be the first."

"Is that an occasion for a party?"

"Hmmph," Cooter said. "That's an occasion to pay off the fertilizer bill."

"What's a bale worth?"

"Not as much as last year. The price was 26 cents a pound Tuesday, and that's assuming top quality. We don't want it to get rained on. There are 480 pounds in a bale."

I picked along, thinking about the Harlan Howard song *Busted* that had been a big hit for Ray Charles and Johnny Cash. In the song, cotton is down to a quarter a pound, and that's not good. Then I did some math. It didn't add up.

"We're getting more than 480 pounds an acre," I said.

"Oh, yeah. The gin don't pay 26 cents a pound for the raw cotton. They gin it first, to take the seeds out. Then we get paid for the lint. That's about 40 percent of the weight of what we're picking. The rest is seeds. We'll get about $120 for a bale of cotton and maybe 20 bucks for the seed. Plus," he paused and turned to look down into my pick sack, "you got some hulls in there. You'll get paid for those when you weigh in, but the gin pulls them out and we just get paid for the lint."

I felt guilty for my sloppy picking. I could see my cotton wasn't as clean as theirs. So, they were going to get $124.80 a bale for the lint and $20 for the seeds, say $150 an acre. For that, they had to pay $36 to get the cotton picked, pay for seed in the spring, fertilizer, fuel for the tractor, Ace McNutt to spray for weevils and to defoliate, and taxes on the land. The profit per acre wasn't that much for a backbreaking business.

I cleaned up my picking, and the last sack I weighed out was a clean as any of the other guys. When Ervin Davis called it a day, I had picked just over 200 pounds, making the princely sum of $6.36.

"Let's ride to the gin," Cooter said, smiling for the first time since lunch, "and spend some of this money on a Coke."

Mr. Davis paid us all off, and we jumped into the back of the cotton wagon while the others were either picked up by family or started trudging down the road to their homes.

Lounging on the soft cotton as we swayed down the road at a stately pace behind the tractor, with the prospect of an ice cold Coke at the gin, my sore muscles began to feel better. I was glad the next day was Monday and I'd be back at Kinder's store pumping gas and flirting with Addie. Cooter and the others would be back at the field, which was only a third picked.

"First bale of the season!" a man called to us as Mr. Davis pulled through a covered loading dock at the gin in Holcomb. A large flexible hose, nearly as big around as my waist, dangled from the ceiling. Cooter stood and grabbed it and pulled it down into the wagon. I heard a pump turn on and Cooter began vacuuming the cotton.

"Which field is that from?" the man asked Mr. Davis as he dismounted from the tractor. They began to discuss the location of the field, condition of the crop and how much more was left to pick. I climbed out of the trailer as the cotton disappeared into the hose.

"Better hurry gettin' that cotton in, rain's on the way," the man said as he and Mr. Davis walked away from the tractor. "Good news is, with the rain in Texas, cotton was up 2 cents Friday."

Cooter vacuumed up the rest of the cotton as I watched, hearing the machinery inside spring into action, sounding like a large fan.

"C'mon, let's go inside," he said when he'd emptied the trailer. "If you're gonna pick it, you oughtta see it ginned."

I followed him inside.

"Hey Cooter!" one of the workmen called out as we entered. "Gonna party with that hundred bucks?"

Our cotton tumbled into a large machine and soon began falling down through two cabinet devices with glass windows in the front, and then down a belt to another vacuum tube that sucked it up and out of the room.

"There's the seeds," Cooter said, pointing below the cotton to another conveyor where the seeds, still with some lint attached, moved in the same direction. Walking into the next room, we saw the cotton falling into a wooden box 6 feet tall and 4 feet deep. A hydraulic plunger cycled up and down, pushing the cotton to the bottom of the box. In five minutes, it was full, and the plunger just cycled at the top.

"Watch out," the workman said, stepping in front of us. He shut off the plunger and, with another man, opened the box. They placed a sheet of burlap on top and pulled the edges down the sides, then roughly sewed them to a sheet placed at the bottom using a large needle and some thick cotton thread. When they were done they pushed the bale and it tumbled down onto the gin floor. "That's Number 1!"

A small crowd, including Mr. Davis, the gin manager and some other farmers, gathered to note the occasion. The gin continued running, and we dispersed.

We walked back through the warehouse at the back, where a few dozen bales were stacked here and there.

"Hardheads held their cotton in here a whole year waiting for the price to rise," Cooter said. "It's a nickel less than last year."

As we walked out the back of the mostly empty warehouse, I saw a galvanized metal duct exit the top of the gin and extend 30 feet into the gin's backyard. Cotton hulls and stems flew out the end, falling onto a pile.

"There's your hulls," Cooter said. "In another month, when they've ginned a thousand bales, that hull pile will be as tall as the gin."

"Then what do they do with it?"

"Burn it. Ain't good for nothin'."

Cooter walked to the pile and kicked it.

"Seems like they'd want to put it back on the land, replace what was taken out," I said.

"Fuel to bring the trailer back, fuel to pull a manure spreader across the field, wages to someone to drive the tractor," Cooter said. "Ain't worth it."

Then he laughed and nodded across the railroad track toward a small building.

"That's our Boy Scout hut. We had our Scout meetings once a month over there and, during gin season, we'd come over here and slide down the hull pile or play king of the hill."

Cooter smiled again and said, "The hull pile is like a big pile of leaves. You can climb up it and sink down to your knees, and if someone knocks you over, you just tumble and slide back down to the bottom. Or, you can get a cardboard box and open it up and slide down like a snow sled."

"Oh, to be a boy again."

"Yeah."

"What's that?" I asked, pointing to a large red machine parked in the gin yard.

"Oh, that's an International Harvester two row cotton picker. You need to see that," he said, leading the way to it. "It's a fairly new one. Dad's is an older model."

The beast had large tires like a tractor and a huge mesh basket behind and above the cab. Four yellow noses stuck out from the front below the cab.

"We plant all the rows the same distance apart, and set these to guide the plant into this entry here," he said, kneeling to look between two of the appendages. "Look down here, see those metal spindles in there?"

"Yeah." I saw two rows of tapered metal spindles about the size of my thumb and twice as long.

"They spin and the cotton sticks to 'em, and that pulls it out of the boll. Then some more spindles inside rotate the other way and pull the cotton off the first spindle, then a blower throws it up into that basket. It'll hold a ton or more of cotton."

"So, you drive it to the gin?"

"No. That basket dumps it into a cotton trailer."

"So, if you could get this into that field we picked today, how long would it take?"

"Well, the dumping and turning is what takes the time, and you'd need three cotton trailers. Before one trailer has gone to the gin and back, you'll have filled the basket twice more. You could do the whole field in less than a day. Dad will do that 160-acre field across from Kinder's in about two weeks."

"Without you."

Cooter's eyes flicked toward me, and I wished I could take the comment back.

"Yeah, without me." We turned and walked back toward the gin. By the time we got there they had ginned the rest of the cotton. Total: three bales.

Chapter 21

"Paint a sign and put it out by the road, 'GAS 25 CENTS.' Sell the gas for 25 cents and everything else for half-price."

He could barely raise his head, and the pallor he'd had the past few weeks was ghastly. When Buck collapsed after Addie's birthday party, we had carried him inside to the bed and Emmabelle picked up the telephone to call the ambulance.

"Ain't goin' to no hospital," he'd said.

"Buck! You're near dead!" Emmabelle said, used to having the last word

"Yep. Doc showed me the X-rays. Cancer in both lungs. No sense going through surgery, he said. Can't take 'em both out. So, I've got pills for pain and whatnot, and if I need any more, just call the doc. I'm stayin' right here."

And so he had. Relatives and old friends from all over the area trooped through to sit by the bed and recall old memories. Doc Tarver came by every couple of days with pills and beer. The family lawyer updated Buck's will and brought a fifth of Old Grand Dad. Emmabelle and Addie cooked and served the visitors while I ran the store.

Then Buck called me into the bedroom for some final instructions.

"Write these off," he said, and gave me a list of people who owed the store money but who were so far down they'd never come up with what they owed.

"Collect these if you can," he said, reciting another list of people able but perhaps not eager to pay.

"Don't let anyone buy anything more who owes money. Some might pay up just so they can get a case of pickles cheap," he said, chuckling. "Take the truck down to the bank in Greenwood every night. There'll be a lot more cash than usual, and there'll be some who will notice that and wonder how to get some."

Buck had another session with Addie and Emmabelle after he talked with me. Lots of tears all around.

That night, they called me to help after he vomited some more blood. By morning, he was gone.

The funeral was two days later, and they buried him by the Presbyterian church. The next day, Emmabelle loaded up all of Addie's clothes and moved her to Jackson to start orientation at Millsaps College.

I made the sign and propped it up by the side of the highway.

"WDIA! Fifty thousand watts of soul power!"

Rufus Thomas and B.B. King were both disc jockeys on the Memphis station that played all colored music – blues, rhythm and blues, and soul. They talked about who was touring the area and pushed music by up-and-coming musicians, especially recording artists for Stax records. The old blues were giving way to more professionally produced music from Chicago, featuring big bands backing up the vocals, and music from Detroit – Motown. Still, it was Delta music.

"Chess recording star Howlin' Wolf will be fronting Sonny Boy Williamson's band at the Satellite Club in Greenwood on Saturday night," Rufus informed his audience one afternoon a week after Buck passed.

Hmmm. Right down the road, I thought, turning the radio down as a white customer pulled up in front of the gas pump. How could I get into a colored club in Greenwood?

"Gas for a quarter? You got a gas war or something?" he asked, getting out of the truck.

"Going-out-of-business sale. Everything inside is half off, cigarettes, coffee, motor oil, shotgun shells, whatever they've got. Even selling the tables and chairs," I said, clearing the pump.

I was becoming a salesman. The locals came in to buy what they needed but didn't have a lot of money. The big sales were people attracted by the cheap gas who loved a bargain.

"Got any beer?" he asked. A quick thinker.

"No beer, but we've got some top quality cigars for half off."

That got him into the store. When he left half an hour later, he had a handful of cigars, a case of motor oil, six cartons of cigarettes, a shovel, a box of Baby Ruth candy bars, five cans of Crisco, the last two pounds of bacon in the store and a case of pickles. That last purchase, accomplished as a suggestion just as he was pulling out his wallet to pay, gave me a warm feeling, like Buck was there with a big smile on his face.

And so it went. The store emptied out, and the deposit bag for the bank filled up. That Satellite Club in Greenwood was the same place Billy Ray and Cooter had taken me to buy the beer before we crashed the annual meeting at the Duck Club on Sharkey Bayou, and every night when I passed it on the way to the bank I tried to conjure up a way to get in without getting arrested or robbed.

Howlin' Wolf was a Chicago blues musician of some renown and had been on some of the same stages as Mississippi John Hurt, like the Newport Folk Festival. And, like all those other guys, he was from Mississippi. There was going to be quite a party Saturday night.

Tap. Tap. Whoosh!

"Cooter," I asked as I took the proffered beer, "ever been to the Satellite Club over by Greenwood?"

I was sitting on the bench tuning up my guitar, and he was sitting in Buck's ladder-back chair that evening.

"Just to buy beer," he said.

"It's just me and you left," I said. "With everyone else gone, it seems like we should have some kind of excitement this weekend. Want to go over there?"

"No. I'm off to Marine Corps boot camp on Monday. The recruiter was by the house today to meet my folks and make sure I was ready. He warned me about getting into any kind of trouble right before leaving. Don't want anything to get in the way of leaving here."

Hard to argue with that. We finished a beer, said our goodbyes and he walked back home. I played the guitar and listened to the tree frogs and the cicadas.

I found Hennis Hurt's account book. Hennis had a telephone, so I called him. He agreed to take me to the Satellite Club. I picked him up in Buck's truck. He was accompanied by Pearl, a 50-ish lady, and they were both dressed in their best. The deal was I would drive and pay the cover.

Hennis was well known at the Satellite Club. Remember, Mississippi was dry, so all alcohol, even the beer with the Mississippi tax stamp on the top, was bootleg. The Satellite Club was the main outlet for Hennis' lightning.

"This here is Doug Spencer from Chicago. He play backup for John Hurt," Hennis said, introducing me at the door as I paid the cover, $2 each. That white lie was, perhaps, unnecessary as he was tight with the owner and we would have gotten in anyway. It caused an issue later.

We were tucked safely in the corner by the bar. I went up to the bar to get a round of beers, paying a buck each. We'd gotten a whole six-pack a month before for two bucks, but now they had to pay the band. The bartender motioned for me to lean over toward him.

"You won't have no trouble. Clarence be watchin' pretty close" he said, nodding toward a large colored man by the door.

Then he added, "You want some pussy later, you come see me."

"OK, thanks."

That lingering virginity problem was still there, and the sheer carnality of the Satellite Club and all that went on there put one in mind of that kind of activity, but this didn't seem to be the time to deal with it.

I took three beers back to the table. I did notice while I was standing there that they were doing a brisk business in shots from under the bar, 50 cents each. I did some quick math and figured the house was pulling in $40 a gallon on

Hennis' lightning. I thought he might want another load of sugar before I shut down the store.

Howlin' Wolf came in through the front door. Like a feral predator, Wolf stared down the bouncer, the owner and anyone in the crowd who locked eyes with him. Dressed in a pressed black suit with a white shirt and tie, he walked to the bandstand. There was no introduction. The band snapped to their instruments like a military unit and stood motionless, waiting for the Wolf. He was big and wide and black and already shining with sweat, and he owned that room.

Wolf adjusted the microphone and stood there for a moment before his wide face broke into an infectious grin and he started to speak.

"How y'all tonight?"

He looked out over the audience like he expected an answer. There was a murmur from the crowd, and the tension of his entrance dissipated.

"We all here to remember our friend, Sonny Boy Williamson," he said, pausing to let the audience respond, like a rural preacher waiting for an "amen."

"We got that jar over there," Wolf said, nodding toward the bar where the proprietor had just put a gallon pickle jar, "and during the night we all gonna be puttin' something in there for Sonny Boy's final expenses."

I believed that "we" all would.

Hennis told me Wolf had come down from Chicago to front Sonny Boy's band to give them a good gig now that Sonny Boy was gone. He'd played Clarksdale the night before and was scheduled in West Memphis, Arkansas, on Sunday night. Wolf was 55 years old and had been playing the blues full time for 40 years, starting out as a teenager in the 1920s playing guitar for Charlie Patton, widely credited as the father of the Delta blues. Patton lived in Sunflower County, just south of Greenwood. Later, Wolf had his own band headquartered in West Memphis and had a radio show there.

"Why West Memphis?" I'd asked Hennis when he related Wolf's background. It seemed to me like the clubs on Beale Street would be the natural base for any blues musician. I'd seen what a barrier that Mississippi River was between Memphis and its counterpart in Arkansas.

"Memphis was a tight town years ago," Hennis said. "They had a curfew for coloreds – 11 o'clock. Be out after that, go to jail. West Memphis was wide open!"

Wolf took off his suit jacket, handed it to one of the band members and pulled a harmonica out of his pocket. With an evil grin, like the Big Bad Wolf, he snaked out his long tongue and licked the harmonica like he was about to swallow it whole.

"Wooohoo! Woohoo!"

A murmur went through the crowd. Wolf had given them his signature wolf howl, and everyone was on the edge of their seats, waiting for what might come next. The band was motionless.

Slowly, he brought the harmonica to his mouth and softly started the introduction to *Bye Bye Bird,* one of Sonny Boy's signature songs. That little harmonica was swallowed up by two huge hands and that big face, but the sound was soft and soulful, just like Sonny Boy's recording I'd first heard from radio station KFFA in Helena the day Sonny Boy died. Wolf did the song slow, alone, without backup, and drew the last note out long and sad. When he finished, all was quiet, like a prayer. Then Wolf nodded, and his guitar player began a slow rhythmic introduction, classic Delta blues, but much more nuanced than the basic twelve-bar blues riff I'd learned.

At eight bars, the crowd knew the song and, like one, they jumped to their feet.

"Wooohooo."

The rest of the band came in behind him, and the song was *Smokestack Lighting.* Wolf's voice was as big as he was, and that falsetto howl introduced the guttural first line, "Smokestack Lightning, shining just like gold!"

You could have heard that call across the highway without a microphone. Oh, and it came from the cotton fields and the chain gangs, and I saw the old steam locomotive with fire shooting out of the smokestack and the whistle screaming through a rural Mississippi night. Then he blew the harmonica for eight bars and went into the next verse, asking, "Where did ya stay last night?"

I felt a hundred years of honky tonks and beer joints and the infidelity and passion they produce. Each time he'd hit the refrain – "why don't you hear me crying?" – it was like Wolf was reaching into my chest with one of those huge hands and demanding to know why I, Douglas Spencer, had not heard him crying. I was thrilled. I was scared. I will never forget it.

After *Smokestack Lightning,* he played *Back Door Man, Killing Floor* and *Spoonful* to finish out the first set. His sound was different than Albert King's, who had been much less talkative, played louder, sang less and tortured the guitar with rhythmic flourishes, a pick, a steel thimble and slide. King was the face of the new rhythm and blues, a dance band with long improvisations. Wolf was the old blues, and the focus was on Wolf, though he was backed by Sonny Boy's band.

With King, I'd felt each song was being played in a new way, never to be repeated exactly the same way again. With Wolf, I knew he'd worked out each verse with the band, and it would be the same way tomorrow in West Memphis.

"Whew, y'all havin' a good time?" he asked, wiping sweat off his face with a white handkerchief. Though his white cotton dress shirt was soaked with sweat, he still wore a tie.

The audience responded loudly.

"Want to introduce this fine band I'm playin' with. They been on radio station KFFA on the King Biscuit Time show with Sonny Boy, but they'll be around even though he's gone. This is Rufus Monkton on bass, Houston Stackhouse on the guitar and Peck Curtis back there on the drums. You be watchin' for these guys.

"Coming down here to Greenwood," Wolf went on, " I had to bring my lead guitar player, Hubert Sumlin. Y'all know Hubert, he's from Greenwood. Been with me for 10 years."

I'd noticed that Sumlin, a studious, younger, colored man, was leading off the songs, setting the pace and playing subtle yet absolutely fabulous riffs backing up Wolf. Their timing was so perfect, he had to have played with Wolf for years.

Sumlin started an instrumental, and the band came in. He played without a pick, with a strong rhythmic line on the bass strings and a light melodic touch on the treble strings, a lot like John Hurt. He did some slide accents, but they were rare, muted, and he used only his fingers. It was odd that this restrained, classy guitar player was backing up a big in-your-face performer like Wolf. As I listened through the night, I realized that Wolf was more like Hubert Sumlin – thoughtful and restrained, and the feral predator was the act.

"We gonna take a break now, but don't y'all go away," Wolf said. "We got some old friends here from up at Avalon. Mississippi John Hurt's brother Hennis is here, and Doug Spencer, one of John's back-up band, is gonna sit in the next set."

Oh, shit! That little white lie had come home to roost.

Wolf was like a truck plowing through a field of wheat as he crossed the dance floor headed for our table.

"Hennis, how you been?"

Sumlin and Stackhouse were right behind him. Introductions were made, and Wolf moved on to the bar and more well-wishers. Sumlin and Stackhouse took a seat by me.

"Mr. Sumlin, I'm just a college student from Chicago. I play a little guitar, but I just met John Hurt last week. We played together for just a little while," I stammered.

I was stuck between weaseling out of embarrassing us all and offending Hennis, who had inflated my presence.

"I sat in on bass with Delta Jim up in Cleveland a couple of months ago, but that's the extent of my professional experience."

He nodded, took a sip of a beer Wolf had set before him on his way to the men's room, then turned to Hennis' companion.

"Is this old man treatin' you OK, Pearl?" Sumlin asked, nodding at Hennis. Pearl smiled and replied that he was.

"She my auntie, my mother's little sis," Sumlin said to me.

They talked for a couple of minutes, then he stood up.

"Come on," he said to me. "Show me what you got."

We walked to the bandstand, while Stackhouse walked to the men's room.

"Gimme some blues in A," he said, handing me Houston Stackhouse's guitar.

I laid down the twelve-bar blues and the riff I'd learned from the street musician in Memphis.

"Not bad. What else you got?"

I gave him the introduction to *Sliding Delta.*

"Oh yeah, you been playin' with John Hurt."

I took that casual remark and the smile that went with it as the biggest compliment I'd ever been given.

"Do this," he said, as he sat down and picked up his guitar. It was a twelve-bar blues riff very similar to mine, only every other note was left out. That made it very slow and stately

"The drum gonna come in right at the first, don't get too fast."

So there I was, standing on the bandstand next to Hubert Sumlin, backing up Howlin' Wolf for the opening song of the second set. There was no introduction, we got our instruments ready, and Wolf walked up there and adjusted the microphone. He said nothing, just nodded and that was my signal. Hubert was tapping his foot with the beat. It was very hard to keep it slow and bluesy; my tendency was to speed it up. The drummer came in right with me with a military sort of cadence on the snare that seemed to be a little faster, but I just stuck with Hubert's toe

The effect was ominous, as if something bad was about to happen. The song was *Forty Four,* and Wolf came in loud and mean, he'd "carried that forty-four so long, it made my shoulder sore." He was looking for his woman, who had been with another man. I just kept up my blues chords, and Hubert came in behind me with a subtle, classy counter-rhythm. I could feel Rufus come in, cautiously at first, then meld around my amateurish effort and make it into something special. I felt like a pro.

Wolf nodded at me during the applause at the end, and I did a little bow and handed the guitar back to Houston Stackhouse.

Sumlin came back to our table after the second set.

"My mama's gonna put out something for Wolf and the boys to eat after," he said to Pearl. Y'all want to come along? She'd be happy to see you."

Chapter 22

Mama Sumlin's house was on a quiet side street in Greenwood. When we got there, it was already half filled with well-wishers wanting to welcome Hubert home and meet Wolf. An old colored man in dirty overalls was carrying a cardboard box in the back door. The box was lined with newspaper and filled with barbecued ribs.

"Oh, my!" Wolf said, hitting those ribs like a man on a mission, the band right behind him. Fortunately, there were plenty of ribs.

Wolf pulled the meat off a rib bone much the way he'd slicked up his harmonica four hours before.

"We got ribs in Chicago, but not ribs like this. Who did these?" he asked, looking around with that feral predator look.

"That's me," the old man said, taking a step into the kitchen from the back porch and giving a self-conscious wave, like maybe the Wolf was going to gobble him up next.

"Hubert!" Wolf called. "This man's an artist! You take care a him?"

"Yes, boss," Hubert said patiently, "he's been paid."

"No!" Wolf said sharply, with mock seriousness. "I mean did you TAKE CARE of him?"

Shaking his head and smiling patiently, Hubert crossed the kitchen, reached into his suit pants and pulled out a roll of bills. He stuffed a twenty into the old man's shirt pocket.

"That's good. We may take him on the road with us," Wolf said as he slid another rib through those big lips.

Playing blues music is hard work — standing on a stage for hours at a time, hot, shouting or drumming or riffing a guitar, and it's frequently done at the end of a long day driving. These guys were hungry.

By the time Hennis and I made it to the kitchen, at the end of the line, the band and guests had ploughed through two big bowls of potato salad and slaw, three loaves of Hart's White Bread and two boxes of ribs. Those boxes had held 15-ounce cans of peas, just like I'd been selling all week. Filled with peas, they weighed 25 pounds; filled with ribs, must have been about the same. Fortunately, just as we got there the old man brought in another box. That's a lot of ribs.

I picked up a slab from the box, looking for a knife to cut off four or five ribs, but it fell apart in my hand. Hot, smoky and sticky. The party was springing to life and, as the only white face there, I felt a bit awkward. I took a plate and stood in the corner of the kitchen, then moved out to the back steps as more guests arrived. The old man came out behind me, carrying an empty box.

"How do you do this?" I asked, holding up a rib.

He set the box down and got a serious look on his face, scratching his bald head preparing to give me a complete answer.

"Well, ribs take the whole day, see. Don't want to get into a big hurry with ribs, burn 'em up. They be dry."

He paused, but he wasn't finished.

"These here," he said, pointing at the ribs on my plate, "I started the fire at 6 this morning, oak and hickory. Then I went to the store and picked up a hundred pounds of ribs."

I raised my eyebrows but didn't say anything. I could see wisdom on the way.

"I wash 'em off, see. Don't know just where they been. Don't want to make nobody sick. Then I put my rub on 'em, rub it all over."

"You make that rub?"

"Oh, yeah. I put in salt and black pepper, and some red pepper, " he said, smiling like he knew I was trying to get his secret formula, "and some stuff I don't talk about."

I nodded agreement.

"Then I put 'em on the rack, let 'em smoke for a while, not too hot. Too hot and they dry out. Want to get that smoke in 'em while they fresh. Won't take the smoke after they're cooked."

"What time was that?"

"That was about 10."

"So your fire burned four hours before you put the meat on? How come?"

"Got to heat up the pit! See I got this block pit, big as that shed over there," he said, pointing to a utility shed in a neighbor's yard built to house lawn equipment. "I get those blocks hot first, then let the fire die back some so it's just smolderin'. Then I put the meat on racks see, but not over the fire. No! The fire be on the back side, and the meat in front. Then, about 2, I threw a couple more logs on the fire and let it warm up some, just enough to make the fat run. Don't want no sizzle! No, sir. Not with ribs."

"Then you put sauce on 'em?"

In addition to being soft and porky, these ribs had a sweet ketchup, vinegar, spicy glaze on the outside that stuck to the ribs and didn't run off onto the platter or drip onto your clothes while you ate.

"No! Not til they're done," he said. "See, that sauce, got sugar in it. Put that on too soon and it burns, gets black all over the meat. Nobody eat it if it looks burnt. No, got to wait. Once they cooked, let the fire die back again and just keep 'em hot for a few hours. That's what makes 'em soft, see. Then put on the sauce, put 'em back in the pit and wait another couple hours. That sauce dry out, make that shine you see there."

I nodded as I took another rib and sloughed off the sweet, tender, porky meat. I smiled.

"That's how you do ribs," he said with confidence, picked up the empty box and carried it back to his truck.

I went back inside to see if there were any ribs left. It was nearly 2 a.m., and the crowd had thinned considerably.

"Well, Doug," Wolf said, " you gonna be takin' a blues band on the road?"

He sat at the kitchen table with a glass of orange juice.

"No, sir. That's a tough life. But I want to thank you for the chance to say I played with the great Howlin' Wolf."

"Well, when you get back to Chicago, you want a lesson, call Hubert. He's the best guitar player in the world. You hear me? The world."

He went from friendly to that Wolf predator look, then softened, all in two moments.

"I'd be honored," I said, " if he had the time."

"Well, we on the road 300 days a year. Hardly get home these days."

Hubert was talking with Hennis and Pearl and his family, and the band was packing up the Pontiac station wagon and trailer for the drive to West Memphis. Wolf seemed content to sit in the kitchen and talk to me.

"That song, *Smokestack Lightnin'*, where does that come from?"

"Well, as a boy I lived along the railroad, and me and my cousin would watch the trains come by at night. I can still imagine that whistle on a cold night, and the fire coming off the boiler is the smokestack lightnin'."

"Where'd you live then?"

He got a soft look on his face as he gazed out the back window.

"I ran away from home when I was 13," he smiled. "I walked all the way from West Point to my father's home in Clarksdale."

Wolf paused and smiled and looked back at me.

"Well, I didn't walk the whole way. I jumped on a freight train at Grenada, then waited in the yard at Cleveland for one to Clarksdale."

"Which railroad?"

"It was the old Y&MV. I didn't know where my father lived, so I jumped off just before the yard in Clarksdale. I asked where he lived and walked the rest of the way. He lived along the tracks north of Clarksdale. We'd get Daddy's pocket watch and lie in bed waiting to see if the night train to Memphis was on time."

"Night train to Memphis, that sounds like a song."

"Oh, it is. Couple songs. *Night Train* is an old honky tonk blues song. I play it all the time, and every time I play it I think about that Y&MV, and those passengers goin' up to Memphis."

I heard the car start outside.

"Wolf, we ready to go!" Peck Curtis called from outside.

"Thank you, Wolf."

"Come see me in Chicago," he said. We shook hands and he was gone.

Driving back to Avalon with Hennis and Pearl in the front seat of Buck's truck, I thought about Lloyd Kinder, Addie's grandfather, who would have been driving the night train to Memphis about the time Howlin' Wolf, whose real name was Chester Arthur Burnett, would have been waiting for his whistle and dreaming about the big city just up the road. Hennis was dozing.

"Hennis, when you and John were younger, did you ride the railroad much?"

He woke with a start. "Uh, uh, what that?"

"When you and John were young, did you ride the railroad much?"

"Well, they sometimes had a car for colored, and we could ride there. Mostly we just jumped on one of the flatcars as they went by. Nobody cared. We all lived around here, knew the brakemen and the engineers."

"So, you could go up to Memphis and wherever?"

"No, just on the Y&MV around here. We didn't get on that main line track over by Grenada. We just jumped on the branch line to ride up to Holcomb or into Greenwood."

"Did they name those trains?"

"Oh, yeah. That one that went from Greenwood to Grenada was the Sliding Delta.'

Chapter 23

"Sounds like nigger music," a fresh faced freshman boy said, trying to show his macho.

"Your name Hoagland?" I asked, pausing the verse of *Spike Driver Blues* I was singing and reverted to just a twelve-bar rhythm.

"Who's Hoagland?" He asked.

"A redneck bigot whose ass I was gonna kick a couple weeks ago, but Addie stopped me," I replied, eyes locked on his.

"He has a temper," Addie interjected with a wide-eyed serious look.

"Uh, sorry," he said, much deflated.

I went back to the song. The rest of the small group of new freshmen, mostly girls, were mystified by the exchange but were delighted to be listening to an upper-classman from some prestigious school in Illinois play the guitar and sing folk music. It was all so *au courant*.

Addie was settling in to college life at Millsaps College very well. She was ensconced in the freshman girl's dorm, with a room on the first floor, had a cute roommate, had met other fresh-faced, naïve, idealistic freshmen and was having a visit by her oh so worldly boyfriend – me.

I was seated with my back to an old oak in front of Addie's dorm, surrounded by a dozen freshmen eager to begin their college experience. I decided to change genres to something more likely to please this audience. I retuned and picked a quick introduction to *Red River Valley*, nodding to Addie as I sang, *"Come and sit by my side if you love me, do not hasten to bid me adieu."*

She moved from the adjacent bench, face aglow as she felt the envy of the other girls. She came in on the second verse and we sang the rest together. Then I ran through most of my college coffeehouse folk repertoire. It was quite a change from playing with Hubert Sumlin and backing up the one and only Howlin' Wolf just hours before.

"How did you and Addie meet?" one of the girls asked.

I didn't think we needed to get into anything about the Bolivar County Jail, or being mugged on Beale Street, or getting off a bus in front of Kinder's store broke and one step ahead of the law, so I did what any enterprising young man would do when asked a dumb question. I made something up.

"I'm in Mississippi on an internship in marketing and promotion with Kinder Enterprises. I'll wrap it up this week and return to Stratmore College to organize what I've learned into a future project on the economic, cultural and entertainment options for the lower Mississippi Valley."

"Oh."

I just couldn't leave it alone. I was on a roll.

"I plan to maintain this relationship with Kinder Enterprises, possibly with future projects in professional and personal development."

That drew furrowed brows and earnest nods, and a quiet snort from Addie.

We finished up the impromptu concert, and I signed Addie out for the remainder of the afternoon. That was an experience. At my college, girls signed themselves out when they left the dorm, merely stating where they would be. But at this college, deep in the Old South, the male escort had to sign a girl out and be specific about where they were going.

I hammed it up by putting my full name, Douglas Spencer III, and stating that we would be "at the home of Miss Emmabelle Kinder" and gave the address. Then Addie and I went over to Emmabelle's to pick up some more of her clothes and have an early supper, and then out in Buck's truck to find a place to park.

"Will you come back to visit?" she asked, sitting demurely in the truck on a dark side road outside Jackson.

"That depends," I said with mock seriousness.

"Depends? On what?"

"Well, a man can't rush into things like this. Emmabelle, uh, Miss Kinder, has agreed to give me regular reports on your comportment."

"Comportment, yes," she responded, catching my mood.

"And, grades of course."

"Certainly. And I will instruct her to keep in close contact with her friend Mrs. Spencer in Lake Forest to get regular reports on your comportment and grades."

"Emmabelle did indicate that, if I was interested, I could visit for Thanksgiving vacation, and I responded that I would be delighted to revisit Mississippi."

"Well, if you maintain your high standards of manners and behavior, I would agree to see you."

She slid to my side of the truck.

Chapter 24

"So, whatcha want for everything that's left?"

The man had been nosing around the store for several minutes, telling me what a great guy Buck had been and how sad he and all his kin were to hear of his passing. It was bullshit. He owned the store five miles down the road, toward Greenwood.

"Don't know," I said. "Guess we could count it up."

We'd sold all the popular stuff, like candy bars and cigarettes, and toilet paper and shotgun shells. We were down to odds and ends: six bottles of ketchup, dozens of partial cases of vegetables, sacks of flour and corn meal, some tools, less popular brands of snuff and chewing tobacco, nails screws and tacks, spices, and bags of chicken, duck, dog, pig, calf and goat feed.

"When you plannin' on wrapping it all up?"

"Oh, no hurry. Buck said to get the best price I could for it," I said, unwrapping one of the few El Producto cigars left and lighting it up.

I leaned back on the stool behind the counter and hiked my feet up on the shelf. My nonchalance hid the fact that when the bus came through the following morning, I had to be on it. If I didn't register at Stratmore by the end of the week, I'd have to face the draft board.

He took another circle and then headed for the door.

"I'd take two hundred."

"A hundred."

"Cash."

I helped him load it.

That night I finished the rest of Buck's beer sitting out on the porch playing the harmonica. It's not that hard to get a tune out of it. The nuance, well that's the trick. Think of all the guys who began to play harmonica around this time while playing the guitar. Bob Dylan comes to mind. He could sing or play the harmonica while he played the guitar. He was very successful at that, became a huge star, wrote a lot of very good music and sold a mountain of records. But what he did wasn't the same thing Sonny Boy and Wolf did.

Tap. Tap. Whoosh.

It was just me and the tree frogs and the mosquitoes. I gave up on the harmonica and practiced my whistling for a while, then went back to the guitar. I went through my expanding repertoire, starting with the simple twelve-bar blues I'd learned in Memphis, then the bass line from Jerome and Delta Jim, then what I'd picked up from John Hurt, and finally the simple rhythm line for *Forty Four* that Hubert Sumlin taught me. I could do it. I could play a competent version of the Delta blues.

That didn't make me a blues musician.

Rain during the afternoon had left it cool and humid, and a mist rose from the wet cotton planted across the road, now showing a dozen green cotton bolls on each plant. Through the gathering darkness, I could see down the gravel road intersecting the state highway, the road on which John Hurt's house had been for most of his 70 years.

In my mind, I saw the ghosts of the shacks that had lined that road and imagined the people who had lived there all those years. What would they be doing on the last night of August? Not much, I reasoned. There wouldn't be cotton to pick for another couple of weeks, and then the money, such as it was, would flow for a while. Cooter had told me when he'd asked me to pick cotton that Mr. Davis was paying 3 cents a pound but that Mississippi farmers typically paid only 2½ cents a pound when it had to be hand-picked. He also told me that up in northeastern Arkansas and southeastern Missouri, where they also grew cotton but where most of the farmhands were white, they paid 3 cents. Why was that? Was cotton easier to pick in Mississippi? No.

The night I saw Wolf play, he'd been playing the blues full time for twice as long as I'd been alive, and more than half of that time he was an unknown local musician playing on the street for tips or in segregated colored clubs within a hundred miles of the Yazoo River. Think of what that must have been like during the Depression, say in 1935.

Virtually all the old blues songs are about sex, love gone bad, jealousy, violence and murder. The words to most of the songs on John Hurt's original 1927 recordings couldn't have been played on the radio that summer of 1965. Forced into submission by the Klan and the lynch mob, trapped on the cotton plantation by poverty, they took it out on each other. Blues are the scream of pain.

I got up early on my last day at Kinder's store. The days were shorter now, the first of September, and the eastern sky was just showing light as I made my way out to the privy for one last contemplative interlude with the first cigarette of the day. I returned to the house, packed my bag, locked up and went to the front porch to wait for Cooter Davis' father to come by and pick up the keys.

"Heard from Cooter?" I asked, stepping down to hand him the keys.

"He called last night. Passed his physical up at Memphis, and they filled a bus going to Parris Island in South Carolina. He's supposed to be getting a lot of shots and his uniform today. Said not to call him a Marine until he's finished boot camp."

"Tell him I'll write him a letter."

"Just send it to Pvt. Ervin Davis, Marine Corps Boot Camp, Parris Island, South Carolina. He asked that we not put Cooter on the envelope."

"A new start."

"Yeah. Well, good luck to you, Doug."

He put the truck in gear and looked behind to back up. His eyes welled with tears.

Old Silversides showed up right on time headed north out of Greenwood, turned onto the gravel from the county road and came to a stop in front of Kinder's store for the last time. I bought my ticket from the driver, stowed my suitcase and guitar and climbed aboard. It was empty.

Chapter 25

"OOMPH!"
A body slammed into me from behind in the Greyhound bus terminal on Union Avenue in Memphis. I had just stopped for a moment to tie my shoe and had one foot on the wooden bench. A middle-age woman in a bright, flowered, cotton dress tripped over my guitar case, bumped into me from behind, tried to regain her balance, broke off one of her high heels, tripped over my outstretched leg as I tried to regain my balance, and pitched forward across the aisle, smashing face first into the wooden seat there. Stunned, she rolled off the bench onto the concrete floor, still clutching an oversize purse, the contents of which were now spilled out in front of her for 20 feet.

"Uh, I'm sorry," I stammered, turning toward her.

Blood was streaming from her nose as she lay on her back on the hard floor. She was dazed, not responding.

"Oh! Oh!" she said, recovering enough to put her hand to her nose and see the blood on it.

"Here, let me help," I said, pulling my handkerchief out and kneeling, sitting her up against the bench and wiping the blood off. A crowd was forming, staring down dumbly at this fashionably dressed woman splayed out in the aisle, her long stocking-clad legs exposed up to her garters. I was distracted for a moment; I didn't know they still made garters.

"Mama! What happened?" A tall young woman rushed up, her head wrapped in some kind of turban that women used to cover their hair when it was in rollers. She was dressed in slacks, flats and a simple cotton blouse. She carried a large suitcase.

"She tripped," I said. "It was all my fault. I'm sorry."

I stood, giving her access to the downed woman, but the young woman just stood there, so I knelt again and pulled the lady, who had slumped back to the floor, back up to a full sitting position.

"Oh, my nose. Is it broken?"

I leaned over to apply the handkerchief again and feel her nose. I smelled whiskey.

"I'll get some ice," offered someone from the crowd, finally coming to the realization that perhaps they should help. Several people rushed to the café in the bus station and quickly came back with a cloth napkin filled with ice. We lifted the lady to the bench, and the crowd began to dissipate.

"Oh, baby," she said. "I was just going to find us a driver. We must get you to rehearsal!"

"Mama, it's early afternoon. The agent said to be there in the afternoon," the young woman responded, sitting next to her mother and lifting the icepack to look at her nose. "It doesn't look crooked."

"It didn't feel broken," I offered hopefully.

"Oh, baby!" The woman on the bench put her hands to her face and wept. The remaining crowd was gone.

"Could I be of assistance?" I asked, standing there, feeling awkward and responsible.

She looked up, tears streaming down her face, blending little blobs of mascara into the pancake makeup on her cheeks. Her eyebrows lifted and she looked me in the eye and asked, as if she were seeing me for the first time, "And you are?"

"I'm Douglas Spencer, ma'am. Uh, from Chicago."

She looked expectantly but said nothing.

"I was just returning to college," I stammered, as my first statement had, apparently, been insufficient.

"I am Marie Louise Fontenot," she said with some formality, offering her hand, "and this is my daughter Camille."

"I'm pleased to meet you," I said formally, engaging my debutante ball gentility, and took her hand in an abbreviated handshake. I gave a slight bow and turned to Camille. "Camille, Doug."

Camille smiled. She was almost as tall as I was and wore no makeup, in contrast to her mother who was heavily done up. She had a youthful vitality and attractive features.

Marie Louise regained awareness and opened the huge purse she had clutched throughout her fall. I bent down and began handing her items from the floor – reading glasses, mascara, eye liner, compacts of makeup, bus tickets, letters, keys, toothbrush and so on. I crawled on my knees down the aisle, leaning under the long wooden bench to retrieve things that had rolled most of the way across the bus terminal. When I returned with the last item, Marie Louise had cleaned the running mascara from her face, reinforced her makeup and sat there composed with Camille. In front of them were two large suitcases, a makeup case – more makeup? – and an overnight case. My guitar case, which had been the cause of the fall, and my small suitcase were stacked neatly beside.

"Thank you, Doug," she said. "We have an engagement at the King Cotton Hotel. Do you know it?"

"I've heard of it." I recalled it was one that my guide Maurice mentioned when I first came to town.

"It's one of the finer hotels in Memphis."

"Yes. Would you like some coffee or something?" I nodded toward the café in the bus station.

"Yes, I think I need that," she said and rose unsteadily. I rushed to grab her arm and, together we crossed the terminal. I kept a wary eye on my guitar case as I got her settled in a booth. I returned three times to lug all their luggage and mine into the café.

"Camille is a performer," Marie Louise announced proudly as I sat to join them, "and tonight is her big debut."

"Oh, well, break a leg then," I said to Camille, who gave a confused look to her mother.

"That's show business talk, it means good luck, Camille," Marie Louise said, patting Camille's hand in reassurance. "When I was in vaudeville, it was considered unlucky to wish someone luck, as the opposite might happen, so we would say 'break a leg.' "

The waitress took our orders.

"Vaudeville?" I asked. "So, you're a performer, too?"

"Oh, yes. Thirty years on the road. It was a wonderful life. I see your guitar case, do you perform as well?"

"I've had a few gigs, folk music mostly, some blues. I sat in with Howlin' Wolf in Greenwood last week."

"Oh, big Chicago blues star. You traveling with him?"

"No, I'm going back to college at Stratmore."

"Music major?" Camille asked, interested for the first time.

"Maybe, or business, or political science. Anything but pre-med. I couldn't stand cutting up that shark."

"Ick! You cut up a shark?" Camille was more interested now.

I went through the ordeal I'd endured with the smelly fish, then the formaldehyde cat I'd been issued for the second semester.

"So you're retired now?" I asked, returning my attention to Marie Louise.

"Actually, no. As a performer, I had to design and make my own costumes, so now I make costumes for the younger performers. I'm no longer on the stage, but my costumes are."

Our drinks arrived. Marie Louise reached into that oversize purse and, without so much as a glance at who might be watching, pulled out a small silver flask and poured whiskey into her coffee.

"A brace for opening night jitters," she smiled.

"What kind of performer?"

"I was a dancer, an exotic dancer."

"So Camille's been studying to follow in your footsteps, so to speak?"

I thought that was really clever, but they didn't seem to notice.

"She has," Marie Louise said, taking a long drink of her coffee and savoring it while looking around the terminal café before continuing. "It isn't just feathers and long legs. Exotic dancing is about poise and promise, and it takes years to get it just right. Camille has studied dance since she was 6."

She beamed with pride at her daughter. There was a strong family resemblance. Entering the café, we had drawn attention, as both women were tall, statuesque and moved with an athletic grace.

"You must have some stories," I said.

"Oh, yes." She was delighted that I had asked. "I debuted in Memphis in 1933, but I was just a beginner. Two years later, I was the headliner, and when our show opened at the Pantages Theater in Hollywood, Milton Berle was the comedian."

"Wow. That must have been something."

"Oh, it was." She took another sip of coffee. "Camille's tired of hearing my stories, but I can still hear the applause."

She paused, thoughtful for a moment.

"Camille, if she is to succeed, needs a debut. We've waited for just such an opportunity. I've turned down several performances this year, but our booking agent in Memphis was very enthusiastic when he called with this engagement. The King Cotton is not as good as opening at the Palace Theater in Memphis, but it is a top hotel, and the agent said the audience would be 150 or more. And it's in the main ballroom. We could get some publicity photos to send out to other venues, to show Camille as a headliner."

"Mama, it looks like it's going to rain," Camille interrupted, looking out the window. "Maybe we better get over to the hotel."

"Oh, yes. Let's go." Then, as she stood, Marie Louise said, "Doug, would you like to see the show?"

Ask a college boy if he wants to see a burlesque show?

"Yes, ma'am. I'd love to see it."

My train to Chicago didn't leave until the next day. I got a baggage cart and trucked everything out to the curb and into a taxi.

"Would you like to join us? Camille needs an entourage," Marie Louise said, refreshing her makeup in the taxi. "First impressions are so important. You can be Camille's musical director. Please, join us for rehearsal."

Oh, yes! Then it got interesting. The taxi took us down Front Street, where I'd gotten my first look at the Mississippi River on June 1st, then turned up Jefferson and stopped at the 12-story, red brick King Cotton Hotel. I helped the driver stack luggage on the sidewalk, paid him and walked into the lobby with the doorman pushing all those bags on a cart.

There was a scene already. Marie Louise stood with Camille at the reception desk, talking with the hotel manager and a younger man.

"Our contract calls for a suite, so that Camille can properly prepare for her performance," Marie Louise said pleasantly but with a certain insistence.

"Your contract is with him," the manager, a middle-age man with wavy dark hair wearing a dark business suit, said nodding toward the plump, younger man whose expanding belly was straining the buttons on his white cotton dress shirt.

"Uh," the anxious young man hesitated, eyes looking up, then, apparently remembering that indeed there might have been something in the contract about lodging.

"Uh, what's available?" he asked the hotel manager.

"We have a nice suite on the second floor, near the elevators," he said. "Performers are able to access the ballroom easily from there."

The manager was all sweetness and accommodation now that he had established who was paying for what.

"Thank you," Marie Louise said, smiling momentarily. "Now as to the musicians. Are they here yet? Camille must rehearse."

The manager, Leonard Crump, according to his name tag, turned to the younger man, a placid smile on his face.

"We have engaged musicians, and some of them are here."

"Good. Is Camille to perform in the ballroom?"

"Yes, it's on the mezzanine level. Would you like to see it?"

"No." She turned to me. "Doug, would you inspect the ballroom and the arrangements? I'll take Camille to our suite to dress for rehearsal. I'll be down in half an hour."

Then she turned back to the two men and said to the younger one, "The booking agent said I was to meet a Mr. Driscoll."

"Yes, ma'am, that's me," he said, still uncomfortable but now eager to please.

"We're delighted to be here in Memphis," Marie Louise said, "and I can assure you your event will be a rousing success. Camille Fontenot is a star, and for good reason. Please show Mr. Spencer, our manager, all the arrangements."

Whoa! I didn't know what I'd gotten into here, but I was going to ride with it. I pulled a five out of my pocket and gave it to the bellman waiting with the bags. Five dollars in 1965 was a grandiose tip, and I made sure everyone saw it.

I'd had another infusion of cash from my grandmother to get my watch out of hock, plus Buck had raised my meager wage for the closeout of Kinder's store. A restrained smile on Marie Louise's face as she turned to direct Camille toward the elevators told me I had caught the gist of where this adventure was going. I noted with a sense of anticipation that my suitcase and guitar case were on the bellman's cart headed for that suite upstairs.

"Oh, I'm so glad you're here," Driscoll said as we climbed the steps to the mezzanine floor, leaving the manager to return to his office. "I've never done this before, and it's turned out to be a whole lot harder than I thought."

"Oh?"

"Look, I'll level with you. I'm Larry Driscoll, by the way." He held out his hand at the landing halfway up the stairs.

"Doug Spencer," I said. We shook. I was going to let Larry level with me, but I was not going to level with him. This pot needed to simmer a bit first.

"I'm the president of the Delta Omicron Gamma fraternity at Memphis State. The brothers thought it would be cool to put on a big rush party right before classes start, something that would really establish the DO house as the party place on campus. Someone said we should get a, a, an exotic dancer."

Yes, college boys would do that. I suppressed a smile.

"Well, it created a lot of excitement, and it kind of got out of hand."

Ah, yes.

"Two other fraternities joined in with us. We're on kind of a limited budget, but we needed a pretty big ballroom. This hotel, uh, I know, it's kind of seedy, but they have a huge ballroom up here. And, uh, just to lay it all out, uh, the other hotels wouldn't let us have an open bar with a lot of, uh, younger guys, you know?"

I knew all about drunken fraternity boys. My caution lights were on, but I said, "Certainly, no problem as far as we're concerned. We're in the entertainment business, after all, and we want to be sure this comes off right."

"Oh, good." Larry relaxed and we continued up the stair.

A clap of thunder reverberated through the building as we opened a set of double doors into the large ballroom.

"They wouldn't rent us the ballroom just for drinks and a show," Larry said. "They said it would have to include dinner."

The hotel staff was setting up tables. A large bar was off to the side, a stage in front. Drums were set up, and two guys were wiring an amplifier.

"Good," I said. "Good. That makes it an event, not just some tawdry fraternity beer bust."

"That's what the hotel manager said!"

At least someone knew what they were doing, I thought, maintaining my confident demeanor.

A flash of lightning lit up the room, and four seconds later a clap of thunder. I looked out the window to see the Mississippi River to the west, with dark clouds rolling in from Arkansas.

"What kind of band do you have?"

"It's a band from out at Memphis State, Bubba and the Clamdiggers," Larry said. "They play a lot of parties. The contract says we have to have a saxophone player, so we got one from the music department. He's a music major. He's cool."

"They ever play together?"

"I don't think so."

"You got a lead guitar player?"

"Oh, yeah. It's his band. He's good. He'll be along any minute."

"Sax?"

"He was here, I think he's gone to the bathroom," Larry said, turning toward the side door that led out to a hall, restrooms and the elevator. "Oh, here he is."

A young colored man in black slacks, black turtleneck shirt, closely cropped hair and dark glasses entered sucking on a saxophone reed.

I was introduced to Theodus Wiggins, a sophomore majoring in music at Memphis State. He had never played with or even heard of the rest of the musicians, who were pointedly ignoring him.

"Bebop, mostly, cool jazz. I don't dig the big band or rock and roll," he said, answering my question about what music he played. "Oh, I groove Rachmaninov or Ravel, too."

Engagement. Booking agent. Performer. Debut. Star. Entourage. Applause.

These were all words I'd heard Marie Louise use that afternoon. The way she swooped into the lobby of the King Cotton was a memory of the glory days of vaudeville, when the headliner blew into town amid excitement and expectation. It was pretty clear that she had carried her daughter along on a fantasy and that the reality of this event could wind up to be something very different.

On the other hand, she'd gotten what she wanted so far and showed no lack of confidence.

"Let's hear you play something," I suggested, playing along as Camille's musical director. I turned to the rest of the band.

"Hey, you guys set up yet?"

"Bubba's not here yet," the drummer said. He and the bass player looked to be barely out of high school and seemed uncomfortable without their leader.

"Hi, I'm Doug Spencer, Miss Fontenot's music director. I thought we'd just warm up some. You guys can back up Theodus here."

Reluctantly the bass player plugged in, and the drummer sat behind his trap. Theodus assembled his sax and ran through some scales, then began some random notes, then nodded his head with the beat and added, "boom, shoo, boom, shoo," to indicate a drum rhythm and went into a cool jazz sax solo. After a few bars, he said to the bass player who sat confused, "It's key of G." They picked it up and, after a while, it became music. Sort of. Useless for the project for which they'd been hired, but music nonetheless.

Lightning struck a power pole right across the street with a brilliant flash and simultaneous clap of thunder, followed by the lights going out. I looked out the window to see it raining so hard I could no longer see the Mississippi River. The musicians stopped abruptly.

"OK, let's see what you guys can do. We don't need an amplifier right now. Play some of your stuff and see what Theodus can make out of it."

"Well, Bubba usually leads," the bass player stammered.

"You guys play *Kansas City*?" Theodus asked.

Every cover band in the world played the song *Kansas City* in 1965. This one did and lurched into it. I told them to work on it and went to find the hotel manager. *Kansas City* has a bluesy bass line, and some bands played it with a saxophone solo. I was thinking of how we might work that into a burlesque act while I jogged down the stairs to the lobby, now dark without power. The manager stood at the front door peering out into the rain. I approached and stood silently by him for a few moments.

"You know what you've got booked up there, Leonard?" I asked quietly.

He pursed his lips and nodded but said nothing.

"You got security?"

He shook his head.

"You need security."

He nodded his head, then said glumly without looking away from the rain, "The previous manager booked the event. He didn't book security."

"Already been paid?"

He nodded. Lightning crashed, followed four seconds later by the thunder. The rain began to let up.

"What if the power doesn't come back on?"

He shrugged.

"You going to cancel it?"

He turned on me, sharply, "Look, I bought the food, called in all the staff, extra staff. They're all here. The food's being prepared."

He fell silent again and resumed looking out into the street.

A Memphis Light, Gas and Water truck pulled up to the corner and began setting up traffic barriers. Two police cruisers arrived and began to divert traffic. A lineman strapped on his belt. We watched as he climbed the pole. A truck with a cherry picker arrived and set up on the next pole toward the city.

"The lights are going to come back on, the guests are going to arrive, they'll eat, they'll drink and then the show will go on," I said without emotion, just stating a fact.

Leonard nodded, pursing his lips.

"Then one of those drunk college boys is going to make a grab for Camille Fontenot, and another one will pull him off, and Marie Louise Fontenot will call the cops."

"No," he said almost absent-mindedly, still looking out at the rain. "No, that won't be the problem."

He turned to me, suddenly focused, as if he'd settled some issue that was troubling him.

"You worry about pulling together that band they hired, and leave crowd control to me."

The lights came on. A moment later, the elevator door chimed and Marie Louise Fontenot and Camille tumbled out into the lobby, having been trapped for half an hour.

"Mr. Crump! Did you not hear me crying in the dark?" Marie Louise asked, coming across the lobby on a mission.

"No, ma'am, the power went out," Leonard said, turning toward Marie Louise and becoming suddenly solicitous. "I'm so sorry. Could I offer you something? A late afternoon libation perhaps?"

Brilliant! And I thought the guy was a dunce.

"Let's go get something to eat," Camille said to me, striding toward the revolving door without waiting for her mother's permission. She slipped off her dancing shoes and took flats out of her purse. Without missing a stride, we were out in the street.

"I'm not new to this life," she said as we skipped quickly between awnings to stay out of the light rain that was still falling. "I travelled with Mama until I was 10. Then my grandmother died, and she retired to take care of Paps."

We rounded the corner, found a café on Court Street and slipped into a booth.

"I've got to get back pretty quick," I said. "Your band is not coming together as planned."

"Nothing is coming together as planned," she said sadly, looking at the menu.

"I'm sorry. I'll do what I can."

"I know you will, and I appreciate it. It's more for Mama than me. This is her dream."

She looked up from the menu and ordered a chicken salad sandwich and a coke.

"What's your dream?" I asked.

"Like yours, it's music." Her face brightened for the first time since I'd mentioned music back at the bus station.

"You play an instrument?"

"Sure," she said. "I played the oboe in the high school band."

"Oboe, that's interesting."

"It is interesting. It has an eerie, spooky sound. I've always liked oboes, and the band at Tallulah already had enough clarinets, so I got an oboe."

"Tallulah?"

"Oh, Tallulah. Tallulah, Louisiana. We came up on the bus this morning. My grandfather has a farm there. I just graduated from high school."

"So, an oboe player from Tallulah, Louisiana, just out of high school, and you're headlining the show at the King Cotton Hotel in Memphis tonight?"

"Yeah. That sounds good. Think we can pull it off?"

"We can try."

We finished our food and hurried back to the hotel. The sun had come out.

"I wanted to start college this fall," Camille said. "I was accepted at Southeastern Louisiana in the music program, but Mama wanted to try to find this one engagement, to see if I might have a career."

"Living your mother's dream."

"Well, like I said, I travelled with her until I was 10. I liked it. I stayed backstage for the shows, but I went to all the rehearsals. Mama gave me piano lessons beginning when I was 4, and when there was a break in rehearsal, I did my piano lessons on the stage or in the orchestra pit. I've been tutored by some of the greats. Lionel Hampton gave me a vibraphone lesson in Chicago when I was 8. Oscar Peterson let me sit on the piano bench with him and play a duet when we played Montreal just before Mama retired.

"He had a big butt," she laughed.

"So, you're excited about this show, too?"

"Oh, yeah. I've been dancing since I was 6, modern dance, classic ballet, I like it all."

We breezed through the revolving door to face Larry Driscoll rushing toward us.

"We've got trouble! Bubba Sikes called from the John Gaston Hospital. He lost control during the rain and ran into a Memphis city bus. He totaled his car and is waiting at the hospital to have his face sewed up and his arm put in a cast. He's out for tonight."

"Who's Bubba Sikes?" Camille asked.

"He's the lead guitar for Bubba and the Clamdiggers, the band for tonight," I said.

Marie Louise came out of Leonard Crump's office, a bit unsteady on her feet but showing a more relaxed look on her face. I rushed past her and up the stairs into the ballroom.

"Could you play it in A major?" Theodus asked loudly, frustration evident in his voice.

The band stumbled into a jazz piece with Theodus embellishing on a theme with a flourish of notes and the drummer and bass player struggling to keep a steady beat.

"OK guys," I said, "take a break. Bubba's not coming tonight. He totaled his car, and he's at the hospital. He called Larry, and he's OK, but no Bubba tonight."

Shock all around.

"Let me see that," I said, reaching for the bass. "Look, guys, this is a burlesque show we're doing tonight. It's not jazz, it's not rock and roll. Can you get that? Burlesque."

I went into a slow twelve-bar blues rhythm.

"Something like this."

I looked at the bass player.

"I can do that," he said.

"OK. Do that."

I handed him the bass and looked at Theodus.

"Do you know any blues songs you can wail on?"

"Don't really dig the blues, man."

"Work on something," I said. "I'll be back."

I left them struggling to cooperate and went back to the lobby.

"You can play guitar, can't you?" asked Larry, who'd been talking to Marie Louise.

"I can, but mine is acoustic. We could rig a microphone, but I have another idea. Can I use your phone?"

Leonard Crump nodded. He had mellowed significantly since the storm. I went through the Yellow Pages and found the pawn shop where I'd pawned my watch and got the owner on the line. We enjoyed a brief negotiation and came to an agreement. He would "rent" me a Fender Stratocaster and amplifier that he had in his store for 20 bucks, plus the deposit of the entire purchase price in case it didn't get back on time. Fair.

"Larry! You got a car?" He did.

"Camille! Rehearsal in 40 minutes."

I ran back up to the ballroom to find the band near fisticuffs over Theodus' concept of blues.

"Stop! Sit down. Theodus, can you play this?"

I took my harmonica out of my pocket and nodded to the bass player.

"Give me that twelve-bar blues again."

I waited for a few bars and came in with one of the three harmonica blues songs I knew, and I wasn't very good, but I had the melody. The song was *Red Rooster,* one of Howlin' Wolf's standards, slow and naughty.

"That's barrelhouse music," Theodus said with disgust, but he put his sax to his lips and played the melody, then followed it with a flurry of improvisations that thoroughly confused the bass player and drummer. We struggled with that for 10 minutes. I was about to give up.

"You play like Coleman Hawkins," Marie Louise said, standing in the door.

"Yes, ma'am," Theodus said, smiling for the first time now that someone appreciated what he was doing.

"He blows cool," she said, coming down the aisle between the tables. She'd changed clothes and freshened up. Camille was right behind her in shorts, polo shirt and dancing shoes, ready for rehearsal.

"When I played the Apollo Theater in Harlem," Marie Louise said, "Coleman blew with the band."

"No, he plays cool jazz."

"That's Coleman's bag, but he's 18 karat on some dirty blues! They started out with a walking bass and, when I came in, he blew a wail they heard in the Bronx."

She came up on the bandstand with a slinky vamp and bumped her left hip at an incredulous Theodus.

"Cut out the noodlin' and let's make it happen," she said.

I blew the melody to *Red Rooster* again and we picked it up. Just then, Larry rushed in with the Strat.

"OK, start slow and bluesy," I said and played the simple intro Hubert Sumlin had played down in Greenwood. "Then the bass comes in after four bars, then the horn."

"Quit noodlin' Theodus!" Marie Louise yelled, right in his face. "That's a cry from the heart, let me feel the pain!"

It worked! It was there, Theodus just didn't know it. He'd suppressed it, but it was there. Simple and lonely and sad, Theodus blew the blues.

"All right, Theodus! Now, you on the drums. When you play burlesque" – oh, she was calling it burlesque now – "every eight beats you hit the snare harder. The dancer bumps or turns or does something in her routine expecting that beat. But, don't hit it too hard at the first. Build to it. Do it again."

Camille came in from the side door and did her routine and, even in street clothes, it was just like Marie Louise said, poise and promise. But with a young athletic dancer, there were some interesting twists and pirouettes. She finished at the door and gave a wave. The wait staff applauded.

"We need two songs," Marie Louise said to me. "Do you have another?"

"I do." I turned to the band. "This one is the same pace, but it sounds faster because it has a kind of military snare beat. Come in with the snare – dot ta dot ta dot ta da, dot ta dot ta dot ta da, dot ta dot ta dot ta bang! Then after eight bars, the sax comes in with this," and I blew the tune from *Forty Four.* Theodus played the melody a couple of times and nodded. Then we went through it once, then again with Camille.

"Oh, that's good, honey, we've got it!" Marie Louie said to Camille, and they marched back down the aisle as a crowd of awestruck college boys crowded up the steps from the lobby. As I followed Camille and Marie Louise to the head of the stairs, I saw three buses lined up along Jefferson Street in front of the hotel.

"Wow! Did you see that girl?" I heard one boy say as the elevator door closed behind Camille.

Chapter 26

The two policemen came in through the revolving doors and stamped their feet on the mat to dislodge the water they'd carried in from the deluge outside. The bellman just inside shot a nervous glance over their heads as they walked casually into the center of the lobby.

"Uh oh," Leonard Crump said, swinging his feet from the top of his desk and standing.

We'd been discussing the sound system and spotlight the hotel would provide for the show while seated in his office so he could keep an eye on the front desk. The desk clerk was waiting tables upstairs. Leonard strode quickly out to the lobby.

"Welcome, gentlemen! Wet night."

I hung back, so I couldn't hear one officer's muffled response, but the visit seemed to be a routine stop on their beat. The other officer systematically scanned the lobby while he stood by his partner.

"How about some coffee, or a snack?" Leonard asked brightly, leading them toward the registration desk, which was out of sight of the doors to the ballroom up the staircase. As they turned, he looked in my direction and jerked his head upstairs. I casually walked up the steps and slipped through the doors to the ballroom.

It was loud but orderly as three waitresses served dinner: Salisbury steak, mashed potatoes, green beans and a salad. Leonard Crump had limited the bar to two kegs of beer, and it had been served in paper cups. Thus, the evidence of nearly 30 gallons of beer having been consumed was the existence of red 16-ounce malt cups on all the tables. I rushed to the bar.

"Cops are here," I said to the bartender.

He nodded without expression as he looked up to the next customer in line. "ID?"

That caused some consternation, as beer had been flowing freely for an hour without concern for any documentation.

"Hey," Larry Driscoll protested..

"Cops," I said. "Keep a lid on things up here. We'll try to keep them downstairs."

Panic crossed his face, but he nodded and turned to walk casually back across the room. Those in the beer line who heard the exchange quickly moved to their seats.

I returned to the entry and looked back just in time to see the bartender standing stately at an empty bar. It's always a pleasure to see a true professional at work. Larry was rushing about telling the boys to finish their beers and stack the cups in front of anyone with an ID. He was assisted by his security detail. In two minutes, we were legal.

Downstairs, at a table at the front of the lobby that looked out into the rainy night, Leonard poured coffee for the two officers.

"You must have heard we were serving up some of Pearlie Eubank's peach cobbler to a big group from Memphis State," Leonard said as a bellman approached with a napkin-covered tray and served the cobbler.

I gave Leonard a reassuring nod and walked to the other side of the lobby and looked out the window as rain swept across the now vacant park across the street.

"Sure you won't have some ice cream with that?" the bellman asked.

"No, but you can tell Pearlie it is reasonable cobbler, mighty reasonable," one of the officers said as he dug in.

I'd given the band an hour to eat and get back with their instruments to a vacant room Leonard had given us for practice. We'd gotten the two blues songs down fairly well, but we still had to perform a general music show for an hour before Camille came on at 9.

"Just slide the snare, like this," Theodus was saying as I entered the room. He held the drummer's brush, demonstrating some different way of playing the snare than he'd been hearing. It was not well received.

"Where'd you learn to play the drums?" the drummer responded sarcastically, taking back his brushes.

"OK, guys," I said. "We need to work up five songs we can fill the hour from 8 until the big show at 9. Let's start out with a couple of those Coleman Hawkins songs you were doing earlier, just a light simple snare, some bass and I'll follow on rhythm with an occasional solo. I'll catch your eye. OK?"

The bass player and I had our guitars without amplifiers, the drummer had drumsticks and brushes and used a coffee table instead of a drum, while Theodus had his sax. He went back to his complex improvisation on *Body and Soul,* a popular song of the day considered to be sophisticated and cool by the college crowd. Then he wanted to play *Mood Indigo,* another recently popular song, but it was so slow and moody I thought it might kill the party. He went to *Smoke Gets in Your Eyes,* one of my parent's favorite songs; not for this crowd.

We settled on *Tangerine.* It was just uptempo enough, and Theodus could improvise on it as long as we wanted. Two of those would be all this crowd would tolerate. We needed more.

"Anybody know *Creole Belle?*" I asked?

They didn't, of course. But it's a simple tune that's been around for half a century. John Hurt just added words to it. I laid down the complex rhythm line I'd learned from John, and the bass player came in behind that. It felt odd playing on the Fender Stratocaster instead of my Gibson J-45, but there was no way to play the acoustic guitar and sing with only one microphone. It came off as sort of a folk-rock song, a little odd but not bad.

I suggested *Memphis,* that ever popular Chuck Berry song. I had practiced the Lonnie Mack cover version since I was a high school senior and could play most of those airy riffs that transformed a good song into a great song. That would be our finale.

"Well, what else you got?" I asked my band.

"Surely you can cover Ace Cannon," the bass player said to Theodus.

Theodus showed irritation but nodded in the affirmative.

"Who's Ace Cannon?" I asked.

They all gave me a look, like, where are you from?

"Hey, I'm from Chicago," I said. "He a local guy?"

Indeed. They filled me in. Ace Cannon was a white jazz/blues/country sax player from Calhoun City, Mississippi, who recorded in Memphis and elsewhere. His songs always hit the top at WHBQ, the pop station in Memphis. He started out with Bill Black, Elvis Presley's first bass player and later a recording star with his own band. Ace's first hit was *Tuff*, a slow bluesy waltz, and Theodus, now with his newfound wailing sax blues sound, nailed it. That would be our show.

We set up the instruments and did a sound check while the tables were cleared. The bartender was finishing off the beer for anyone with a cup, so the police must have moved on. The room came to order, and we went into the first song without introduction. It was just right for the moment. I could see guys nodding with the beat, liking Theodus' improvisations on the Coleman Hawkins song. The restrained bass and drum background was just right, and I stayed well in the background with some rhythm.

"Welcome to the Delta Omicron Gamma Rush Extravaganza!" I said after the first round of applause. As the frontman, it was my responsibility to introduce the show and the band. Things were going well so that, on a whim, I decided to give the band a name.

"We are Theodus and the Cool Blues!"

That got another round of applause. If this worked out like it was starting, this pickup band of last resort was going to get a lot of gigs at Memphis State. And, if it didn't, then they would drop from sight like innumerable combinations of musicians had in the past. I'd seen how musicians play with one band tonight and another tomorrow. It's an uncertain, cash-only business.

Just as I'd expected, interest in cool jazz began to wane with the second song, so when it was done, I went right into *Creole Belle*. Looking up from the frets I saw every eye on me, watching my fingers pluck that light countermelody, and when I came in with the words, smiles broke out. Performing taps into something that rehearsals don't. I felt the thrill I saw in Addie with her solo in church and understood why Albert King and Wolf were able to explode on stage.

Oh, what a feeling! I wanted it to go on forever, but Theodus caught my eye, so I backed off and let him wail a verse. It was good, and the nods continued from the crowd.

Tuff starts out with the sax, and Theodus blew naughty and mean, like Beale Street late after too many shots of lightnin', or the parking lot at the Stardust Club in Cleveland, Mississippi, after that midnight mandatory closing time. I came in working the bass strings with a counter-rhythm that, with the bass, gave it a darker feel than the hit recording, which featured a Hammond organ backing Ace Cannon's sax. During the applause, I noticed the bartender carting out the empty kegs on a hand truck. I also noticed it was 8:50. Camille was probably leaving her suite at that moment.

I took a step forward and went into the introductory riff of *Memphis*. This was no ordinary song. Not in Memphis. Not in 1965. Four treble chord strikes and the entire audience leaped to their feet. They knew it even before I hit the bass strings for that hard driving, totally unique, up-from-the-gut melody. Every cover band in America played *Memphis* in 1965, though most of them played the Chuck Berry/Johnny Rivers version with vocals, which is a rock and roll dance song. I was playing the instrumental Lonnie Mack version, which has a challenging 12-bar blues solo that only a virtuoso could reproduce.

I wasn't that good, but I copied Albert King's style and did some string bending and fret sliding and came up with a pretty good facsimile. Finishing out with the same four treble chord strikes that started it, I stood there to howling applause. I felt better at that moment than at any moment in my life.

It was 9 o'clock.

"Gentlemen!" Leonard Crump had the microphone to the main sound system in the back of the room. The audience, mostly adolescents used to being told what to do, came to order. Then the service door opened beside the stage, and a large, dark presence entered.

"There will be no photography during the performance."

Leonard paused, and all eyes were on the large colored man standing in the service door. Wearing white pants and a white shirt, he had taken off his apron for this duty. He was at least 6 feet 7 inches tall, and he was thick.

"Mr. Pearlie Eubanks, chief of security, will eject anyone who leaves their seat during the performance."

Leonard paused again, and Pearlie gave a slight wave. There was a murmur through the audience. Now I knew why Leonard had not worried about someone getting out of hand.

Coming down from the high of my solo, I stepped back and looked to the band, struggling to recall what the first song of Camille's routine was. Then the lights went out.

"The King Cotton Hotel takes great pride in presenting, direct from Bourbon Street in New Orleans, Camille Fontenot!"

The spotlight came on, and there she was, standing in the side door. There was a collective gasp and a moment of silence. Like a statue she stood motionless, wearing a low-cut, form-fitting, full-length, white satin gown. She wore long white gloves. Her right hand rested on a long jeweled walking stick, left hand on her hip, and beneath a huge-brim lavender hat topped with white plumes her fresh, youthful face scanned the stunned audience.

Red Rooster! I remembered. I hit the sultry introduction, and a smile crossed her face as she stood, letting the audience wonder what was next. When Theodus came in with the sax, she began to move to the center of the stage. Poise and promise. It seemed as if she would strut like an unapproachable model at some high-class fashion show – until the first snare hit at eight bars.

She gave a subtle bump and made a quarter-turn so the left side of the audience could see part of what I could see all of from the bandstand. That full length, slinky, satin dress was cut so low in back you could see butt cleavage. Oh, and a fine butt it was, as a wave of smiling faces swept across the audience as she swept across the stage.

The sax wailed and the melody intensified as she walked to the other side of the stage and turned with the next snare hit, letting the right side get a look. A howl went up and a few jumped up, to be quickly pulled back to their seats by their neighbors. Pearlie stood silent and stern.

She wore impossibly high heels. Those heels made her walk even more stately, her backside even more evident, though we only saw just the very top of her gluteal muscles. "Promise is the foundation of exotic dancing," Marie Louise had told me a dozen times that day.

Camille began to pull the gloves off as she strutted across the stage, making eye contact with individuals in the audience. Each guy felt she was dancing just for him. The next snare hit sent one glove soaring over their heads, to be retrieved by one of the waiters.

After the second glove came my way, she strutted back to center stage and, while she walked to the right, the lowest seam of that satin dress began to break away. As her bare leg emerged, the seam continued to open, and by the time she'd walked back across everyone was transfixed by a long bare leg. She circled around her walking stick a couple of times and then the other seam began to unravel, leaving her with the front and the back of the satin dress hanging down with the sides open.

One quick jerk and the front was gone, flung back to the entry door, and the next eight bars brought another jerk and the back was gone. The satin dress was now just a bustier with tight satin panties.

That was our signal to end the first song, so I nodded to Theodus and we closed out in eight bars, which gave Camille enough time to get back to the door and pose with her walking stick and hat.

"More! More! More!" they shouted, more excited now than if she'd run naked around the room from the very beginning.

We let them stew for half a minute, then started in on the intro for *Forty Four,* which had the 12-bar blues with every other note left out and the military-style snare beat making for an ominous, or promising, mood. When Theodus came in with the sax, she began to move back toward the stage, and I thought Pearlie was going to be needed. She kicked off her high heels and danced barefoot around her walking stick, then danced over to Pearlie at the service door.

She leaned seductively on the wall by him, then turned like she was going to kiss him but blocked from view by the huge hat.

With the next snare hit, she turned quickly back to the audience and yanked off the hat. Her long black hair spilled out, and she strutted back to the center, holding the hat in one hand and the stick in the other, then used the stick as a vault to leap across the stage, cartwheeling around it to leap the other way, then pulled the hat in front of her and teased the audience by raising her eyebrows as if to say, "Should I do something else behind this hat?"

"Yes!" they shouted, catching the meaning.

The bustier went flying, and she flounced across the stage with her top hidden by the hat, returning to the center and again circling the walking stick.

We were eight bars from the end, and I looked over to confirm that Theodus was blowing all that that saxophone could muster as panties flew into the audience, hat flew into the band, and Camille Fontenot did a handstand cartwheel off the stage and out the door.

Chapter 27

"I polished it up for you," the pawnbroker, a man named Saperstein, said as he slid my watch across the counter and put my $65 in his cash register. "How did the Stratocaster work for you last night?"

"It worked great," I answered as I put the watch back on, admiring the shiny gold on what looked like a new watch. "We were a big hit. Larry Driscoll has the guitar, he'll bring it back later today."

"I hope he keeps it. He paid for it," Mr. Saperstein said with a twinkle in his eye.

The deal I'd negotiated on the phone was to leave a cash deposit of $150, the price of the guitar and amplifier, which would be refunded, less the $20 rental fee.

"If you believe that instruments have a personality, and most musicians do, that one should have practically played itself."

"Oh?"

"It's been in and out of my shop a dozen times, pawned or sold by three different owners, and played here on Beale, in the Stax recording studio, and in most of the honky tonks and juke joints in Arkansas and Mississippi."

"Really?" I thought for a moment, recalling the high point of my life, up until that time, standing on the stage after the final chord of *Memphis*. I had already told him when I called the night before about Bubba Sikes' accident and having to take over as lead guitar for a group that had never played together and had vastly different interests in music. I gave him a brief on the seven songs we put together and added, "I guess that Stratocaster had been there before."

"Most of my instruments have a story," he said, pointing to walls filled with guitars, upright basses, saxophones, drum sets, fiddles, banjos, trumpets, trombones and organs. He also had jewelry, guns, household items, some clothes, and assorted bric-a-brac and objects d'art. But mainly he dealt in musical instruments.

"Take this Gibson ES-335," he said as he turned and pulled down a guitar with a thicker body than the Stratocaster. He walked around the end of the counter to an amplifier at the side of the shop and plugged it in. He ran through a scale and tuned it up quickly. He knew his way around a guitar.

"When B.B. King started playing a Gibson, because he thought the bass sounds were deeper, more visceral, all the young blues players wanted the Gibson."

He ran through a 12-bar blues rhythm and went into *Sweet Little Angel*.

"You're good," I said with surprise.

"Musicians and their instruments are my business," he said, still rolling with the rhythm, then breaking into an improvisation off the simple melody. He finished up the song and laid the Gibson aside.

"I can't buy and sell instruments if I don't appreciate their worth. That's a fairly eclectic set you played last night. Most cover bands want to sound like the Beatles, or stick to what's popular on the radio. You played cool jazz, traditional blues, and rock and roll."

I related my blues sojourn over the summer and the lessons I'd had from various guitar players. I had a couple of hours to kill before the Illinois Central's City of New Orleans pulled out at 1:15 in the afternoon. I'd be in Chicago sometime after midnight. I wanted to hit the Arcade café for another plate of fried chicken and biscuits before going back to the grind at Stratmore College.

"Hubert Sumlin, that's impressive," he said, handing me the Gibson. "Let me hear that introduction to *Red Rooster*."

I played it for him and said, "This Gibson has a mellower sound than the Stratocaster, but it's bigger and a little harder to play."

"That's what most of the guys say," Mr. Saperstein said. " I think it depends on how much you plan to work the strings. You mentioned Albert King, he's all over a guitar, so he uses that Flying V because it's smaller and easier to pick.

"You mentioned Mississippi John Hurt, let me hear that *Creole Belle.*"

I played it for him.

"It's harder on the Gibson," Saperstein said as I finished.

"Yeah, I learned that song on my Gibson J-45 acoustic. I thought of it as more of a folk song. Never thought I'd play it with a sax and bass backup. But last night it was all I had."

The bell on the front door tinkled, and Larry Driscoll came in lugging the Strat and the amplifier.

"Doug! I've been looking all over for you! We've got to talk."

He set the guitar case on the counter and produced the receipt. There was a protracted negotiation as Larry had lost the connecting cable to plug the guitar into the amplifier.

I hoped he wasn't expecting me to pay for the cable.

I thought back to the night before. When we finished the last song and Camille cartwheeled out the door, the audience went wild, stomping and yelling for more. The lights came up, and Pearlie moved to the stage and stood impassive, blocking access to the band and the door Camille had just exited. Leonard announced that the show was over. The bar had already been closed and dismantled. Then Larry announced that the buses were leaving and everyone had better get down to the street or walk back to Memphis State, some 10 miles to the east. Reluctantly, they began to file out. I put the Stratocaster in its case and put the connector cord in an open compartment in the back of the amplifier.

"You guys were great!" Larry said, coming up to the band.

He handed me the agreed upon payment in cash, $50 for the Clamdiggers and $15 for Theodus. This was at a time when the minimum wage was $1.25 and a hundred bucks a week would support a middle-class family. Then a couple of friends helped Larry carry the Stratocaster and amplifier out to his car.

So, it was Larry who lost the connector, not me. And he'd left me with the touchy task of divvying up the money.

"What about Bubba?" the drummer asked, looking at the $65 in my hand.

"Bubba didn't show," I said, holding on to the money until we had this settled.

"It's his band."

"No. It was my band."

"You work for Camille," the bass player said.

"Yes."

I let them argue and haggle long enough to learn that the drummer and bass player had agreed to work for $10 each and that Bubba was to get $30. That was instructive.

"Does Camille need a road band?" the bass player asked after I agreed to let them have all the money the Clamdiggers were owed and let them settle up with Bubba. I had everyone sign a receipt. I told them I didn't think Camille needed a road band, but I got their telephone numbers just to be sure.

"Compliments of the King Cotton," Leonard Crump said, putting a six pack of Bud on one of the tables.

Just at that moment, Camille, changed back into her shorts and polo shirt, came back through the side door and bounded over to me, throwing her arms around my neck and giving me a big wet kiss.

"Oh, thank you, Doug!"

Marie Louise was not far behind, carrying a celebratory bourbon and sporting a happy face. The congratulations and hugging went around as the band popped some beers and packed up. I'd sensed it at the barbecue in Greenwood at Mama Sumlin's house that coming down from a successful gig is a very mellow, pleasant feeling.

"We put your things in the extra bedroom," Camille said quietly out of earshot of her mother. "It's the least we could do after all you've done for me."

"Well, I am homeless, so to speak."

"We couldn't leave you out on the street on such a night as this."

"I would hope not."

At the pawnshop, Larry had come to the end of the negotiation on a new cord and was about to settle up.

"Doug!" he called, breaking my reverie. "Look again in your guitar case to be sure that cord isn't in there."

"OK, OK." I opened my acoustic guitar case; no connector cord. Just to be sure, I opened my suitcase; no connector cord. Larry and Mr. Saperstein came to an agreement, and the pawnbroker counted out the rest of Larry's deposit.

"OK, now the big news," Larry said. "There was a guy in the back last night from the Blue Note Lounge to hear Bubba and the Clamdiggers. After hearing your band he wants to hire you weekends for the next two months!"

"I've got to get back to Chicago," I said. "I'm a college student, and if I don't register by Friday, I'll lose my student deferment and get drafted. They can get another lead guitar player."

"No, he said you and Theodus had to be part of the band or no go."

"Have you talked to Theodus?"

"That was my first call, I couldn't find you. He's in."

"No, I couldn't do that …" I paused, walked to the front of the pawnshop and looked out on Beale Street. There was another factor.

The suite Leonard had given Marie Louise and Camille had a wide hall off the second floor corridor that served as a small sitting area, with the bathroom at the end and a bedroom on either side. They settled into the larger one, which was quite large and had its own sitting area, and I was in the smaller one, which just had a double bed. After the show was over and we returned to the suite, we talked for a bit and then Marie Louise announced it was bedtime. I washed up first and went to bed. I went right to sleep.

Click! The latch on the door opened. I clawed up from a deep sleep.

"Doug?" she asked. "Are you awake?"

"Uhh. Yeah." I saw a white apparition float into the room and close the door. I sat up. It was Camille in a long white peignoir. She floated to the side of the bed as I regained consciousness. Light from the streetlight on the corner showed me it was just Camille underneath.

"Hi."

"Hi."

She just stood there. My eyes were adjusting. What I saw was more than just poise and promise, way more.

"Where's your mother?" I asked. I didn't want to have Marie Louise burst in from across the hall and make a scene.

"She left."

"Left?"

"After she thought I was asleep, she got dressed and left. I think she went to meet Leonard Crump."

"Lucky me."

"Yes, lucky you," she said as that peignoir slipped and fell silently to the floor.

I was the luckiest man in Memphis, Tennessee, and I mean man — a boy no longer.

But when I awoke in the morning, they were gone. No goodbyes, no note, nothing. I rushed downstairs to ask the desk clerk where they'd gone. He said they had checked out. The room had been paid for by the Delta Omicron fraternity, so he had no address for Marie Louise or Camille. Leonard Crump wasn't in yet.

"Uh," I said, coming back to the present. The prospect of enrolling in an as-yet-undetermined major at Stratmore College and going to monthly fraternity meetings and playing folk music at beer busts and coffeehouses held no appeal at all. None.

"Registration is still open at Memphis State," Larry said hopefully.

On the other hand, there were blues bands in Chicago, and lots of saxophone players, and fraternity parties all over northern Illinois. Plus, my tuition at Stratmore was already paid, and my grandmother, who had financed this sojourn, expected me to report back.

"Uh, let me think about this," I said. "I've got a couple of hours before my train leaves."

I got Larry's phone number, and he left, assuring me once more that with his connections, we would be getting gigs at all the fraternities at Memphis State. I could tell he was beginning to think of himself as the manager of a band.

"You need that Stratocaster," Mr. Saperstein said quietly as the door closed behind Larry. He carried it around the counter, plugged it into the amplifier and handed it to me.

"When was this made?" I asked, looking at it, really for the first time.

"They came out with standardized colors in 1960, but this one is older than that."

He stepped back around the counter and came back with another Stratocaster, also red.

"This is a newer one, in Fiesta Red. See, the colors don't match."

Indeed, they were both red, but the one I held was darker with less gloss. The fretboard was worn, as was the pick guard. Turning it over, I could see through the red paint at the edge of the contoured back where the instrument would ride on the player's body. I tuned it up and sat down, running through the 12-bar blues. I closed my eyes and for a moment, smelling stale cigarette smoke and beer and hearing people laugh. Where had this guitar been? Who had played it? Where were they now? The pawnbroker leaned on the counter and said nothing as I played the Strat for 10 minutes.

"They all come from Mississippi," I said, eyes still closed, still in my reverie and thinking about all the blues artists I knew.

"Yes."

"How long have you been here?" I asked Mr. Saperstein.

"Thirty years."

"Since the Depression," I said, eyes still closed, fingers picking a blues rhythm on the bass strings.

"Yes."

"You've seen 'em all," I said, picking up a simple melody on the treble strings, stretching them a bit at the end of a phrase.

"They've all been here."

"Where does it come from?"

I pulled the pick from under the E string at the tuning head and moved from John Hurt's style to Hubert Sumlin's, imagining Wolf barging in the door like he was going to eat the first person that got in his way.

"They learn it."

"Learn it from who?"

I went back to the simple 12-bar blues and imagined Sonny Boy coming in sly and low on his harmonica, then wailing and dropping off at the end of a phrase.

"The audience."

"Hmm."

With Sonny Boy wailing along I saw a line of dark-skinned people moving down a row, stuffing cotton into pick sacks. He went into the next verse, and I improvised eight bars and then, in my vision, looked up to see a man sitting on a horse. Watching the work. After a week of that, people would not be in the mood for any Mozart happy music. A man, and that woman working right down the row from him, would want a shot of Hennis' lightning before letting loose their anger and pain in song and dance, followed by what I'd had the night before. They were forbidden virtually everything else.

Chapter 28

"Get a musician's union card," Mr. Saperstein said. "The manager of the Blue Note Lounge will assume you're nonunion because you're from Memphis State. He'll offer you a three-month contract at less than union scale. If you're a big hit, he's got you cheap for all that time, if you don't draw a crowd, he'll fire you at the end of the first week. Show him the card and agree to work for one month at minimum scale, then talk again when you've seen what the crowds look like."

"Good advice. You manage bands?"

"No. I used to. It's a dirty business. I'm just a pawnbroker."

"What other advice do you have?"

"Well, buy that Stratocaster," he smiled, adding, "there's something special about that guitar."

"There is." I walked to the front of the store again and looked out at a deserted Beale Street. Instead of dread at going back to Chicago, I was feeling anticipation. There was a great appeal in the thought of transferring to Memphis State and playing the blues in the home of the blues. I didn't even know where Memphis State was or what kind of school it was — or if they'd take me on such short notice. But, I didn't know what I wanted to study, so it should do as well as any other school for the time being.

And if their music department could keep a musician as good as Theodus happy, I could learn something there, too.

"Can I use your phone? I need to call Chicago. I'll call collect."

⸺

"THEODUS AND THE COOL BLUES!" was on the marquee of the Blue Note Lounge two days later on Friday afternoon when we pulled up in my just pur-chased, way used, beat to shit 1960 Volkswagen minibus. It had belonged to a Baptist church and had been driven a tough 100,000 miles carting its youth group around the state. But the drums and amplifiers and guitar cases fit in it.

"I'm with the band," I announced as I entered the medium-size club on Poplar Avenue, just east of downtown. It was the white equivalent of the Club Handy, a place where people went to drink, dance and party, and the club tried to have the latest band – as long as they were cheap.

"Go around back," the waitress said without looking up from clearing beer bottles from the first round of happy hour.

That took some of the spring out of my steps as I retraced them back out front to tell Theodus and the other two we needed to move the van. It turned out to be good advice; the club had some parking and the back door led right onto the small stage.

We loaded in and set up. I had the red Strat Mr. Saperstein had first rented me, and I'd sprung for a better amplifier than the one I'd used at the King Cotton. It had plugs for a guitar and a microphone. We were three hours early.

We bombed. We were awful, and everyone knew it. We're lucky they didn't throw us out. During the three days of intense practice between our triumph at the King Cotton and our opening at the Blue Note, several painful truths emerged.

First, Bubba and the Clamdiggers were not a Memphis State band. Bubba was a used-car salesman at Courtesy Rambler on South Bellevue who played guitar on weekends and used whoever he could pick up cheap for backup. The drummer and bass player were just out of high school. The drummer could keep a beat, but he had nothing else; no drum solos or fancy intros or endings. The bass player couldn't keep a rhythm unless I nodded my head or tapped my foot where he could see it. Theodus was good, but he kept throwing in superfluous notes that were off the rhythm and off the key, and it confused the rest of us, causing all sorts of mistakes.

We opened with Theodus playing the Coleman Hawkins songs and, just like at the King Cotton, the audience got bored after the second one and started talking over the music. We switched to the *Creole Belle* I'd worked up with the fancy picking; it fell flat. They hardly noticed. We came on with *Tuff*, and a couple got up to slow dance. We went into *Memphis* and they seemed to like it, but nobody danced. Then we went into *Kansas City,* the old standby with me singing lead and a saxophone solo. They perked up some and that ended the first set.

The manager came over as we broke and said, "Say something about taking care of the waitress. They don't work for free y'know."

"Right. So, pretty good so far?" I was hoping for some positive feedback. I didn't get any.

"Yeah, well, this is the happy hour crowd. We need to keep 'em here if we can. That's why we wanted you guys to start early. They don't like much slow stuff. Maybe right at the end, if there's anyone still here. Don't break for too long, they'll start to leave."

"OK."

"Oh, and don't do no Beatles songs."

"OK."

Memphis, like Mississippi, had some weird liquor laws. Beer was legal, no problem. Wine and distilled spirits could be served only in private clubs, but people could bring a bottle to places like the Blue Note and leave it with the bartender, who would sell them drinks out of their own bottle if it needed mixing, or they could keep the bottle at the table and buy setups, which were glasses, ice and mixer at inflated prices.

After the first set, the happy hour crowd left and people started coming in groups with bottles they kept on the tables. These people had been to dinner someplace and now wanted to dance. We started to get requests to play songs

I'd never heard of. We'd only rehearsed 10 songs, and we had to make do with those.

"You boys need to relax," the waitress said after the first song of the second set, and she placed a tray of shot glasses on the amplifier. "Compliments of the house."

"I don't take alcohol," Theodus said with a derisive sneer.

The drummer and the bass player giggled like two adolescents sneaking their first taste of hard liquor, which they were. I downed my shot and Theodus' shot.

This was a hard crowd. Unlike the college boys at the King Cotton, who were high from their first taste of college beer, these were hard-working people used to some raucous fun on the weekend. We had no exotic dancer waiting in the wings to add anticipation, we'd played nine of our ten songs and we still had two more sets to go. Then the bourbon kicked in.

I let Theodus flutter along with a long sax solo to get us through the second set, then turned and got my face right into his. I tried to imagine Marie Louise Fontenot when she took him down during rehearsal at the King Cotton.

"Listen, Theodus, if you don't quit noodlin' around, these people," and I jerked my head back toward the audience behind me, "are going to throw us out into the street!"

He looked shocked. In true cool jazz form, he'd been in his own little world behind those dark glasses, blowing whatever weird thought came to mind.

"I ..." he started to say.

"Shut up! We're gonna close the set with *Stagger Lee,* and you're going to play it straight. I'll sing it through to the last verse, then throw it to you, and you play the whole thing again, wail on the tune No noodling. Then I finish."

I bumped his forehead with mine.

"Got that? Blues, Theodus, just like at the hotel!"

Stagger Lee was our 10th song, saved for a big close, but we had to use it now or the crowd was going to leave. It's an old blues song that's been around since the early 1900s and sung by nearly every musician. John Hurt played a folk version in 1927 that described the hanging of "cruel Stagger Lee" for the murder of Billy after a misunderstanding over a Stetson hat. Lloyd Price had a big hit in

1960 using the same tune but changed the words completely, making it a wailing lament over the fate of poor Billy. I used those words.

"Stagger Lee! cried Billy, please don't take my life!" I wailed out into that smoke-filled room, with all the misery and pain I could muster and, finally, Theodus caught it. All the faces in the audience were on us when he came in and he took them back into that alley where a man begs for his life with a .44 pistol in his face. Then, "Stagger Lee shot Billy!!" in the last verse, and I cried as if that bullet were going through me and then went back to the basic blues rhythm and turned up the volume on the Stratocaster while nodding my head, the signal for Theodus to come in with something on that beat to walk it out.

I fired the drummer and bass player at the end of the night. With my third shot of whiskey I decided I'd rather renege on the contract and go back to being an ordinary college student than have to spend another night onstage with incompetent musicians. I was incompetence enough for one band.

Fortunately for me, Mr. Saperstein and the musicians union found replacements by the next afternoon, and one of them was a big surprise.

Rufus Monkton, the bass player backing up Howlin' Wolf down in Greenwood, was not the regular player with Sonny Boy Williamson's band on the King Biscuit Time radio show. Wolf had picked him up on his way through West Memphis just for that three-show trip, and he was now available. But not at minimum scale.

"My name's on the marquee!" Theodus protested late the next morning when I called him with news of the new pay arrangement.

We'd signed on for a month at minimum scale – $15 each plus double that for the headliner or the bandleader. It was my band, but I let Theodus have the double scale that first night.

"You have a choice," I told Theodus. "You can be a one-night headliner and go back to playing Ravel and Coleman Hawkins by yourself, or you can play with professional musicians for three weeks at minimum scale and have a chance to be something special."

He agreed, then whined and pouted until I finally told him he could be at the practice room at 1 or not. I didn't care. It was a hollow threat. Being a music major, he had a key to the practice room at Memphis State. Without him, we didn't have a room to practice in, or a band. He was there, and he shut up when he met Rufus Monkton.

Monkton was a laid-back, rangy colored guy in his 20s from West Memphis. He'd been on the fringe of the music scene in Memphis and West Memphis since buying his first bass from Mr. Saperstein while still in high school. He worked on the loading dock at the Sears distribution center and played bass wherever he could on weekends. He had some distant family relationship to Howlin' Wolf, or maybe it was somebody who knew Wolf. But he was a good bass player and had played a few times as a session musician at both the Sun Records studio and the Stax Records studio as well as with most of the bands around town. He was looking for the big break.

"OK, guys," I started in while they were setting up, "we almost got fired last night, and might get fired tonight. We've got a one-month contract, at the end of which we might not have a job, or we might get a raise. It depends on how good we are. Theodus is our headliner, but this is my band. You all work for me. Got that?"

They all nodded.

"Theodus?" I wanted to be sure.

He nodded.

"OK. We play blues. No pop. No Beatles stuff. Blues. That Coleman Hawkins stuff is fine for a while, but this market doesn't want Coleman Hawkins. It wants Memphis blues."

They nodded.

"Last night, we played some rock and roll, but it was Memphis rock and roll, and that's R&B, and that's OK. By tonight, we need to have 20 songs we can play."

They nodded, and we started in with *Red Rooster*.

Right off, it was different. Rufus had played that one with the master, and his shuffling bass line anchored Theodus when he came in playing the melody on his sax. Like at the King Cotton, we played it as an instrumental, and now I felt Theodus begin to move with the beat. He hadn't done that before. Although his sax expression was good during the debacle of the night before, I'd sensed what a muddle a band can become without a steady beat.

Rufus could sing, though no better than I could. Neither of us had anything distinctive about our voices, but letting him sing let me be better on guitar. He sang *Smokestack Lightning,* and it was decent Delta blues that got better when Theodus came in for solo. Then Rufus sang *Walkin' the Dog,* a big hit in Memphis by Rufus Thomas, one of the DJs on WDIA. Monkton had filled in with Thomas' band and knew the song well. Plus, it was an important transition from the old Delta blues to the new Memphis soul style, which was dance music, so our Blue Note Lounge customers could shake it out when the bourbon began to hit home. Then we ran through our initial 10 songs.

"Theodus, why you do that?" Rufus asked at the end of a song.

"Do what?" Theodus was defensive, rather than annoyed, which had been his usual response to any questions or suggestions.

"You get off the beat like that, we all think you lost the beat, then we cover. You know, change what we doin' to cover you. Then you change back to the beat, leave us hanging."

"That's my thing."

"Your thing? Makin' me look like a fool is your thing?"

I just stood there, letting this play out.

"You in a band, Theodus! Got that, a band! You don't change the beat and the key just in the middle of the song!"

"That's improvisation."

"That's bullshit!"

Rufus got up, set his bass against the amplifier and stormed out the door, lighting a cigarette as he slammed it behind him.

For a moment, I thought he was going to step in the other direction and have a physical confrontation with Theodus, which would have been a bad thing for Theodus.

Theodus turned to me and then Ben, the drummer, with a questioning look.

"He's right," Ben said. "You're playing with professional musicians in a band, you stay on the beat and in the same key or you make us all sound like fools."

I thought Theodus was going to break down in tears. He got a look of desperation on his face and then sagged onto the stool behind him.

Rufus came back in from the side door, flicking a cigarette out into the yard. He took in the situation as he crossed the room. The scowl on his face had become a bemused grin.

Theodus stood up, as if to meet a confrontation. He looked scared.

"You ain't learned yet," Rufus said, incredulous. He'd come to some kind of insight about why Theodus wouldn't stay on the beat.

"You ain't stupid, and you blow good horn, you just ain't learned yet," Rufus said, picking up his bass and plugging in.

Theodus looked puzzled.

"Look, you playin' music in your head, just like we all do," Rufus said. "You playin' that music in your head, like it was just you. Like you solo on the stage. That's why you like that Coleman Hawkins guy, cause he plays alone. But, we all here, too, see?

"And the bass," he said, holding it, "be your best friend."

Rufus started a blues shuffle.

"Look, hear this first. I keep the beat for you, so this is first, then think of that tune you gonna play, but think of it on top of what I'm givin' you. It ain't you out there alone on the stage with us followin' you, it's you playin' that tune and followin' us. Now play that song again and stay right on my beat."

The song was *Matchbox,* an old blues standard made into a hard-driving rock and roll song by Carl Perkins. Perkins, born to sharecroppers in Tiptonville, Tennessee, just north of Memphis, he recorded the song at Sam Phillips' Sun Studios on Union Avenue in 1957, the same studio that recorded Howlin' Wolf's breakthrough song *How Many More Years* in 1951. The Sun recording of *Matchbox* has a piano giving a boogie-woogie background beat, just like Howlin' Wolf's first recording. We were trying to use Theodus' sax in that rhythm role while Rufus sang the lyrics and I tried to match Perkins' guitar.

Rufus started playing, and Theodus reluctantly picked up his horn. Ben and I came in behind Rufus. Theodus watched Rufus and stayed right on the beat. This was a complex undertaking, using the sax, bass, drums and lead guitar in an integrated, beat-centric rock and roll song. For the first time, we sounded good.

Chapter 29

I knew something was up when the manager rushed out of his office and crossed the dance floor to meet three men standing at the door. We were in our third week, and Theodus had learned to stay on the beat, we had thirty good songs, and I was beginning to fancy myself a rock and roll singer.

The Blue Note was crowded that night, a Saturday, but not overflowing. We'd been getting a steady flow of free drinks and, because Theodus and Ben didn't drink, Rufus and I were flying high.

It was a real love fest at the door. A handsome colored man was first to give the manager a hug and a handshake, obviously old friends. A shorter white man with light brown, curly hair, and then the third, older man got a somewhat more formal greeting. Leading them through the crowd to the front of the room, the manager waved to the bartender, who stepped to a storeroom and brought out a folding table. With fanfare, the manager set that right by the side of the bandstand and brought four chairs.

"That's Booker T. and Duck," I heard Rufus tell Theodus behind me.

Booker T. & the M.G.s were the hot band in Memphis that year, having just scored a major national hit with *Green Onions,* a rhythmic instrumental featuring Booker T. Jones on the Hammond organ.

"Heard you guys were layin' it down hot and cool here," Booker T. said, signing a young woman's leather purse with a Magic Marker as I approached at the break. Half a dozen well-wishers and autograph seekers were lined up behind her. Rufus went right to Duck Dunn, the curly-headed bass player, and began a conversation as if they'd just been speaking earlier in the day. They had. Rufus was an occasional session musician at the Stax Records studio where Booker T. and the M.G.s were the house band. Rufus had filled in for Duck earlier in the week when Duck had gone out of town to his grandfather's funeral.

"This here's the hot sound I told you about," Rufus said, turning from Duck to Theodus, who was standing awkwardly by the drummer behind us. Introductions were made while Booker T. finished greeting customers.

"Let Duck play the bass, you give me the Strat," Rufus whispered from behind my right ear. It is customary for a band to ask visiting musicians to sit in for at least a song, if not a set, especially when the visitors are well known.

Booker T. sat at an old upright piano beside the bandstand, a place he had occupied many times; they played the Blue Note as often as they played the Club Handy. Booker T. and the M.G.s were the first mixed-race band to perform widely in Memphis. Theodus and the Cool Blues were the second.

Giving Rufus my Strat made me a spectator, though they planned to call me up to sing after they warmed up on some instrumentals. I didn't mind. Well, a little. It was my band. But I was never going to be any kind of headliner, and Rufus and Theodus were good. So for the start of the third set, I sat with the older man who'd come in with Booker T. and Duck. Turned out he was the entertainment reporter for the *Memphis Press Scimiter*. Somehow, word had gotten out, and the house was now packed.

They started out with Booker T. laying down a boogie-woogie beat on the piano, then Duck came in with a complex bass line, then the drums, then Rufus on lead while Theodus, dark glasses back on, nodded his head, taking in the background. Then Theodus joined the others with a monotone rhythm — no countermelody or beat, just driving boogie-woogie. The song was *Last Night*, the first hit song Booker T.'s group had when they were known as the Mar-Keys. Predating *Green Onions* by a couple years, this was an early example of the Memphis soul sound.

By changing the rhythm to boogie-woogie from the traditional blues shuffle, and using all of the instruments together, they created a much more danceable song, and the audience at the Blue Note got the message right away. The dance floor was packed. The only words to *Last Night* were just those, spoken by Duck during a break at the end of the first verse. After the second verse. Theodus came in with an improvised sax solo that was much closer to Coleman Hawkins than Howlin' Wolf – closer to what Theodus wanted to do but locked into that driving dance rhythm. Booker T. took a solo, then Rufus came in with some lead, then they went back to Theodus, then walked it out.

"Wow," the entertainment reporter said, turning to take in the energy of the packed house. "They own the room after one song."

"Maybe you ought to get a picture," I suggested.

"Good idea," he said, turning toward the bar.

The manager thought he wanted a refill and brought him one, with a shot for me. He nodded enthusiastically when the reporter yelled in his ear asking for a camera. The band was playing *Red Rooster* with the faster beat. The manager returned with an Instamatic as the song ended.

The band called me back up to play lead while Rufus sang *Matchbox*. The audience, still dancing, cleared a way in front of the bandstand so the manager could take some pictures. We jammed on *Matchbox*, each taking a solo, then walked it out. The third set was over, and the crowd had grown so large there were people waiting on the sidewalk outside and listening to the music through the open door.

We got some good ink in the Sunday paper. The picture was from the Instamatic shots the bartender had taken of Theodus blowing all out in front of the band – well, the band except me.

HOT HORN AT THE BLUE NOTE

Booker T. Jones and Duck Dunn sat in Saturday night with Theodus and the Cool Blues at the Blue Note Lounge. This hot new band had the spillover crowd dancing down Poplar Avenue, and Theodus Wiggins, with his hot sax, is the new pied piper of the Memphis blues scene.

Chapter 30

The cotton was all picked, and the bare plants with their open, empty bolls were skeletal reminders of the hard work done during September and October. The soybeans had been harvested, and the combines had shredded and scattered the plants so that nothing was left but a bare field. Every small town along the route had a cotton gin, and the hull piles were as tall as the gin buildings, just like Cooter had described. In my reverie, I imagined Cooter as a young Boy Scout standing at the top of one playing King of the Hill.

The Illinois Central's City of New Orleans slid smoothly down through Senatobia and Batesville to stop briefly at Grenada. As the stations at Duck Hill, Winona and Durant passed with no stops, I imagined Lloyd Kinder driving the troop train south in 1944, trying to make up time. As he slowed at Pickens, did he think about his son Buck, somewhere out in the Pacific with the 4th Marine Division preparing to assault Saipan? Vaughan was less than five miles away.

It's a long left turn into Vaughan. I stepped to the other side of the nearly empty passenger car to see it from the fireman's point of view inside the curve. I tried to imagine the dark, rainy night and the frantic lights of the brakeman signaling the wide-open troop train to stop. We roared through Vaughan without slowing down, and I stepped to the other side to see the remnants of the passing track that wasn't long enough to hold two freight trains, and the last embankment before the station where Lloyd Kinder died a sudden, scalding death protecting a thousand young soldiers like his son. None of the other riders paid any attention.

Addie was at the station in Jackson. Emmabelle stood back a discreet distance, allowing a measure of privacy for our first meeting in three months.

As we gathered my suitcase and headed out to the parking lot, Addie breathlessly brought me up to date.

"… And my roommate will sit with us, she's from Florida and won't be going home until Christmas. She wants to meet you. I just finished my last midterm this afternoon, but we've been cooking all week. I made you a pie."

It turned out that transferring colleges isn't that hard; a couple of phone calls registrar-to-registrar, a promise of a mailed transcript, and it's done. It took less than an hour. Political science was a lot easier major for me than premed with its mandatory comparative anatomy, and poli-sci had no labs, no dead animals, no bad smells.

Theodus was in my music theory class, and some days the two of us showed up bleary-eyed from a night wailing and rocking on some stage. Our contract at the Blue Note Lounge was renewed with a modest pay raise and, for the first time in three years of college, I was earning my own expenses.

"How are your parents?" Addie asked as we got into Emmabelle's car.

"I don't think they'll miss me for the holiday," I said.

My father had moved out and was living with my grandmother until he found something in Lake Forest he could afford. He was now paying two white-shoe law firms to settle a nasty divorce from my mother. They'd seemed relieved when I told them I was going to Mississippi for the Thanksgiving break.

My task for the feast on Thanksgiving Thursday was to boil a pot of sweet potatoes, mash them with some butter, spread them into a baking pan and cover them with little marshmallows, and bake it again until they melted and got brown on top. I was very proud later as the melted marshmallows stuck to the serving spoon and added a decadent sweetness to an already elegant treat.

Emmabelle presided over the turkey and gravy while Addie put together the cornbread stuffing to go inside. Addie's roommate, Judy, from someplace in Florida, mixed some green beans with canned mushroom soup and spread French fried onion rings over the top and baked it. Pumpkin and pecan pies had been made the day before, along with cranberry sauce made from scratch. Frozen Parker House rolls were thawing on the table while we worked, rising to be popped into the oven at the last minute.

Finally finished, we took a break to sit in the parlor and talk while the turkey rested under a foil tent. Emmabelle opened a bottle of champagne, and we all had a glass while Emmabelle told the stories of Grandpa Kinder's sad demise at the Vaughan station and Addie's polio.

Then we remembered Buck, with Judy serving as the audience while we told anecdotes and poignant memories. I told of our cigarette and beer front-porch sessions and heard again about Buck coming back from the war to raise his infant daughter, the time he turned the tractor over plowing beans, and the big deer he killed in Sharkey Bayou.

Judy told of her family in Florida and why she wanted to go to college in Mississippi. Then we told about the snake on my first fishing trip, Mississippi John Hurt's concert on Addie's 19th birthday and our brush with the Klan. I filled them in on my success in the Memphis music scene.

"You've had such an interesting life," Judy gushed, clearly happy to be included with Addie and her suave boyfriend.

"Oh my, look at those rolls," Emmabelle exclaimed from the kitchen, where she'd gone to get some beer after the champagne was gone. The Parker House rolls had been set on the top of the stove when we set the table, and the heat had caused them to rise extravagantly. They looked like little balloons. She popped them in the oven, and we gathered in the dining room.

"Our Heavenly Father ..." Addie began, giving a detailed grace remembering Buck and Lloyd Kinder, her roommate's recently deceased grandfather, and mentioning my grandfather, Dr. Douglas Spencer, who'd been dead half a decade. I thought she was just trying to be polite by not leaving anyone out. It was a bit long, but we got through it. The dinner was great.

Ensconced in the guest bedroom, I had visions of diaphanous peignoirs and floating apparitions visiting me in the night, but nothing happened and I slept undisturbed.

The next day, we drove up to Avalon to retrieve Buck's truck from Ervin Davis, who'd used it during the harvest. He reported that Cooter was nearly finished with Marine boot camp and would be home for Christmas. He already had orders to the Marine base at Okinawa, Japan, after advanced infantry training at Camp Lejeune, North Carolina. Addie sat close during the drive back to Jackson.

Chapter 31

"We lost the gig at the Blue Note," Theodus, who'd kept my car over the holiday, announced when he picked me up at the train station in Memphis. "The manager booked Carla Thomas beginning next week."

"We have a contract!"

"He says it's cancelled. He said look at the contract, he can cancel at any time."

"But ..." I was thinking of how I was going to make my next car payment.

"He said not to worry, he'll bring us back after Christmas and New Year's."

We were well-known at Memphis State and had no trouble getting parties on weekends, but not at union scale. Sometimes we played for tips. Then we got a break.

Larry Driscoll caught up to Theodus and me as we left our music theory class.

"The Rebel Club in Osceola, Arkansas, wants a band with a saxophone to back up a stripper they have next weekend," he said. "It's a two-night gig at union scale."

It seemed simple enough. We'd gotten a reputation backing up an exotic dancer, and we could do it again. Osceola is 65 miles north of Memphis on the Arkansas side of the river. No problem, just drive up there, do the gig, put money in our pocket.

I had thought the Club Handy was rough. I had no idea.

Elvis, Jerry Lee Lewis, Johnny Cash, Albert King, B.B. King, Conway Twitty, Howlin' Wolf and Booker T. & the M.G.s had all played the Rebel Club, and they told stories. The club is not within any city or town; therefore, no police. It's out in the country on old Highway 61 in Mississippi County, Arkansas, an area notorious for "selective" law enforcement.

Though there used to be a large colored population in the area to work the cotton plantations, they mostly left after the mechanization of cotton, and the remaining sharecroppers were white, poor and accustomed to wild times on the weekend. In addition, there was a large Air Force base just up the road west of Blytheville, home to 3,000 young Airmen.

Enter Theodus and the Cool Blues.

The first thing we noticed when we got there early in the evening to set up was the chicken-wire fence set up floor to ceiling in front of the bandstand. We'd never seen that before.

"Why the fence?" I asked the bartender while I was carrying in an amplifier.

"Well, the stripper draws quite a crowd. Don't want nobody to get hurt."

What does having a stripper have to do with anyone getting hurt? I wondered.

The club was a bit nicer than the Satellite and Stardust clubs I'd played down in Mississippi, but not much. Looking at the wire from the back, it was pretty clear that it was there to protect the band from the customers throwing beer bottles, or anything else, at them.

"You start at 8, the stripper comes on at 10," the bartender said. "The house will start filling up by 7:30. They'll start yellin' as soon as they get their first beer. Ignore that. Play loud. I'll give you a nod when the stripper is ready. Do some kind of intro. Her name is Krystal Keene. She'll come in from the back, by the bar. Randy, the bouncer, will stay right behind her. She'll come up here by the bandstand and do her dance, then mingle with the customers, and then run back out by the bar the way she came in. Randy will block the door. We pay her to dance for 20 minutes. If she gets some cash from the customers, she may dance longer. When you see her work toward the back, play some kind of climax."

That had an ominous feel to it.

"Who's that?" the bartender asked as Theodus came in.

"That's Theodus," I said. "The band is Theodus and the Cool Blues."

The bartender muttered something, and I went back to setting up.

The crowd was mostly male. I should have figured that. They came in groups, and it was clear from the start that the music was incidental. We dispensed with the Coleman Hawkins stuff and went right to the rock and roll. The waitresses served the beer in paper cups, which was reassuring. We finished the first set to smattering applause and took a break

"How about a round for the band?" I asked one of the waitresses, who went back to the bar and returned with some beer.

"So, is the stripper here yet?" I asked, wondering whether she'd have any special instructions. Marie Louise Fontenot certainly had some strongly held opinions about how the band should play.

"She's here," she smiled. "It's me."

"Really?" She was a cute, shapely young woman. Well, a few years senior to Camille, but attractive. "Uh, any special instructions?"

"Well, play music, I guess."

"You ever done this before?"

"No."

"You have a costume?"

"Just something I made," she said. "A dress with a seam that opens, then a bikini, then me."

"Uh, come back here a minute and let's make some plans."

I gave her the basics Marie Louise had taught the band: a snare shot every eight beats; poise and promise; strut, tease, give some, promise more; then, well, then it was up to her.

The soon to be Krystal Keene went back to the bar, and I saw the bartender hand her a shot glass, which she threw back and made a face like it was medicine. I guess it was medicine.

The crowd filled the club during our second set – young, male, white and loud. Oh, where was Pearlie Eubanks when we needed him?

The crowd was growing more restless as we took up our instruments after the second break. I saw Krystal emerge from the door behind the bar. There was no spotlight or dimming of the house lights to give her a bit of momentum, so I did what I could with the introduction.

"Ladies and gentlemen!"

The room grew quiet in anticipation.

"The Rebel Club takes great pride in presenting, direct from Bourbon Street in New Orleans, Krystal Keene!"

We started in on *Red Rooster* as Krystal strutted down the aisle in a high school cheerleader's uniform. The crowd was on its feet in an instant, and the collective cheer that built as she came to the center of the room told me that, in this locale, and with this crowd, the fantasy of a high school cheerleader shucking her clothes was sufficient to merit the $3 cover and the long wait. No fancy costume, no gymnastics routine needed.

Randy the bouncer followed her down the center of the room, staying just enough behind so he wasn't too much of a distraction but signaling by his presence that grabbing at Krystal would be dealt with. He wasn't nearly as intimidating as Pearlie, but he was a large, solidly built man of middle years.

That performance light was in her eyes. No longer just a waitress bringing beers and clearing tables, she now was the center of attraction, and she enjoyed it. Her routine was a simple dance with some flouncing of the skirt to show she had just a bikini underneath. Then she unzipped the side and showed her bust, sat on a few laps, rubbed against an old man in one corner igniting general hilarity and merriment, and then paused.

They screamed for more. We went into *Forty-Four.*

"Watch that bouncer," Rufus warned from behind me.

In his right hand, Randy had a sap, a leather hand weapon weighted with lead that is as effective as a billy club in taking out a rowdy assailant but less noticeable. I would never have seen it, but Rufus did.

Krystal Keene unzipped the cheerleader's outfit and flung it back toward the band, standing there for several moments in her bikini before making the rounds again. This time, Randy stood closer, and she got pats and squeezes but no grabbing. When she got to the old guy in the corner, there was a general cheer. He seemed genuinely embarrassed, as if he'd come just to get a glimpse of a young honey gone starkers but now he was up against her and at center stage.

Theodus blew hot and bothered and right on the beat. Krystal went back to the center to unsnap the top and wait for the next eight-beat snare. There was no tease. The beat came, and the top came off, and there she was. She let them look for four beats then twirled around to shake her backside at the howling mob. She gave the band a wink and a big smile. Everyone in the Rebel Club was having fun at that moment.

"Uh oh," I heard from behind me eight beats later as she turned to face the crowd and pulled off the bottoms. She wore a G-string, which covered very little, as 50 excited young men surged toward the middle of the room to get a better look. Krystal did a pirouette and, as her face flashed our way, I saw the smile was gone. Randy moved closer and, when she finished the circle, she lost her nerve and rushed toward the back of the room and the door to the bar. Like a rabbit she ran through the door with two spectators in hot pursuit. Randy was suddenly there in the door, and for a moment it looked like the pursuers planned to storm over him like two linebackers taking out an offensive lineman.

Randy took a half step backward, deftly transferred the sap to his left hand, then stepped forward and punched the first pursuer square in the face with a full-force right cross that stopped the teenager cold. He dropped like a sack of boiled cabbage. The sap in his left hand was right behind the right cross. Fortunately for him, the second pursuer veered off to the side and was grabbed by friends to save him from serious injury. The smile on Randy's face told me why he worked at the Rebel Club.

The downed boy sat up, dazed, rubbing his jaw. Friends helped him up and slapped him on the back. He was a sort of hero, as if he'd done some daring feat, which I guess he had. Now that Krystal was safely behind closed doors, Randy approached and inquired whether the boy was OK, and he was. They spoke briefly and shook hands as friends helped the teen out the back. Get drunk, watch a local girl take off her clothes, mix it up with the bouncer, get your face busted, talk about it all week. Fun in the Delta.

We packed up, keeping a wary eye on the dwindling crowd.

"Good job, guys," the manager said after we were done and the crowd was cleared out. "We'll settle up after the show tomorrow night."

"No," I said. "We'll settle up now or we won't be back tomorrow night."

That was the other thing I'd heard about the Rebel Club. Don't work on credit.

"We usually pay off on Saturday nights."

"Seventy-five dollars, in cash, now."

Rufus and Ben were standing right behind me. Randy was there, but he wasn't standing right behind the manager. Theodus was loading the bus.

He paid us in cash from the cash register, and we were gone.

"We gonna go back there?" Rufus asked as we pulled out onto Highway 61.

Mr. Saperstein, Booker T. Jones, and Duck Dunn had all warned me about the Rebel Club. It was a place people went to get rowdy.

"Well, we got twice what we've been getting at Memphis State," I said.

"I've got a rent payment due Monday," Ben said.

We rode south in silence through Osceola and a couple of miles west to the new Interstate 55, which was open as far as the Missouri line 30 miles to the north and all the way through West Memphis to the Memphis-Arkansas Bridge.

"Really," I said "it was just the girl they were after. They didn't pay much attention to us."

When there was no response, I added, "We can decide in the morning."

The next night, we showed up just before we were due to go on, and the place was full. The kid who'd gotten his face busted the night before was back, the left side of his face puffy and bruised. He sat at the back. He'd apparently been the beneficiary of several free rounds from friends and was already glassy-eyed. The bartender nodded, and the manager said he'd laid in some additional security "just in case."

During our first set, a tough-looking group of five guys in their early 20s came in and sat up front to one side. They had a stern look and didn't seem to be enjoying the show or the prospect of a naked cheerleader. We opened with Theodus doing a Coleman Hawkins song, just because Theodus liked to play it and we knew the audience wasn't paying much attention to our music. During his solo, I heard the word "nigger."

We took a break, and one of the waitresses brought us some beer. A few patrons approached to chat or make requests for the next set. The five toughs sat stern-faced.

"You see them guys?" Rufus asked quietly.

"They got another bouncer," I said, to reassure.

"That look like trouble. You and Ben stick up here with me and Theodus."

"Ladies and gentlemen …"

My theatrical enthusiasm attempted to pull the room into a happy group of comrades on a lark, an adventure, and most of them were there with me, but not all. Krystal Keene made her entrance, all innocence and enthusiasm. That honest smile belonged somewhere else. She couldn't have put on a convincing act of innocence if she'd been associated with this den of iniquity for long, yet she was peachy fresh as she strutted toward the bandstand in her cute little cheerleader outfit.

Where did they find her? What did they pay her? Why did she do it?

She made the rounds, sitting on a few laps and rubbing against a few guys. The old guy from the night before had apparently had enough and was not in the corner. She avoided the five at the front. The crowd was better behaved than the night before, and the two jokers who'd rushed the bouncer kept their seats. I felt a flicker of optimism.

She dropped her top, and they loved it. She worked out most of her 20 minutes topless, then did the pirouette and dropped her pants.

"Lookin' on a naked white woman," I heard, and a cold grip of terror stopped my breathing. This was serious.

Krystal ran out to the front to wild cheers, with Randy right behind blocking the door. There were no pursuers this time.

"I just seen a nigger lookin' on a naked white woman!" one of the five stood and shouted.

The room was silent in an instant.

"You gonna let niggers look at white women with their clothes off? Are you? Are you men or nigger lovers?"

The five stood looking around the room.

"Wait!" I shouted. I did still have a microphone.

"This is just a party, a good time. We don't need some kind of confrontation here."

My voice of reason went silent when one of the five pulled the power cord to the amplifier.

"We need to teach some niggers a lesson," the ringleader said, stepping in front of the bandstand and he and his friends approached.

I looked to the back and saw Randy heading back toward the bar. If he was going to call the police, we'd all be dead by the time anyone responded. That chicken-wire fence in front of the band seemed wholly inadequate.

"Keep 'em off the bandstand," Rufus said, unplugging his bass and holding it by the neck like a club. Ben grabbed his cymbal stand and pointed it forward. I jabbed the first guy to come around my side of the fence with my Stratocaster; he retreated, and I reversed my hold on the guitar like Rufus had. Theodus cowered in the back.

To their credit, most of the audience backed away from the fight, but they didn't help. A couple of people joined the five, and they came all at once around both sides of the fence. I swatted the first guy, and Rufus blasted another hard enough to lift his feet off the floor. He went down and another tripped over him. I swung again, missed, and the Strat was pulled from my hands.

"Get 'em!"

A swell of humanity overwhelmed our defenses, and we all fell into a big pile on the bandstand, kicking and punching and biting. One arm was pinned under me, but I got in some good licks with the other, punching the same guy in the face over and over. His arms were pinned behind him. I was getting an elbow to the family jewels while another guy was trying to get his teeth into my ear. There was a metallic crash as Theodus finally came to his senses and swung his sax down onto the guy who was biting my ear.

Then the whole universe exploded in a flash of blinding light and searing pain in my eyes, nose and throat, and choking spasms that stopped all respiration for half a minute. All of the combatants in that pile on the bandstand gasped and screamed and rolled away from the fight, animosities and injuries forgotten, blotted out by something so terrible, so threatening to our very existence that we crawled and stumbled to distance ourselves from the bandstand.

Randy had thrown two 12-ounce beer cups of household ammonia into the fight, and it was over. Oh, was it over!

Randy then waded in with his fists, focusing on the five, and he was backed up by the other bouncer with the sap in case anyone jumped Randy. No chance of that. We were all incapacitated. The fight was over. This was character building, a tutorial in behavior modification.

Randy dragged the two biggest of the five out through the bar, pulled them upright, busted them in the mouth and pushed them out into the parking lot, still gagging and choking. When he came back, the other three ran out the fire escape behind the bandstand.

Chapter 32

"It's been broken before, see?"

Mr. Saperstein pointed to a broken dowel and the remnants of glue as he examined my damaged Stratocaster.

"The factory attaches the neck to the body with a dowel so that the dowel will break instead of the neck," he said. "Dowels are easy to replace, necks are expensive."

"So I'm not the first guy to use his guitar like a battle ax to fight off a mob."

"No, and especially not at the Rebel Club." He turned it over and pointed to some new scratches, then showed me that the screws that had attached one end of the guitar strap were pulled out.

"I have a man who works on guitars," he said. "I think he could fix it for about 30 bucks. Want me to give him a call?"

He looked at me for a moment while I considered my financial situation, then added, "Want to trade it in on something else?"

I considered that option while I looked over the other guitars on his wall. The bloom was certainly off this whole blues music adventure. I ached all over from the beating, I had a constant wheezy cough, and my nose was running some nasty green stuff. Ben, the drummer, quit on the way back to Memphis. Rufus said he would continue but never again for a strip show, and he reserved the right to refuse to play at any place he deemed unsafe. Theodus was in the midst of a family conference regarding his future.

On the other hand, I enjoyed music, and performance of improvisational music is music in its purest form. Musician and audience joined in the moment, and that moment unique in all of time. I liked blues music in all its forms – Delta blues, R&B, Memphis soul, Rock and Roll. I enjoyed the kaleidoscope of other musicians as they came and went, each adding something and taking something away from our sessions, lifting tunes, words, styles from other artists and making them their own in performance.

Recording took a song, musicians, a style, a moment and framed it unchanged forever. As tastes change, that song would sound old, copied, less interesting. But, I could listen to John Hurt's 1927 recording of *Stagger Lee* and then compare it with Lloyd Price's 1960 version and then craft my own version. That was fun.

Then there was the lifestyle. The moving from place to place, the setting up and taking down, working disparate musicians into a cohesive unit capable of actually producing music people would pay to hear; that was a challenge but fun when it worked. There were girls, of course, and parties after the parties, especially at Memphis State. But most of the time, we packed up and went home exhausted. The performance was the thrill.

"How soon can he have it ready?" I said to Mr. Saperstein. "They want us for a fraternity party Friday night. Oh, and can I have a loaner until then? I have to break in a new drummer."

<hr />

The next week, we made a record. Sam Phillips made the famous Sun recordings of Elvis, Johnny Cash, Jerry Lee Louis, Albert King and Howlin' Wolf at the Sun Studio, 706 Union Avenue in Memphis, but he'd moved to a larger facility in 1960 and rented out the old building to an independent recording company that made a lot of demo recordings for aspiring musicians.

We were contacted that week to work a studio session backing up a singer/songwriter from Southeast Missouri who had a song he wanted to promote.

Ken Williams performed in the Memphis market, but he didn't want to bring his own band. Instead, he wanted some of that Memphis soul sound, and he didn't want to pay union scale. We agreed to two hours after class one weekday for 10 bucks apiece.

Theodus' family agreed to let him continue performing but suggested we get a colored drummer. I disagreed. We played to mostly white audiences and were known as a mixed-race band, which increased our appeal in that market. Having a colored drummer would make it a colored band with a white front-man. That would be odd. Reluctantly, they agreed but insisted that Theodus would not play any gig without Rufus. Charlie Peck, a white guy and fellow Memphis State student, was our new drummer.

"Here's your band," the recording engineer announced to Williams as he showed us into that hallowed room.

Williams had been running through his music on the old upright piano, the same one Jerry Lee Lewis used to play the Boogie-woogie rhythm on Carl Perkins' recording of *Matchbox*.. He briefed us on his simple tune and asked us to try it with a blues shuffle beat and a sax solo while he sang and played piano. We went through it a couple times, then the engineer suggested we do it straight through first, then listen to it and then do it again, and he'd try some echo sound effects.

"Three, two, one, recording," the engineer said, and Ken nodded the beat and we started in.

The studio was about the same size as my bedroom at home. It had a window into the control room, which was just a cubicle off the reception area that opened onto the sidewalk along Union Avenue. We used our regular amplifiers with the sound turned down from performance level, and the drummer muffled his bass with a towel. There was a microphone for Ken and one for the rest of us.

We did a couple of takes, then listened to them, and did a third. This time, the engineer ran the sound through a section of garden hose coiled inside a soundproof box with a third microphone at the other end. The slight delay as the sound traversed the garden hose sounded like the echo of a performance in a larger space. It gave the recording a more professional sound.

"If I buy dinner, will you stay for one more song?" Ken asked when he and the engineer were happy with the music. More money would have been nice, but we settled for dinner. He ran down to the Loeb's barbecue stand on Union and came back with a sack of tasty, slow-roasted, pork shoulder sandwiches.

We did his second side, a syrupy ballad that Theodus greatly improved with some Coleman Hawkins-type background.

I got home in time to study for a poli-sci test the next day on the evolution of public law and contracts since Roman times, ironic in that we'd just violated our contract with the musicians union to not work for less than scale.

During my weekly phone call with Addie the next night, she said, "I've been asked to sing a solo in church on Christmas Eve. Will you accompany me?"

We had talked about my going to Jackson for Christmas, but events back in Chicago had taken my family relationships to a new low. The lawyers handling the divorce had agreed on a settlement, and both my parents had signed the papers. The divorce would be final when the judge got around to reading it and approving it. In the interim, my mother had decided to "retire" to Florida and had leased a condo in Sarasota. Dad was planning to take Ethel to Las Vegas to "get away from it all" over the holiday.

"Uh, what's the song?" I asked, stalling while I tried to find a way not to hurt Addie's feelings. I absolutely could not leave my grandmother alone on Christmas.

"*Little Drummer Boy*, it was written for a soprano, and I've found an arrangement for guitar accompaniment."

We sparred for 10 minutes as I outlined some of the events back home. There was no way to put a happy face on this ugly situation. I invited Addie to Chicago, but Emmabelle refused to let her travel alone, and there wasn't enough time for me to take the train down there and pick her up. My car was not an option. I didn't trust it across the bridge into Arkansas, much less all the way to Chicago in the winter. The call ended in tears and hurt feelings.

It was barely light out two days later on Saturday morning when the phone rang and I struggled to wake up. We'd played the Blue Note the night before, and there'd been some after-party action. They'd sacked Carla Thomas and booked us back for weekends through the holidays. Her style was more

Motown and appealed more to teenage girls, way wrong for a hard-edge club like the Note.

"Douglas?" a voice said.

"Yes?" I struggled to recognize the voice.

"Douglas, is this a bad time?"

I fought back my impulse to answer that question while I sat up and looked at my watch. It was 7:30.

"Uh."

"Douglas, should I call back later?"

It was my grandmother.

"No! Uh, no, not at all. I was just, uh, brushing my teeth."

"Liar. You were asleep. I'm sorry, but I wanted to let you know. I'm coming down to hear you perform."

"Really?"

"Yes. I've heard so much about your music. I want to hear it for myself."

I had a vision of my grandmother at the Blue Note for the last set of the night. We'd matured as a band as Theodus had learned to work closely with Rufus. The night before, our last set had ended with a 30 minute jam on *Matchbox,* featuring Theodus rocking the house with his solos.

"Uh, we'll be playing the 28th, 29th and the 30th. Uh, it's a kind of blues club. It's not really..."

"No, Douglas. I mean on the 24th, Christmas Eve. My friend Emmabelle Kinder has invited me to Jackson to attend services with her. I understand her niece, Adelle Kinder, has been asked to sing and that you have been invited to accompany her. It sounds charming."

And so it was. But it wasn't easy. The Southern Presbyterian Church was a bastion of tradition. Christmas Eve services were an occasion for reading the relevant scriptures – all the relevant scriptures – and singing the traditional songs. That would be limited to the music in the Presbyterian hymnal.

Little Drummer Boy was not in the hymnal, so it was considered secular, even though it's about the birth of Christ. That's the Christmas story, and much more consistent with the scriptures than some of the traditional church music.

Still, singing a song that had been recorded by popular folk singers of the day was a break with tradition. That was the first hurdle.

The second hurdle was having a guitar accompaniment. There were those who felt that only organ music should be heard in church.

The third hurdle was unspoken, but there was a bit of hesitation about putting a crippled girl in front of the congregation on Christmas Eve. Addie was a member, everyone loved her and supported her, but, well, it was awkward. But Emmabelle Kinder was an elder in that church, and the first female elder in recollection. And she was forceful in her opinions in a way only an old-maid schoolteacher can be forceful. Who was going to confront her?

Reluctantly, they approved having me, a nonmember, play that accompaniment.

Little Drummer Boy is about a boy asked by the Magi to give a gift to the new baby Jesus, but he has nothing to give, so he plays a drum solo. Set to an old Czech folk tune, it has been an enduring favorite Christmas song for a long time, sung solo and in ensembles by all types of musicians.

But it sounds best sung by a soprano. The guitar accompaniment used a lot of bass string to simulate the drum, and I improvised some percussion on the face of my Gibson J-45 for additional drum sounds.

Addie was decked out in a new white Christmas dress with red ornamentation that looked a little Eastern European, appropriate for the tune's origin. The acoustics in that large church were excellent, and the purity of her voice and the innocent sincerity of her delivery awed the First Presbyterian Church of Jackson, Mississippi, and my grandmother.

That led to another delicate situation. My grandmother was so taken by Addie and enjoyed the company of Emmabelle so much that she decided to extend her stay, rent a car and drive them all up to Memphis to see us play the last night of our three-night gig at the Blue Note. But, no lady would go to a bar or nightclub unaccompanied by a male escort, even as the guest of the bandleader. Emmabelle did have gentlemen friends, but this was an overnight trip; another bit of awkwardness. It became my problem.

I called my music professor, but he was out of town. My poli-sci instructor agreed to go and asked his wife to join us. It would not be a problem to have one

man and four women, but she had other plans. I called the entertainment reporter from the *Press Scimitar* who had given us such a good write-up the month
before, but he was busy covering the Memphis Symphony.

So, it came to pass that on Thursday the 30th of December, 1965, Mrs.
Douglas Spencer of Lake Forest, Illinois, and Miss Emmabelle Kinder and her
niece Miss Adelle Alice Kinder of Jackson, Mississippi, came into that den of
sin, the Blue Note Lounge, and took their seats at a reserved table near the front
of the room, escorted by Mr. Abraham Saperstein.

Mr. Saperstein and I seated the ladies, and he discreetly handed a small
leather liquor caddy to the waiter, who took it to the bartender and returned
with three Scotches and a Coke for Addie.

All this studied decorum occurred as the Blue Note filled up the night before New Year's Eve. The hardcore partiers don't save it for New Year's Eve,
they build to it, and they'd been building all week. The next night, they were
going to get Booker T. & the M.G.s with Isaac Hayes, or if they wanted to go
down to Beale, they could see Albert King at the Club Handy.

We started the first set with our usual Coleman Hawkins songs, then *Tuff,*
that waltz with the naughty sax to set the mood for the night. I did my virtuoso
guitar work on *Memphis,* and we closed out the first set with *Stagger Lee,* which
included an extended sax solo, and then we walked it out, literally shuffling off
the stage behind Theodus wailing away with the audience continuing that driving backbeat for us.

As we crossed the dance floor, I looked over to my grandmother, who was
standing next to Emmabelle chanting "go Stagger Lee, go Stagger Lee" with
the rest of the crowd. They stayed for all three sets, including our by-now-
signature extended jam on *Matchbox.*

Chapter 33

Theodus quit the band the next week.

Distracted by my grandmother's visit, Addie's performance on Christmas Eve, the surprise visit of all of them to Memphis and impending final exams, I had failed to find any bookings for January, and I missed an important undercurrent within the band that had been going on for some time. If I had gone back to the Blue Note for New Year's Eve, I would have seen Theodus Wiggins playing with Booker T. & the M.G.s.

Booker T. Jones had gotten Theodus some session work at the Stax Studio and, in the process, worked his sax into some of the M.G.s' music. Rufus and Isaac Hayes had worked up an arrangement of an old blues standard, *Spoonful*, with a boogie-woogie rhythm. They'd practiced at the studio, Booker T. liked it, Duck Dunn liked it, and Steve Cropper, the lead guitar player for the M.G.s and, more importantly, the chief producer for Stax Records, liked it. They'd cut a demo and shopped it to Jerry Wexler, partner in Atlantic Records in New York. He liked it, and they agreed that Stax would produce it and Atlantic would promote and distribute it.

Theodus Wiggins signed a record contract with Stax the first week in January, took his finals early, took a semester off and was added to a monthlong promotion tour starring Otis Redding, Booker T. & the M.G.s, and Wilson

Pickett that left the second week in January. They took Rufus Monkton with them.

"I made that guy!" I complained to Mr. Saperstein the next week when I went by the pawn shop to pick up my Strat, which was back from the luthier.

"No, Doug," he said, softly delivering the painful truth. "You rode the rocket for a while is all."

"Yeah," I said, plugging in the Strat and sitting down by the amp to see whether it would still play. "I need a rest, anyway."

I started with a scale, then chords, then a blues shuffle.

"I've got finals this week."

I thought of Theodus and Rufus on the road, playing three sets in a club every night, and remembered how tired I'd been after just three nights at the Blue Note.

"I guess musicians come and go," I said, going back to John Hurt's style, without the pick.

For a moment, I saw John's shy grin that night on the porch when he played for Addie's birthday. That seemed so long ago.

"Music changes," I added, picking up the pace. "There's no loyalty."

I slid up the fretboard and stretched the string, mixing Albert King's style into John Hurt's song.

"That's the music business," Mr. Saperstein said.

———

Camille Fontenot called the next week.

It seems Leonard Crump, the manager of the King Cotton Hotel, had made a couple of trips down to Tallulah to see Marie Louise, and Camille had asked him to get my number.

"Doug?" she said. "It's me, Camille."

"Well, hello old friend," I said. I had been warned by Leonard that she was going to call.

"Old friend, indeed. I owe you an apology."

"About disappearing at the hotel?"

"Yes. An explanation, at least."

"I figured it was all a part of that show business life, to move on when the show's done, new town, new show, new friends."

"No, Doug. That's crass. I don't hop into bed with just anyone. There's more to it than that."

"Well, it was quite the letdown to wake up alone after, uh, well, after we did what we did."

"Leonard Crump's wife got a passkey from the desk clerk that night and walked in on him and my mother."

"Ooh."

"Yes, it was ugly. She knew the King Cotton had an exotic dancer that night, and when he said he had to work late, she assumed she was going to catch him with the dancer. It wasn't the dancer, but it didn't matter. She had a camera and made a big scene."

"Did your mother know he was married?"

"I don't know. She grabbed her clothes and ran down the stairs to our room while they were yelling at each other and throwing things. We were gone in an hour."

"Ran down the stairs naked? I thought only guys did that."

"I've been teasing her about it ever since. It's funny."

"It is funny."

I had a vision of nude, middle-age Marie Louise Fontenot hotfooting it down the stairwell with her fashionable dress, hose and garters in her arms.

"She left her shoes behind," Camille said, and we both laughed.

"But, she's still seeing him," I said.

"He's not married anymore."

"You certainly have a, uh, mature relationship with your mother. I can't imagine discussing something like that with my mother."

"Well, Doug. That's show business. Remember, I traveled with her on the road for 10 years."

"So, where are you now?"

"I'm in Hammond, Louisiana, at college. I registered at Southeastern Louisiana University like I planned. Which is why I'm calling. I'm going to be in Memphis at the end of the month. Our Reed Trio will be performing at the Memphis State Chamber Music Festival."

"Reed trio?"

"Oboe, clarinet and bassoon. We'll be playing *Trio* by Auric, and *Largo* from *Xerxes* by Handel. I'd like you to hear me play, if you can."

The Memphis State Chamber Music Festival was a big deal, at least to the Music Department. Proud of what they had, they'd planned this festival to enhance their reputation regionally and had invited other universities to send musicians to a day of workshops and performance in Memphis State's newly completed auditorium named after some generous alumnus. The festival was mentioned in my music theory class the next week, and we were strongly advised to attend at least one performance during the all-day event.

The Southeastern Louisiana University Reed Trio and Chamber Orchestra came by bus in the morning and spent the day in workshops and attending other performances, so I saw Camille only briefly. I escorted Marie Louise Fontenot to the evening concert, at which the Reed Trio was the opening presentation. This was a coat and tie event for me, and Marie Louise was statuesque in a perfectly tailored suit. As we walked down the aisle to our seats, I couldn't suppress recalling the story of Marie Louise abandoning her shoes in Leonard Crump's hotel room.

"Lovely venue," she said as we sat and looked around the slowly filling room.

"Yes, the university is quite proud of it," I said, but what I thought was, "Buck naked down the stairwell."

"They were just sandals," she said simply.

"Sandals?"

"That I left in Leonard's room."

"Oh."

"She told you about it."

"Well, she did, uh, fill me in on, ah, certain details that, well, answered a lot of questions I had about that night."

"Yes." She smiled. "Did she tell you the whole story?"

"She didn't give a lot of, uh, detail."

"Yes, the hasty exit, the lack of decorum down the stairs, all true. But there's more."

Where was this going? Did she know about Camille coming to my room? Surely the candor between them didn't extend that far. Camille was legal, over 18, so they couldn't send me to jail for diddling a minor. Shotgun wedding? Was she pregnant? We'd taken the customary precautions.

"Camille didn't know, until this week."

"Uh, yes?"

"I don't jump into bed with just anyone," Marie Louise said. "Leonard Crump and I are old friends. I've known Leonard for more than 20 years."

"Really?"

"Yes, old friends, but nothing more. Leonard's eye is on the sparrow."

I wrinkled my brow.

She looked at me patiently, then added, "Or the chickadee."

"Oh."

"Yes. Always looking ahead. But, I, we, all owe Leonard. He was the one who recognized an opportunity for Camille's debut and called me."

"With all this candor," I said, "could I ask you a question?"

"Certainly."

"In the bus station, was that an accident?"

"You are a bright young man," she smiled. "Yes, it was an accident. I saw you tying your shoe, and your guitar case, and on impulse thought it might be interesting to meet you. I didn't expect you to react so quickly and thrust your leg out, and I didn't expect to break my heel and fall into the bench."

"Lucky accident."

The lights dimmed, and the performance began. The Reed Trio was wonderful, of course.

And that was the night I almost got evicted from my apartment.

"What is that awful noise?" shouted Mrs. Gottfried, my landlady, who was pounding on the door of my garage apartment well after midnight.

"Oh, good evening, Mrs. Gottfried," I stammered, opening the door. She and her late husband, a mathematics professor, had rented this small efficiency to Memphis State students for 30 years. It was two blocks from campus, and the rent was the same as the dorms. During my five months living there, she had never climbed the stairs by the garage to knock on my door. But she did this night.

"Won't you come in?"

Perhaps I'd had a beer too many.

Mrs. Gottfried's scowl softened as she looked into the room and saw Camille, still dressed in the formal black gown she'd worn for the Reed Trio performance three hours before, standing in front of a music stand holding her oboe.

"Mrs. Gottfried, this is my friend Camille Fontenot from Southeastern Louisiana University. Camille is part of the Reed Trio that performed at the Memphis State Chamber Music Festival tonight."

A very faint smile broke upon Mrs. Gottfried's face.

"Camille, this is Mrs. Gottfried, my landlady."

"Good evening, uh, morning, Mrs. Gottfried. I hope we weren't too loud."

"Yes," I said, "we were going over *Trio* by Auric, experimenting with guitar and oboe instead of clarinet and bassoon. It's a spirited piece."

The smile broadened

"We found that not a good combination, it needed something else, so I tried harmonica. That was the sound you heard, oboe and harmonica."

It isn't often you see a blue-haired old Jewish lady dissolve into uncontrolled laughter.

Chapter 34

The transmission in my VW went out. While I pondered whether to sell it to the junkyard, where it so richly deserved to be, or to find $300 to fix it, I was afoot. The heater didn't work, the back window fell out, the shocks and springs, if it ever had shocks and springs, were ineffective. It was a piece of junk. So, I alighted from a Memphis city bus just before noon on a weekday in April, one block from Court Square.

I hurried toward the pleasant, tree-shaded park in the center of the city's legal and financial district. I had a competitor, and whichever one of us got there first could play to the lunch crowd, while the other had to go a block down to Confederate Park overlooking the Mississippi River and play to a smaller group.

He was a strummer, hacking chords and singing folk songs. I picked Delta blues.

I opened my guitar case, threw in some quarters and a dollar bill in case someone didn't know they were supposed to contribute, tuned up and started to play. My voice is not that great; reedy and thin, it doesn't project well. I'd found I sounded better just humming a melody, and that works great for the blues, because the words aren't that important. All the old blues guys switched lyrics around freely. Hubert Sumlin told me Howlin' Wolf couldn't remember some of the lyrics of songs he'd sung for 30 years, but it didn't matter because he'd just throw something else in there or play the harmonica. Houston Stackhouse said the same thing about Sonny Boy Williamson.

Moanin' at Midnight is that kind of song. I played the blues shuffle until I saw someone walking my way, then started the moan, just like Wolf. After 16 bars, I went to the harmonica. I had one of those harmonica braces that fits around your neck, like Bob Dylan used. I could blow some harp while I continued to pick a driving rhythm with Hubert Sumlin flourishes, and it sounded good. But I needed to move the harp around in my mouth to get that Sonny Boy Williamson/Howlin' Wolf expression, so sometimes I'd take it out of the brace and just play the harp, or move quickly between the harp and guitar.

The man sat down and opened a sandwich. I alternated the moan with a falsetto moan, then harp, then some words: "Someone's knockin' on my door!" Then back to rhythm with some hot licks.

By the time the first man finished his sandwich, six people were sitting on the two benches or standing by listening. He dropped in a half-dollar and went back to work.

Avalon Blues was next, one of the John Hurt songs that brought me south. I saw heads nodding as my fingers worked the strings. My right hand looked like a spider wrapping up a fly; a lot of activity in a small space.

"Pretty mama's in Avalon sho' can spend your change," I sang, bringing a smile from a lady on the bench where the first man had eaten lunch. Like Wolf, John Hurt was free with his lyrics, inserting the several phrases of a song in no certain order, especially after he'd had a shot or two of that Old Grand Dad.

I saw my rival slink by from the bus stop on the way down to Confederate Park. Just beyond, a barge was laboring upstream and throwing off a pillar of thick black diesel smoke, and beyond that dust billowed up from a tractor plowing a cotton field across the river.

I had a dozen in my audience now, and heads began to bob as I went into another song. It isn't the lyrics; they're interchangeable. It isn't the tune; blues songs are all pretty much the same tune. The 12-bar blues shuffle is part of it. That's unique to the blues, a totally American invention. Some music theorists assert it has origins in African music, and we'd played some African music in our music theory class. I didn't hear anything that sounded like the 12-bar blues.

So, what are the Delta blues, I wondered, as I sat there playing and connecting with my small audience. Heads bobbed, people put money in my guitar case.

I decided to keep picking until I found out.

EPILOG

Thirty years passed. It was snowing. Though it had been spitting snow all morning, the weatherman said there would be no accumulation. It was cold and dark and damp. That fit my mood exactly.

We lost Cooter in Vietnam, but Billy Ray showed up for Addie's funeral. I was supported by our son, Lloyd Kinder Spencer, sitting tall and straight next to me in the front row.

He'd gotten word a couple of weeks before that he would follow in his old man's footsteps and attend the University of Mississippi School of Law. I could hardly wait to order the sign: Spencer & Spencer, Attorneys at Law.

His mother lived long enough to hear the news, and it was a glad day. Polio is a cruel disease. First, it crippled her, condemning her to a life on crutches. Then, years later, it came back for a second helping. Muscles Addie had rehabilitated withered, then others spared the first time around were lost. Fatigue kept her mostly at home the last year, and then in the bed. But that spirit was there to the end.

The crowd was a lot smaller at the cemetery. The minister gave a simple prayer and then turned it over to me. I pulled the harmonica out of my shirt pocket, the same three-dollar harmonica I had bought at Sterling's Department Store in Greenwood 30 years before. Addie laughed at me when I first tried to play it, but I had reminded her that she'd been moved as much as I had been that day Sonny Boy Williamson died and they played his song on KFFA in Helena.

The harmonica seems natural in the soft fragrant air of Mississippi, and those mournful blues we learned from the masters were not just an expression of their pain, but of their faith in a better time.

AUTHOR'S NOTE

Delta blues are more popular today than ever before. Every city has a blues club, or a blues and barbecue club done up with rusted corrugated siding and a bunch of old farm implements nailed to the walls where they sell pulled pork and ribs, and some of it is pretty good. There are thousands of musicians making their living playing "blues music." They're playing Delta blues, R&B, rock and roll, and soul music, and there is a lot of improvisation on the twelve bar blues shuffle. The King Biscuit Blues Festival is celebrated every October in Helena, Arkansas, and you'll find three stages of constant blues performance for a long weekend. Driving into Helena from Memphis, Jackson, or Little Rock you'll go right through the Delta during harvest season. They'll be picking cotton with six row cotton pickers that drop 5000 pound rolls of cotton wrapped in plastic off the back every ten minutes or so; no rows of black men and women stuffing cotton bolls into canvas sacks.

In 1977, Memphis changed the name of the Cotton Carnival to Memphis in May and it became the world's premiere barbecue contest. It's down on Riverside Park by the Mississippi River the first week in May and will have 200+ contestants. Go the night before the judging to see how it's done.

If you want to see what Sharkey Bayou looked like in 1965 without getting your feet wet, you can go to the Bass Pro Pyramid on Mud Island at the Memphis waterfront. They've re-created a Delta bayou complete with live bass, crappie, giant catfish and alligators and a hundred foot tall cypress tree. Take the elevator to the top, 32 stories high and right on the Mississippi River. It has to be one of the wonders of the world. Step out onto a glass balcony and look down, if you dare. Or, take a table in the bar up there and sip an Old Grand Dad straight and watch Ole' Man River roll by. Look across the river and imagine chopping a couple rows of cotton.

Beale Street is bigger than it ever was. The Fedex Forum sits where the old Club Handy was, and Beale is blocked off from Main to 4th St., making a mall now filled with blues clubs, bars, barbecue and soul food restaurants, and music stores. Lansky's is still selling flamboyant clothes, and all the big name hotels have clustered nearby. The Peabody is still just a short walk over to Union and the Sun recording studio is a couple blocks to the east. The last time I was there I saw an afternoon show at B.B. King's and came back out onto the street about nine o'clock. It was packed with revelers and looked just like Bourbon Street in New Orleans with bright lights and blaring music from half a dozen clubs. At the Main St. end they had metal detectors screening anyone going down Beale for weapons.

"Do you ever find anything?" I asked, sauntering over to a policeman, thinking weapons screening to be overkill.

"Every night. Got one already tonight."

Delta blues can still be risky.

The Lorraine Motel, a couple blocks to the south on Mulberry is now the National Civil Rights Museum, and that red brick boarding house across the street is gone.

Avalon, Mississippi was pretty much gone in 1965, and there's nothing there now but a roadside sign and some abandoned buildings. Don't look for Kinder's store, I made that up. John Hurt's house is a couple miles east of Higway 7 down a gravel road. Not much to see, but the family opens it up one day each spring.

I was at Buddy Guy's blues club in Chicago a few years ago. It was a weeknight and the crowd was sparse. The band was the same as Theodus and the Cool Blues in my story; lead, bass, sax, drums. They opened with *Sweet Home Chicago,* an old blues standard recorded by Robert Johnson in 1938. I loved it, and it was done well. The next song was something more recent and they improvised and jammed through the first set. As a younger crowd came in the music got more contemporary. At the break the leader, a late twenties black man who played lead guitar very well came to our table for a chat. He had tortured strings and slid frets like Albert King, moaned like Howlin' Wolf, and generally hit all the genre high points.

"You're good. Where'd you learn?" I asked.

"Right here," he said, nodding at the stage. "I grew up two blocks from here. I've been coming here since I was twelve."

They don't teach the blues in music school.

My brother Warren, to whom this book is dedicated, was a very talented, self-taught guitar player; for twenty-five years a road musician who played blues and rock and roll in every honkey-tonk and dive from Ft. Lauderdale to Buffalo, Wyoming. He got all the musical talent in the family, made a record in the Sun studio, and was a regular at the Rebel Club.

The cover is adapted from a photo of John Hurt taken by Joe Alper in 1964 and used by permission from Joe Alper Photos. The cover art is by Steve Meosky, the same cover artist who did the cover art for my Boyd Chailland adventure books. Editing was done by Barry Gilbert, who noticed that my description of John Hurt's picking style wasn't correct.

If you enjoyed my story, find my other work.
Bookman *http://www.amazon.com/dp/B00AQ98NUE* is a novel about a door to door salesman. **The Other Pilot** *http://www.amazon.com/dp/B008WAX99E* is Boyd Chailland's first adventure. **The Devil on Chardonnay** *http://www.amazon.com/dp/B00E67L8S6* brings Boyd back in a sailing adventure. **The Mingrelian** *http://www.amazon.com/dp/B00K60KGIA* is Boyd's diplomatic espionage adventure in Central Asia. In **The Fourth Domain** *http://www.amazon.com/dp/B00ZUYNMW* is even more international intrigue, thievery and malfeasance featuring now Major Boyd Chailland. These aviation based thrillers draw from my military career as an Air Force flight surgeon. I'm currently working on **Mingo River,** a multi-generational saga that follows two white and one black families from the Civil War through the largest drainage project in America where the impenetrable swamps in Southeast Missouri and Northeast Arkansas were transformed into the best farmland in the nation.

www.ingramcontent.com/pod-product-compliance
Lightning Source LLC
Chambersburg PA
CBHW060914180626

46817CB00004B/1247